KILLER PAST

She was heading back to her cabin after a visit with Aaron. Taking her time. Tossing stones into the creek, picking wild-flowers like a schoolgirl.

She rounded a curve in the trail and there stood El.

Unmoving.

Staring at her through those damn glasses.

The part of her brain that had nothing to do with logic or reason screamed at her to run. Her subconscious kept telling her that El was the same man who had followed her through room after room of her family's shop. Hunted her like a wounded animal; the same man who had trundled on fifty pounds of Kevlar body armor and pursued her down that terrible narrow corridor.

The same man who haunted her dreams.

He had stalked her from her youth, from her past, from the flatlands and burning heat of south Texas to the high passes and frigid cold of rural Alaska, and now here he was, wearing those same damned glasses.

She wanted to scream at him to take them off.

COLD HEART

Chandler McGrew

BANTAM BOOKS
New York   Toronto   London   Sydney   Auckland

COLD HEART

A Bantam Book

PUBLISHING HISTORY
Bantam paperback edition / April 2002

ISBN 0-553-58371-9

Published simultaneously in the United States and Canada

Bantam Books are published by Bantam Books, a division of Random House, Inc. Its trademark, consisting of the words "Bantam Books" and the portrayal of a rooster, is Registered in U.S. Patent and Trademark Office and in other countries. Marca Registrada. Bantam Books, 1540 Broadway, New York, New York 10036.

PRINTED IN THE UNITED STATES OF AMERICA

OPM 10 9 8 7 6 5 4 3 2 1

Oh hell, they're all for Rene.

A first novel elicits a great deal of appreciation on the part of the author. Accordingly, I would like to thank Scott and Sandy Dennis, Jen Richardson, and Marcy McCormick for their unflagging support and for reading various drafts of this and innumerable other manuscripts. Further thanks to Irene Kraas, my stalwart agent. And to Kate Miciak, the best editor in the business—never suffering fools gladly—for devoting far more time and energy to this work than might have been expected of her. Last but not least, kudos to Caroline Miller for the courage of her convictions; may she bring uncounted new talents to the surface.

Let me not pray to be sheltered from dangers
     but to be fearless facing them.
Let me not beg for the stilling of my pain
     but for the heart to conquer it.
Let me not look to allies in life's battlefield
     but to my own strengths.
Let me not crave in anxious fear to be saved
     but hope for the patience to win my own freedom.

—PRAYER OF THE BODHISATTVA

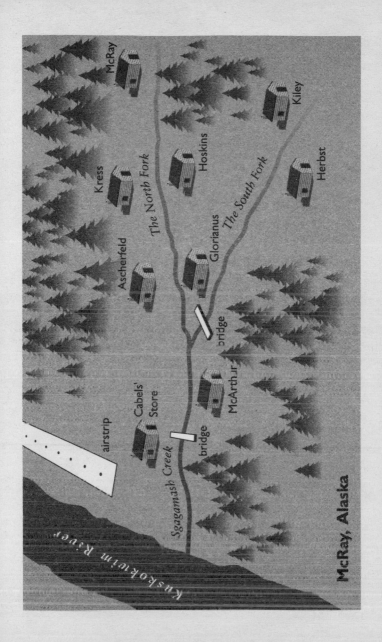

McRay, Alaska

Cold Heart

HOUSTON, JULY 23

DEATH WAITED THREE BLOCKS AWAY.

Micky Ascherfeld watched the streets through the cool barrier of the cruiser's passenger-side window. Her partner, Wade Smith, hummed a country tune, nodding his head like one of those perpetual-motion birds in the Taqueria shop windows.

They stopped at a red light and Micky glanced at two teenage boys, hectoring each other on the corner. But the kids were mouthing, not doing. Micky knew potential violence when she saw it.

Heat waves transformed distant buildings and pedestrians into mirages. As the cruiser pulled away from the intersection, Micky imagined the tires lifting melted asphalt. It was only one o'clock. By three, the temperature was expected to go over 110. She held her hands in front of the air-conditioner vents.

They coasted along, letting traffic pass them by.

The order of the day on their beat was to be on the lookout for a pair of salt-and-pepper suspects who had been pulling hit-and-runs on local electronic shops. The pair, a teenage white male and a black female in her twenties, would burst into the store armed with pistols, grab all the money in the cash register and whatever appliance was handiest, then flee on foot. But Micky didn't think the pair would be doing any running on a day like today.

She spotted a florist shop and her heart pounded. Suddenly it was cold in the cruiser and she tucked both hands under her thighs. As the shop passed, she tried to erase the memory from her mind, reciting the mantra in her head.

No problem.

No problem.

Until the florist shop was left well behind. Until the hateful image it had conjured faded.

Wade stopped at another stoplight.

"You okay?" said Wade.

"Fine."

"Having the trouble again?"

She shook her head.

Her parents' murders were public record. But as far as the Houston Police Department was concerned, Micky had overcome any psychological damage the trauma had caused. By the time she got to the academy, the murders were four years old. She had buried the hurt and the fear so deeply that even the departmental shrink couldn't find enough of it to disqualify her for hire.

But you didn't hide things like that from your partner. Not when you had been working the streets together for four years. You certainly couldn't hide them from your lover and they had been lovers for three, although the department didn't know about that either.

"Just a glimpse," she said.

"The florist?"

"Yeah."

"Why don't you talk to the doc?"

"I'm all right," she replied. But she avoided florists, funerals, graveyards, and weddings. And as long as she didn't go into dark, tight places, she was okay.

No problem.

"You're not all right." Wade watched an overloaded plumbing truck weave through the intersection. "You're thirty-one years old and you're a nervous wreck. You can't fix this all by yourself."

"I know that," she said, trying a smile. "But I've worked my way through it this long. I can handle it." An image of her father, lying in a pool of blood on a white-tile floor, flooded her mind. She could smell the flowers scattered around his body. She was crawling through their shop again. The sound of rubber soles padded somewhere behind her.

"You ought to let other people help you once in a while." Wade sounded petulant and that struck her as funny, the childish tone in a man his size. She let out a hollow laugh and knew instantly that she had hurt him. She touched his arm but he drew back.

"I'm sorry, Wade. I wasn't laughing at you."

"What then?"

What do I have to laugh about?

I'm a nutcase masquerading as a cop.

"How did you ever make it through the armed search course at the Academy?" asked Wade for the thousandth time. The course required the recruits to search a building for armed perps. The trainees went through in pairs, at night, with blanks in their pistols. Officers in disguise appeared at random. Some with guns, others portraying innocent bystanders.

Micky shivered, remembering.

"I don't know," she said.

Not even Wade would ever find out that she had made it through the course with illegally purchased Valiums and by repeating her mantra over and over through the entire thirty-minute ordeal.

Wade pulled across the intersection. The office buildings and shops opened up to parking lots in front of minimalls. Searching desperately for shade, pedestrians in sunglasses shielded their eyes with their hands.

"You had that nightmare again last night," said Wade.

Damn.

She didn't remember having the dreams anymore. The only inkling she had of anything wrong was the gray haze she experienced the next morning, as though the rest she had gotten had done her body no good.

"I'm sorry," was all she could manage.

"It's all right. I held you and you finally went back to sleep. But it's scary. I feel so damned useless when you have one of those things."

"You're not useless," she said to the window. "I love you."

"I love you, too," he said, easing around a Ryder truck as it pulled into a parking lot. "Maybe we ought to get out of town for a couple of days."

"How could we do that?"

"We have time coming. Why not head up to the lake? We could go next week."

She did like it out on the lake. It was a man-made pond really. A group of avid fishermen, including her Uncle Jim, had purchased the land up in East Texas when it was dirt cheap and excavated their own backwoods fishing hole.

"I'll never understand why you stay here in Houston," Wade said. "Why don't we just say to hell with it and find a job on some hick PD?"

"You'd do that?" she said. Wade was slated for detective. It was what he'd always wanted, his goal since childhood. "You'd move to the country for me?"

"In a heartbeat."

"You'd hate it and so would I," she told him.

"Why would you hate it?"

"I'd hate it because you did. I'd hate it because I was giving up."

"So you'll live like this for the rest of your life, fighting your demons valiantly, and never being content?"

"Content is overrated."

"Sometimes you remind me of one of your stained-glass pieces," said Wade. Stained glass was Micky's passion. Two of her works hung in a local gallery and the year before she had sold a piece for over a thousand dollars. "You're so beautiful I want to hang you up on a wall somewhere."

"Uncomfortable," said Micky.

"You know what I mean. There just seems to be something broken in you and no matter what I do, I can't fix it."

"Some things no one can fix."

"I wish sometime you'd finish one of the abstract pieces you start."

"The abstract stuff isn't any good."

"It is good. And just about the time a piece gets interesting you pull it apart and go back to the old stuff."

"People like the old stuff."

"But what do you like?"

"It's just a hobby," she said.

He tapped the wheel with his fingertips and she watched the heat rising from the engine compartment, stirring up the day.

Stirring up my past.

"You're not responsible for what happened," said Wade. They eased up to yet another red light.

"You seem to hit every one," she said, nodding up toward the stoplight and smiling.

"You in a hurry?"

"Not if you're not."

Tires squealed and horns blared as frightened-looking drivers raced through the light before it turned. Wade craned his neck to see what was causing the excitement. As the light changed he eased out, watching.

The Brinks truck, built like a land battleship, was four cars back, moving fast toward the intersection. Power steering screeched as cars fought to pull out of its way. Those drivers not quick enough were blasted aside by the big truck. Sparks flew and the air reverberated with the sound of grinding metal, horns, burning rubber, and curses.

"He isn't stopping," said Micky, as they reached the center of the intersection.

Wade pounced on the accelerator just as the big truck cleared the last car.

As Micky gaped, the front of the metal monster bore down on them. The huge grille looked like the face of an evil, grinning giant, intent on devouring the two of them. The impact was sudden and fierce.

Wade's head struck the driver's side window when the huge bumper slammed through it. Both airbags exploded impotently and disappeared, as the cruiser was lifted off the ground. When the car struck pavement again, with a sickening groan, the top crumpled. Three tires blew out as the weight of the big truck bore the cruiser up over the curb, across the sidewalk, and onto the parking lot of a topless bar. Metal grated on asphalt. The truck's screaming engine and its grinding gears completed the chorus of chaos.

Wade slumped onto the steering wheel as Micky desperately tried to figure out where she was and what she was supposed to do. Blood slickened her hands and stung her eyes. She didn't know if it was hers or Wade's. Blood dripped from his nose, his mouth, and his right ear but she couldn't reach for him. Her hands wouldn't obey her and her hearing and vision were skewed.

Another hard thump and the car wrenched sideways.

Micky blinked as a small tree draped across the hood of the cruiser, then vanished.

Wade turned toward her, confusion in his eyes. His head wobbled but he clawed at his holster.

Is he going to shoot the Brinks truck?

With a hand shaking so badly that it slapped the window, she reached for her own pistol, a blocky Glock automatic. She couldn't get the leather snap undone.

"Stay with me, Wade!" Micky shouted over the roar of the truck.

Instinctively, she jerked the pump shotgun out of its stand between the seats. Wade's eyes had gone glassy and there was too much blood seeping from the side of his head.

The cruiser hit a pair of parked cars. Metal crunched as the truck downshifted and lifted them up over another curb, onto the walkway in front of the minimall. Ahead pedestrians pointed and screamed and Micky prayed that they would stay well away from the lunatic driving the truck. Whoever was behind the wheel of the big rig wasn't going to be satisfied with just a hit-and-run.

"Stay with me!" she shouted as her window blew out and the front window of the Baby Doll Topless Bar burst inward.

Screams and crashing glass.

Groaning metal and crumbling concrete.

And then they were abruptly trapped in a cave that stank of alcohol and cigarettes and overripe hormones mixed with air-conditioning and money. Tires churned hot asphalt and fan belts screeched; the cruiser dropped again and shuddered like a dog, shaking off a cold bath.

The big truck receded slowly, backing across the parking lot. Micky groped for the radio mike. But she stopped in midreach as the truck creaked to a halt. One of its headlights hung from a thin black cable. The other seemed to be leering at Micky.

Grinding gears again.

"Oh, my God," she whispered, watching the truck roll forward.

This time they had nowhere to go. This time they would be crushed between six tons of armor-plated truck and the immovable mass of concrete-block building. She grabbed Wade by the shoulder of his uniform and tugged him toward her. Deadweight. He fell across her, pressing the shotgun painfully into her breast.

The truck punched them sideways through the bar window. It also drove Micky's head into the doorframe. Lights flashed across her eyes and she fought for consciousness.

But there was no real pain. Not yet.

Pain would come later.

If she lived.

Again there was the sound of shrieking tires as the truck tried to shove them on through the building. The truck's motor revved wildly and the cruiser rocked.

Who the hell is driving that thing?

Where are the cops?

Blood warmed her chest and stomach and coated her fingers. The side of Wade's head felt strangely soft, as though there were no skull beneath his bloody skin. The front of her uniform was splotched crimson.

The truck shifted into reverse and shook itself loose from the cruiser again.

They had to get out of the car. The next time the big truck would crush right through the cruiser and smash them both like overripe melons. Micky fumbled for the door handle.

Jammed.

What a surprise.

She was pressed against the door by Wade's weight and the shotgun and the door itself was crimped and twisted, wedged against the remains of the wall. She was never going to open it. She glanced over her shoulder and stared directly into the eyes of one of the dancers.

The girl was thin and pale with unbelievably large breasts. She would have been underdressed for a bawdy honeymoon night.

"Help me!" Micky rasped, trying to push Wade's weight off of her so that she could twist in the seat. A bolt of pain shot up her back.

So I am hurt.

"Help me! Now!" she screamed.

There were other patrons in the bar but none ventured forward, through the sea of overturned tables or downed chairs. The girl gnawed at her lip but took one tentative step, her high heels clicking in the shattered glass.

Micky managed to twist around. She passed the shotgun out to the girl, who grimaced but set the gun gingerly in a booth and quickly returned.

Micky glanced over her shoulder; the truck was still backing up. But they had only seconds at best. Reaching through the window toward the dancer, Micky kicked back.

The car's safety glass had disintegrated into a million harmless crystal pebbles and, as she tried to slide through the car window, her upper body broke away the last of them. But the bar window had splintered into long silver swords with razor edges and dagger points. Micky stared at one of the wicked, curved pieces of death that pointed directly at her heart.

Scalpel glass.

Sharp enough to cut me in half.

Hesitantly, the dancer reached across the nasty piece of crystal wreckage. She clasped both Micky's hands in her own soft palms and pulled.

Good girl.

When I'm nearly out I'll have to roll to my left.

If I sag, or drop straight down, I'll be skewered like the priest in The Omen.

Micky was praying that the attack had stopped. That the insane or drunken driver was having second thoughts or changing his game plan. But she pictured the guy behind the wheel of the truck, shifting and crunching, shifting and crunching, pounding over and over into the cruiser until the cruiser was an unrecognizable mass of crippled metal and Wade was . . .

Was what?

"Get me out!" she hollered.

"I'm trying!" shouted the girl.

Micky's knees scraped across the doorframe and Wade slipped between her legs. She rolled to her left and dropped to the tile floor, scattering glass. The girl fell with her. Micky sucked in a deep breath. Her legs shook as badly as her hands. She could already hear the terrible sound of the truck revving its engine again.

"Get back!" screamed Micky, shoving the girl into the nearest booth and scooping up the shotgun. She turned back into the terrible light of the Texas sun, glinting off the truck's windshield, burning her eyes.

The shotgun weighed a ton. But she tripped the safety and automatically checked the chamber for a shell.

The truck wasn't moving yet.

Maybe the driver had seen her, seen the gun, and was panicking.

No way.

He had to know the shotgun was useless against the heavy armor plate and bulletproof glass of his truck. The first sirens screamed.

Help was on the way.

"Can you get out?" she shouted to Wade.

He didn't answer.

"Hang on," she told him. She reached into the cruiser and gently ruffled his hair, sticky with blood.

He was slumped across the seat.

But he was breathing.

She rested the shotgun on the hood as the truck driver got his act together and caught first gear.

"Shit," she whispered.

The truck rumbled forward.

The sirens got louder.

The ground shook.

Micky edged sideways, crunching glass beneath her feet. She lifted the shotgun to her shoulder. As the armored car built up speed, she hammered off all five rounds into the windshield and grille of the monster. The bulletproof glass shattered but held, a maze of spiderweb cracks, and the grille blasted out water and steam from a tortured radiator and slashed hoses.

Nothing that she could do would keep the truck from pounding down like a huge battering ram into the side of the cruiser again and Wade wasn't going to survive another on-slaught.

The empty shotgun hung slack at her side.

The big grille swelled. Plastic and paint and steel.

God's fist, intent on crushing the cruiser.

Soft hands gripped her sleeve. The sudden jerk caught her off guard and she stumbled, falling on top of the young dancer, crushing the girl down into the booth and knocking the wind out of both of them, as the truck exploded into the cruiser.

Caught on steel-reinforcement bars and broken concrete, compressed between both ends of the front window, the police car crumpled like tissue. The bumper blasted through the driver's door and a section of the wall fell, smashing the cruiser's roof down into the seats.

The girl trembled beneath Micky, clutching her tightly, and Micky scrunched up instinctively into a fetal position, as the entire building vibrated with the impact. It wasn't until the insane bastard put the truck in reverse again—metal screaming against metal as the cruiser fought valiantly to hold on—that she pushed herself to her feet and witnessed all the horrific damage.

Wade was dead.

There was nothing alive in that car. His hand stuck out the shattered window and she stared at it numbly.

No ring.

She knew that he wanted to marry her. She had an idea that when he suggested the lake, he was thinking about popping the question while they were there. She hadn't been sure that she was ready, if she'd ever be ready. But with all her might she wished at that instant that she had a ring to put on his finger.

Grinding gears again. The bastard was ripping the teeth out of the truck's sprockets.

Who taught you to drive, you son of a bitch?

She ripped her holster open and managed to get the Glock in both hands.

The truck was now centered in the parking lot, reflecting the sun in a dull battleship-gray gloss. The windshield sparkled like diamonds where her buckshot had fractured the glass. She aimed for the spot where the driver's head should be, braced her legs, and waited.

Two cruisers shot past, lights flashing, sirens blaring. The uniformed officers would be taking in the scene, exiting their cars, and using them for cover. Other cars would arrive fast, cordon off the area, shepherd bystanders out of the field of fire.

"You in the truck! Throw down your weapons and come out with your hands up. This is the Houston Police Department. Come out with your hands up!"

The truck sat immobile, the engine idling.

Nothing moved.

No one breathed.

The thought struck Micky that the truck itself might be insane. It might be sitting there empty, deciding what to do next. At the moment, that idea made as much sense to her as any other. The other option was that the madman behind the wheel didn't give a goddamn that the entire Houston PD was about to come down on him like a big bad ball of toxic whipass. And that thought was too frightening to consider.

The truck rolled forward again. Not as fast as before. As though the driver didn't even realize that he was moving.

"Take out the tires!"

The bullhorn grated on her ears.

A volley of small-arms fire erupted, then the sound of exploding rubber. The truck stopped. But the tires of the armored car were designed to withstand small-arms fire. The bastard could have kept coming on the bare rims if he had wanted to.

But apparently he didn't want to.

The truck rolled ever so slowly to a stop in the middle of the parking lot.

When its engine shut down the silence was deafening.

"He turned it off," whispered the dancer.

Micky glanced at her, started to say that the girl had a firm grasp of the obvious. But the dancer was huddled in the booth, her face bone-white, her arms crossed tightly across her bare boobs. Her one act of bravery had taken all that she had to give. Micky wanted to tell her that her business was pretty much exposed for free the way she was sitting with her knees up to her shoulders.

But the girl had saved her life.

"Yeah," Micky said instead, steadying the pistol and wiping blood out of her eyes with her sleeve.

"Maybe he's going to give himself up," said the girl.

"Maybe he is," said Micky, sighting on the windshield. The bullhorn was still blasting. Hopefully someone was going to work his way around the truck and come to relieve her and Wade.

That thought sickened her.

There was no relieving Wade.

She staggered back to the car and one hand dropped

from the Glock, testing for a pulse she knew wouldn't be there. She stroked his wrist, fighting the tears that blurred her vision. She needed to have clear aim when the bastard climbed out of the truck. If he made one sudden move, she knew she'd be supported in calling it a clean shoot. A police officer was down.

When both truck doors opened at the same time she gasped. She'd been so focused on the driver, the person who was trying to kill them, that she hadn't considered the possibility of a passenger. Behind the broad doors with the bright blue Brinks emblem, she caught a glimpse of a thick, black-gloved hand and one black sleeve.

The bullhorn blared.

"Throw down your weapons! Put your hands up!"

Fat padded legs dropped beneath the doors and a chill shot up her spine.

Small-arms fire popped and the snare drum roll of two machine pistols rattled through the bar.

There was a loud roar, like a gas tank exploding.

Metal and glass crashed onto asphalt.

A sharp concussion drove her back.

The dancer screamed.

Doors behind Micky slammed and shoes slapped on tile. Apparently the bartender and the rest of the business had split.

The boom of a shotgun joined the pistol and machine-gun fire.

Micky aimed the Glock at one of the fat legs, realizing her shot would be wasted. She knew exactly what was happening. It was a patrol officer's worst nightmare.

The men in the truck were clad from head to toe in heavy Kevlar body armor and bulletproof plastic. They had machine pistols and, though she had no way of knowing it at that moment, she was sure they were using armor-piercing shells. They were cop killers.

But other cops were taking the brunt of their attack. And she was a cop.

So, she fired anyway.

The man's right foot kicked up and slammed back down. Good.

She hadn't pierced his body armor. Nine-millimeter ammo

wasn't powerful enough. But the impact would leave a nasty bruise on the back of the bastard's calf. He'd felt it.

The man turned and stepped ponderously around the truck door, moving to place the open door between himself and the cops out on the street. He was searching, turning slowly left and right with the long-magazine, short-barrel murder machine held at hip level. But the sun had him blinded. Micky was in darkness and she didn't move.

The man trudged directly toward her.

"Shit!" whimpered the dancer, edging out of the booth.

"Be still!" shouted Micky as the man swung the barrel of the gun in their direction. Micky dived toward the girl, her hand out to catch the dancer in the midsection, but the bullets got there first. They whizzed over Micky's head like hornets, ricocheting around in glass and metal and burying themselves in vinyl and flesh.

Three neat red holes appeared in the dancer's torso. She pitched back against the table in the booth, her eyes staring blankly down between her tiny, delicate hands, at her own blood, and then there was another explosion outside. Another gas tank.

More sirens.

Above the din, as though her ears were directional microphones attuned to the man with the machine pistol, Micky heard the distinctive sound of the last round being fired, the pin falling on an empty chamber. The used magazine clattered on the pavement, a full one clicked into place, and she knew that she had only seconds to live.

She considered taking cover behind the heavy oak bar. But that was the first place the bastard was going to look. She needed to make her way out back where she could double around and join up with the rest of the cops. The restroom doors were behind the horseshoe bar. But there might not be a window there, and even if there was, she didn't like the idea of getting caught half in, half out.

The pistol shook in her hand, and she slammed it down hard on the floor. A ribbon of pain careened up her arm and into her shoulder.

The shaking stopped.

No problem.

She didn't kid herself that this guy was going to give up and go away the way her parents' killer had years before. This was no drugged-up kid looking to get rid of witnesses. This was a pair of armed psychopaths bent on murdering cops.

She kept crawling.

All the people in the bar had disappeared.

They got out somewhere.

Where?

Behind the third booth was another door, with panic hardware. She raised herself to a kneeling position in order to push the brass bar down. She was barely strong enough to wedge her way through. But when she crawled inside—the pneumatic door trying to bite her butt—she found herself in a long, narrow hallway, lit by two small fluorescent fixtures high up on the grimy walls. Four wooden doors lined each side.

She struggled to her feet as the door clicked shut behind her.

Stop panicking!

No problem.

She reached out with both hands, placed her palm on one wall, the pistol against the other, and rested the back of her head against the cool door. Sweat and blood made the walls slick. Inside the corridor the gunfire was muffled.

She'd definitely taken a wrong turn.

This wasn't an exit.

It was an illegal massage setup. And there would be no windows in any of the massage rooms. Just a table that doubled as a bed where the dancers could make themselves and the owners a lot of money in the shortest period of time. But no windows. The last thing she'd find in any of these rooms was another way in or out.

She was trapped.

Just like before.

And terror was sapping her strength.

She checked the door, but there was no lock, of course. The management wouldn't take a chance that some drunk would get rowdy with one of the girls and barricade himself in. And there was nothing in the hallway with which to wedge it shut.

She turned and faced the corridor again, refusing to let the scene before her become something it wasn't.

There were no flowers here.

No worktables.

No walls lined with dried plants and glass vases, no rolls of green floral wire.

She wasn't sixteen.

And her parents weren't lying dead on the floor.

But she was going to be if she didn't get moving. She opened the first door to her right.

Darkness greeted her.

She groped inside for the light switch. Another fluorescent fixture blinked on in the suspended ceiling.

The room was spartan, barely five feet wide. Against one wall sat a surgical-looking table with the same paper covering that doctors used in their examining rooms. The black-and-white tile floor was worn and dingy and the walls were dented, as though elbows or knees had made violent contact with the cheap surfaces.

She considered rolling the table out into the hallway to block the door into the bar. But with its stainless-steel walls and shelves it was too heavy for her to move and too wide to fit through the door. Evidently it had been assembled in place. And the way it was wedged into the far corner, there was no place for her to hide.

She stepped back out into the corridor.

Another blast of gunfire sounded close at hand.

The bastard is inside the bar.

She closed the door to the massage room quietly. She was reasonably certain that, inside his bulletproof helmet, with the noise from outside and his own movements in the bar and the closed door between them, the man couldn't hear anything. But reasoning was one thing, blind terror another. Every footstep, every breath, echoed down the hallway as though it were amplified by the entire equipment setup for the Grateful Dead.

No problem.

She hurried down the narrow corridor, moving from one side to the other, opening each door, flipping on each light, flipping it back off, closing each door as silently as possible. Every room was the same.

All I have to do is survive long enough for the cops to get the firepower to take this guy out.

But officers on the beat didn't carry armor-piercing shells. More than likely someone would have to be sent to the nearest gun shop to purchase or requisition some. In the meantime the pair outside would be pretty much unstoppable. And that meant that sooner or later, the bastard in the bar was going to discover the door into the corridor.

Micky reached the last cubicle on her right. The room was identical to the rest. But she had nowhere else to go. And just like her, the bastard would have to search every room.

But she couldn't make herself go in.

She was hyperventilating. If she didn't control her breathing, she would faint on the floor and the son of a bitch would wind up shooting her in the back while she was passed out. But she had no more control over her breathing than she did over her hands, which were again shaking like leaves in a high wind. She put her left sleeve in her mouth and bit down hard, inhaling through the constricted opening.

She glanced down the length of the corridor, at the thin metal door between her and the killer, and suddenly it was as though the metal were dark glass and she could see the bastard through it.

He's looking at the door
He's turning toward it.
He's lifting the machine pistol.
His finger is fumbling for the trigger.

She dove into the tiny room.

A burst of automatic weapon fire ripped jagged holes through the center of the metal door between the corridor and the bar, and blew out the lights in the hallway. Micky cowered against the wall of the tiny massage room, slamming the flimsy door shut while the bastard was still firing.

Far away, there was the sound of more sirens and gunfire.

So they still haven't been able to subdue the bastard's partner.

The room squeezed around her like a boa constrictor.

It was dark as pitch but she was certain that the walls were closing in. The ceiling was lowering. She bit her sleeve, gagging for air.

Now, I suppose I'll piss my pants.

Anger welled up, tempering the fear that bound her.

He still isn't through the damn door.

And he had to get into the room to kill her.

Well, not exactly.

The walls were paper-thin drywall, and the door into the massage room was a bargain-basement, hollow-core type. All the bastard really had to do was establish where she was and then blast right through the wall. She leaned on the tissue paper on the table and nearly fell off when it slid across the slick vinyl.

Setting the Glock on the tabletop, she moved to the far end of the room. The wall behind her seemed to be right against her back. The claustrophobia was driving her mad but her fear of the gunman and her growing anger buffered it. She bent and gripped the end of the table with both hands, wedging her knee against the rear wall.

The table gave an inch, scratching across the filthy floor.

The cry of the blasted metal door screeched against the tiles outside and echoed down the hallway.

The gunman was entering the corridor.

She took a shaky breath and tugged again.

The table gave another inch.

The metal door in the hall crashed, as though it had been kicked viciously.

Micky tugged harder.

The table gave a little more and she wedged her knee between it and the rear wall. Placing both hands on the top, she levered with her leg at the same time. The table crept along the wall enough for her to slip in sideways behind it. But not enough for her to crouch and hide. And it still didn't block the door.

She shoved with her legs, her hips, and both arms. The table slid a bit easier, just as one of the wooden doors crashed in down the hall.

She shoved harder. Another couple of inches.

But now she had less leverage.

Every jerking effort seemed barely able to move the table.

Another door crashed.

Almost there.

Another door shattered.

She eased down the wall, pressed both feet against the table, and using all her might, shoved it firmly against the door. She retrieved the Glock, then hunkered down with the table on her right side and the rear wall on her left.

Another door crashed in. Then another.

She was shaking all over. Again she slammed the hand

holding the Glock onto the floor but the shock treatment didn't work this time.

Another door.

She shivered with each crash.

Another.

Seven down.

One to go.

She rested both elbows on quivering knees and held her finger as light as possible on the trigger.

No problem.

But there was a problem.

She was losing it.

She was no longer in the massage parlor.

She was starting to see things in the darkness.

And she could smell flowers.

Mums and roses. And the chemical odor of the extender they put in vases to make the blooms last longer. The gunfire outside was dulling, getting farther and farther away again.

Micky wasn't certain anymore if she was a Houston cop or a sixteen-year-old girl.

The gunman was so close she could hear his rasping breath through the thin door.

But she was no longer sure if the man on the other side of the door was a homicidal maniac clad in black body armor or an eighteen-year-old kid with a pump shotgun, ski mask, and mirror sunglasses.

She wasn't functioning as a cop.

She was barely able to function as a human being.

The jittering sound of the doorknob being tested and the door rattling against the heavy table echoed in the stripped-down room. Then ominous silence . . .

Gunfire tore through the corridor wall and needles of sunlight pierced the back of the room as bullets chewed through the Sheetrock. Micky stared at the tiny beams of light and wondered why the builder had chosen wood here and not concrete.

But, miraculously, the multiple layers of the steel table deflected any stray bullets from her. She ducked her head down between her legs, keeping the Glock pointed forward.

No problem.

It's the black-suited man.

It isn't the kid.
The kid's gone.
Maybe he's back.
The kid was never caught, never brought to justice.
What if this is him?
What if he came back for me?
If they couldn't stop him the first time, how are they go-
ing to stop him now?

The firing ceased, the remains of the door crunched against the table again. The table moved a millimeter. She leaned against it, pressing her full weight toward the door.

Something rattled on the corridor floor.

Another clip. Maybe the bastard was out of ammo.

Snick.

The sound of another clip ramming home.

Cachack.

The bolt slamming shut.

She jerked as more holes blossomed in the wall inches from her elbow. Dust from disintegrated drywall and insulation and siding filtered across the room, making the shafts of sunlight look like high noon in an old Peckinpah Western. To her right Micky heard the sickening crash of breaking timbers.

The bastard's using the gun to blast his way right
through the fucking wall.

Outside, tires squealed. The cops must have discovered that they had lost one of the perps and figured out where he was. But she had no hope now that any of them would get to her in time. They didn't know where she was and they were just as likely to kill her, firing through the back wall. She tried to scrunch down even more but she was as small as she could get.

Pistol and shotgun fire erupted down the corridor.

The machine pistol answered.

My God! Are the cops inside the bar?

Two-by-fours shattered as the gunman burst through, into the cubicle. He was only a couple of feet from her, firing out into the corridor.

She knew what she had to do.

She hurled herself up over the top of the table.

The hulk looked more like a gorilla than a man in the thickly quilted body armor.

The room overflowed with sound and dust, the odor of

gypsum and old sex and gunpowder and sweat. The space swelled around her where before it had been constricting, crushing her in its stifling embrace. The entire building seemed near to bursting, unable to contain so much violence.

She had to leap up and get her hands around the bastard's head. Had to expose something vital. As it was, the man was impregnable. She had to rip his helmet off, press the Glock against his neck, and blow his fucking brains out.

Unaccountably she found herself staring at her knees, right in front of her face.

But I'm standing.

Aren't I?

No.

She wasn't.

She had only been imagining leaping up and attacking the man.

But it was a good plan!

Yes. It was.

Unfortunately her body wasn't in agreement.

The Glock nestled in her hands, resting on top of her knees. She could just see the back of the man's helmet now, over the tabletop. Sooner or later he was going to turn around and spot her. Or the cops outside were going to start blasting through the back wall.

Either way, I'm dead.

Get up!

Get up and do something!

Now!

While his back is turned.

Her mind raced but her body was a shivering mass of jelly.

She *had* pissed her pants.

Embarrassing warmth coated her bottom.

The acrid odor of urine assaulted her nostrils.

The gunman moved toward the back of the cubicle. Toward her. The table provided less and less cover. She could see the man's shoulders and torso as he stepped directly in front of her. She tried to squeeze the trigger but even her trigger finger was paralyzed with fear.

No problem.

A shotgun roared in the corridor and insulation and bits

of suspended ceiling showered over her in slow-motion snow.

She jerked and the pistol fired.

The sudden movement and noise jolted her out of her paralysis and she pumped off shot after shot. The bullets didn't penetrate the padding, but the bastard was knocked off-balance, shuddering against the wall.

But she was running out of bullets.

She had only a split second to live.

When her firing pin clicked on an empty chamber, she dropped the pistol between her legs and sat still, tears on her cheeks, blood on her face, piss on her butt, and fear and hatred welling in her chest.

The man shook himself off and twisted toward her.

For the first time she saw a face behind the bulletproof plastic helmet and the eyes that focused on Micky would haunt her forever.

There was nothing in them.

They were the same lifeless eyes she had first seen on her sixteenth birthday. She remembered staring into her attacker's mirror sunglasses, waiting for the bastard to pull the trigger. She had been lucky that day. The ski-masked killer hadn't seen her through the louvered door where she cringed in the tiny storage closet. She could never forget the painful feel of the rough terra-cotta pots pressing into her back. The knowledge that the slightest movement from her would cause them to sound against each other in one of their back-shiver grating noises.

But now her luck had run out.

The snub-nosed barrel of the black machine pistol swiveled in her direction.

The nasty hammer of automatic weapons fire erupted.

But it wasn't coming from in front of her.

It was tearing more glimmering holes through the rear wall of the room.

The bullets drove the man toward the corridor. He looked as though someone had slapped him on the back.

He turned toward the rear wall, ignoring Micky, as though she were already dead.

The gun bucked in his hand, ratcheting out a three-second burst that emptied the magazine again.

She knew that this was her last chance.

But all she could do was sit stupidly, watching the man reach for another clip.

Waiting her turn in front of the killing machine.

He slapped at the back of his suit with his free hand, looking like a big old bear, trying to brush away a swarm of angry bees. She realized that he was fumbling for another magazine and the only one left was strapped on his shoulder just an inch out of his reach. Until he could free it, he couldn't reload.

It's now or never.

She sucked in a breath as dry as desert cobwebs and tried to shake off the fear that was paralyzing her.

A giant of a uniformed cop burst out of the corridor and landed on top of the man like a cougar dropping on a sheep. Then another. The gunman was powerful and probably hopped up on drugs, but he was encumbered by the unwieldy suit. The two officers pinned him between the table and the wall, struggling to rip the helmet off his head. One of them turned to her and the shock on his face was almost humorous but he quickly went back to subduing the man.

It was over so fast that Micky was still sitting frozen in place after the gunman was led handcuffed from the bar. One of the officers stayed with her until the paramedics arrived.

No problem.

She managed to walk out with the medic's help; into the daylight.

Past the dead dancer.

Past the wrecked cruiser.

They hurried her by that, though she couldn't help but notice that Wade's hand was still sticking out of the window.

But as the blazing sun burned her eyes, she wasn't seeing Wade or the girl or the scene of violence and confusion out front.

All she saw was empty, lifeless eyes.

HOUSTON, JULY 26

THE MAN WAS TALL and whipcord thin and his skin was weathered from the sun. But only his white hair revealed his years. He wore faded jeans and worn boots. An oval silver buckle the size of his fist graced his belt. "There's an armed guard in the corridor."

Micky stared at the suspended ceiling of her hospital room.

A bullet had passed through her shoulder, just missing the collarbone. She'd gotten that wound at the same time the dancer was shot. Another bullet had creased her cheek and her doctor said she'd have a hairline scar. She had a slipped disc, three broken ribs, and a concussion.

"They had armor-piercing shells," she said.

"So does the guard."

She turned on the pillow.

"I checked," said the big man.

"I don't know what to do now, Uncle Jim," she whispered. He took her hand.

"First we get you out of here. Then you come back home. We'll figure it out from there."

"It was the same man," she said, turning back to the ceiling.

"Who?"

"The same man who killed my parents."

He squeezed her hand. "That was a long time ago, sweetheart."

"I don't know what to do," she repeated.

Silence hung in the room. Micky knew that Jim would stand like that, holding her hand forever if she needed him to.

A nurse clattered a tray onto the bedside table and glanced meaningfully at Jim.

"I think she's here to give you something," he said.

"Wade said I was like one of my stained-glass pieces. He said he wanted to hang me on the wall."

"Wade loved you," said Jim.

The nurse withdrew clear liquid from a vial, then inserted the hypodermic into a plastic valve in Micky's IV.

"You're all I've got," said Micky.

Jim squeezed harder.

When she awakened, Jim was smiling down at her and she wondered whether she had only dozed briefly or if he had left and returned. The sun blazed through the thin curtains behind him.

"There's someone here to see you," he said.

She turned her head.

Damon Kress stood on the other side of the bed, his big hands resting on the stainless-steel rail. He had a two-day growth of blond beard. His icy blue eyes were bloodshot.

"I came as soon as I heard," he said.

The sight of Damon shattered her defenses. Tears welled in her eyes and she choked down a sob. "Wade . . ."

"It's all right," Damon said, bending to stroke her cheek. "Jim told me what happened."

"I couldn't do anything. I just ran."

"I know," said Damon, leaning to kiss her cheek. "There was nothing you could do. Don't beat yourself up."

"You don't understand," she said, turning away. But Jim was there. There was nowhere to hide.

"I'll leave you two alone," said Jim.

When he was gone, Micky forced herself to look at Damon. She and Damon had met the year Micky joined the force. Micky had to testify in a murder case and Damon, as a psychologist, was called on as an expert witness for the defense. Even though they were on opposite sides of the fence, initially Micky and Damon had been attracted to each other. But they quickly realized that their personalities were too different. Damon was driven, goal oriented, and ambitious, while Micky tended to be more introspective and undecided about any future beyond her job.

Still, Damon had been the person she turned to when she began having nightmares about her parent's death again. Damon had treated her confidentially and with the kindness of a friend, not a doctor. The nightmares became fewer. Less intense.

She told him they were gone.

Damon had made a name for himself after that, working with severely disturbed patients. Micky sometimes wondered if her own past ever intruded on his diagnoses. But she and Damon had a long-standing pact.

Damon never mentioned her past.

His days of analyzing her were over.

"I don't have to understand," said Damon. "It's me. Remember?"

"I haven't seen you in a while," she said, at last.

"Been traveling again," he said.

"Doing?"

"Working with severely disturbed patients mostly." His frown was more in his eyes than on his lips. Damon was eight years older than her. But she had never noticed his age before.

"That's me," said Micky.

"They haven't locked you up yet."

"Maybe they should."

Silence hung over them.

"The patients inside are there for a reason, Micky. Believe me, you don't belong there." His voice was cold, withdrawn. His face suddenly ashen.

"What's the matter, Damon?"

"A lot of things happened, Mick. None of them good. When you do the kind of work I do you start to get a little hard, that's all."

"You were never hard."

"People get hurt when they're locked up. More than they already were. Let's talk about you."

"Let's not."

"You're not going to get crazy on me, are you?"

"I thought you head doctors didn't like that word."

"We use it among friends." He tried smiling again.

A bedpan hit the floor in the corridor.

Jim glanced in, shaking his head. He closed the door.

"I can't think straight, Damon."

"Are you all right?"

"I'm not going to kill myself."

"Promise?"

He leaned down until she had to look directly into his eyes. His face was more chiseled than she remembered it, cheekbones closer to the surface. But it looked good on him. He was getting better with age.

"Promise?" he repeated.

"I promise."

"Good. Want something to drink? There's some water." He nodded toward the blue-plastic pitcher.

She shook her head. "Are you going to keep working with your patients?"

"I thought we were talking about you."

"I'm changing the subject."

"I don't have patients, per se. I consult. I have consultations. One of them was about a man named Melrose, in Cordelia, Mississippi. He tried to commit suicide with a dinner spoon."

She winced.

"That was the good one," he said.

"There were worse?"

"Vegler."

"Oh, my God," she said. Martin Vegler had started splashing the headlines across the country three months ago. He was a quiet, unassuming man who lived in a suburb of Chicago. None of his neighbors knew him at all but they seemed genuinely surprised to discover that the innocent-looking little guy had twenty-two bodies neatly buried beneath his crawl space.

"How did you end up with him?"

"I was hired by his attorneys."

She frowned. "To say he was insane? So he could get off?"

"Basically."

"And did you?"

"I quit."

"Good."

"It takes something out of you. Just being around someone like Vegler." He poured himself a plastic cup of water and took his time drinking.

"I wish you wouldn't work with people like that. You aren't the kind of person who can deal with things like that and not be hurt by them."

There was an unfamiliar edge to his voice. "And you are?"

"You have too much heart," she said. "Even if you don't show it."

He sneered.

"I don't know if that was ever true, Micky. It isn't now."

"You can't do anything for people like that. You've said so yourself."

"I don't think I can help a man like Vegler. But if someone had seen it coming earlier, they might have controlled his episodes."

"Controlled? You believe that?"

Damon shrugged. "I don't know what I believe anymore." His eyes were distant, his face harder than she had ever seen it.

"Some things nobody should experience."

Damon's face softened. "You're going to move in with Jim. Right?"

"I guess. For a while."

"Good. It'll kill him if you don't."

She shut her eyes.

"Sorry," said Damon. "I shouldn't have put it like that."

"I just feel lost."

"You aren't lost. I found you."

Damon was there every day for the six weeks that she was hospitalized. He visited her at Jim's every day for three weeks after that. Micky still wore a bandage on her shoulder but the wound was healing. Her back was getting better too.

But not her heart.

She didn't cry every day. Not so anyone could see. And she didn't walk around bumping into walls anymore. She supposed that was an improvement. She was getting better at covering up her grief again.

One day she and Damon sat on the veranda, not speaking, watching Jim tend the horses.

"Don't you need to be back to work?" she asked. The

sun had fled and storm clouds climbed to impossible heights over flat expanse of Texas prairie.

"One of the few benefits of being a consulting psychologist," said Damon, studying the thunderheads. "I come and go as I choose."

"So you're independently wealthy now."

"Like the Kennedys."

"Seriously."

A frown replaced his usual smile. "I'm kind of in flux right now."

"In flux? What the hell does that mean?"

"I don't want to leave you."

"I'm all right."

"Is that why you carry your gun around with you?" The Glock lay on the earthen tile, close at hand between them.

Micky refused to follow Damon's eyes to the pistol.

"Is that why you haven't left this house in three weeks?" he said.

"I'll leave when I'm ready."

"Jim says the police department offered to put you back on limited duty."

"A desk job."

"A desk job might be what you need."

"Don't patronize me."

"I'm not patronizing. I'm trying to be a friend."

"If you're my friend, then tell me why you're giving up on yourself."

"Is this an argument?"

"Sure," she said, smiling. "Let's argue. Now tell me why you're not working. You used to love your work."

"I did," he agreed. "I don't anymore. I need something I can *lock* onto. I just don't have any idea what it might be right now."

"Why do you want something else?"

"Because a psychologist has to tell the truth. And the truth doesn't set you free. Not anymore. The truth will kill you."

His face had a hard edge she'd never seen before; his eyes stared out at something in the distance she couldn't see. "I used to think that people cared about one another. Now I don't. Is that explanation enough?"

She laid her hand on his arm. "I care about you. You care

about me. Jim cares about both of us. He loves us. You know that."

"Yeah. There's Jim."

"Knock it off," she said. "You're turning maudlin in your youth."

"Two cripples," he said, turning at last to smile at her. "And we can't even heal each other."

"You need to get back on your horse."

"So do you."

"No," she said. "Not yet."

"Well," said Damon, rising. "We sit here talking of horses and Jim does all the work."

She watched him saunter out to the corral and she wondered what she had missed in the conversation. Damon's wounds seemed as deep as her own but, like her, he didn't want to discuss them. Maybe their friendship was more hindrance than help. They were so accustomed to each other's long silences that neither of them could open up and release their grief in front of the other. And in a strange way, Damon's feelings irritated Micky. They intruded on her pain. How dare he be enduring his own pangs when she was the one who had suffered?

She picked up the Glock and went back into the house as the first raindrops splattered on the patio.

"You got a letter from Damon," Jim shouted from the hall

Micky rushed to meet him. Jim wore a cockeyed smile, holding the envelope out at arm's length, teasing.

"Give it to me!"

"Thought you didn't miss him."

She and Damon had continued their fight that final day and it had gone from hurtful banter to something darker. Something that had never risen between them before. It was as if their feelings for each other were forcing them apart. Damon walked out and she hadn't heard a word from him in six months.

She snatched the letter from Jim's hands and ripped it open.

Mick,

I know you're sorry for everything you said to hurt

me. I'm sure you're abject. (Look it up.) So I'm writing to tell you that all is well.

Better than well.

I think I found what I was looking for. And you won't believe where.

Alaska.

A friend of a friend had a brother who knew an old man who used to live way up in the mountains. The friend talked me into renting the old man's cabin here for a couple of weeks. The weeks ran into months. I ended up buying the cabin. Now I'm thinking of staying here.

Alaska? God's Icebox? you're saying to yourself.

But McRay's the most gorgeous spot on earth. Moose the size of elephants wander around here like they own the place. (I guess they do, come to think of it.)

I would have called. But I was too embarrassed. I'm sorry we fought. I've had a long time to sit all alone and think about just what that fight meant. Being alone sucks. You're the only real friend I've ever had.

I know you, Mick. I've been thinking a lot about this, so listen up and see what kind of mind reader I am.

You aren't back to work. Are you?

You're still living with Jim. Right?

You say you're better but you know you're not.

How am I doing?

Mick, come see me. Get off your ass and just do it. I'm not joking.

I'll call.

Love, Damon

Micky glanced over the letter at Jim.

"You've been talking to him," she scolded.

Jim smiled. "He told me not to tell you he'd called."

"Alaska?"

"Pretty damned cold, I guess."   •

"Pretty damned crazy," said Micky, slipping the letter back into the envelope. She headed back into the house.

Jim followed her. The living room was wide with a high-beamed ceiling. Buttery morning sunlight shone through the windows. Navajo rugs covered the tile floor and wood furniture gleamed darkly against the stucco walls. Micky dropped into a leather recliner, the letter in her lap.

"You need to do something." Jim sat on an ottoman at her feet.

"Alaska? What the hell is he doing in Alaska? Analyzing Eskimos?"

"Getting away from other people's problems for a while maybe."

"You think that's what I need? Alaska's not going to help me."

He shrugged. "You've moped long enough, girl. Grief is good. In its time. But what you have now isn't grief. It's a sickness."

"How can you say that?" After all she'd been through? How dare he?

"I can say it because it's true. Because I care about you. And because I'm getting old and I'm not going to be here forever. You can live here as long as you like. You know everything I have is going to you. But you can't hide here. Not anymore, Micky."

She couldn't believe it. Of all the people in the world that she trusted, Jim, she'd believed, would never betray her.

Now he was kicking her out?

Sending her to some wilderness?

"Alaska? Are you nuts too?"

"You're sick, Micky, and you won't get help. You don't listen to me or to Damon or your friends on the police force. You won't even talk to a doctor. You're always so damned determined you can handle everything. Micky Ascherfeld is too God-a-mighty tough to need help. Maybe you got that from me. If you did, then I'm sorry."

"I just need a little more time."

"Jesus Christ," said Jim, shaking his head. "Listen to yourself. I swear you make me want to slap you."

She couldn't believe what she was hearing. Jim had never lifted a hand to her, even during the worst of her teenage years.

He rose to his feet. "Damon's going to call. Talk to him. At least do that."

She nodded, shaken by Jim's seriousness.

But when he stopped in the doorway his face had softened.

"He sounds a lot better than when he left," he said. "I don't know what magic he found up there. But magic is what you need too."

"I need more than magic," she whispered after Jim had gone.

But the idea bubbled in her head all morning.

She had kept her problem to herself after her parents' murder. Even Wade had not been allowed to intrude on her grief beyond being there to comfort her in the night. Now Wade was gone but nothing had changed except the depth of her despair.

No one could help her before.

No one could help her now.

The phone rang and she waited for Jim to answer it as usual. But after eight rings she picked it up.

"Jim's out of the house," said Damon.

"You arranged that?"

"Cunning?"

"Machiavellian." It was like Damon. He had a way of getting what he wanted.

"How are you?" she asked.

"I'm fine."

"I liked your letter."

"Come see me."

"And live in an igloo?"

He laughed. "It's not like that at all. More like Switzerland. Without the assholes running around waking you up with those damned ten-foot horns all the time. Seriously though, Micky, you'd love it here."

"Freeze my ass off."

"Nah. It's weird. Not like Texas cold at all. You get used to it fast and you'll love the snow. You wouldn't believe what I've been doing."

"So tell me."

"Well, everybody here is holed up for the winter now. But I have been learning to pan for gold."

"Be serious."

"I *am* serious. There's an old-timer and a couple of middle-aged hippies here who pull the stuff right out of the streams. I've even filed my own claim. Like John Wayne in *North to Alaska*."

"Unbelievable."

"I love it here."

"You sound good."

"I *am* good."

"Who's this old-timer?"

"Aaron McRay," said Damon.

"Like the town?"

"Named after him. He lives way up by himself at the head of Sgagamash Creek. The story is he's spent most of his life poking around looking for a Lost Dutchman mine in the valley here. But you can't get anything out of Aaron. He's a real hermit. Hates everybody. But he's got a cabin for rent."

"Why does he have two cabins?"

"You'd have to meet the old coot. He moved out of his cabin down by the store and built another one so far up in the canyon light only comes in once a year probably. He doesn't much like people."

"So you're going to get rich," she said.

"It isn't about the money," said Damon.

"So what is it about?"

"It's hard to explain. Like I said, I have my own claim now. That kind of does something to you. Looking for the gold. Finding it."

She shook her head, smiling. If there was gold on his claim, then God help it. Damon never gave up on anything he set his mind to.

"And Marty and I are working on something," he said.

"Marty?"

"One of the miners. Marty and Stan. Wild pair."

"Break a leg," she said. "Or whatever you're supposed to say to a gold miner."

"Come up," he said. "This valley will make you better, Mick. The place is medicine."

"Maybe."

"Really?"

"Maybe," she repeated firmly.

"That other cabin is sitting empty. Just downstream from mine."

"I'll think about it."

"Say yes. Just for a visit."

"Yes. Just for a visit." She stared at the phone, wondering what had gotten into her. "I need to talk to Jim, though."

"I'll call again tomorrow."

By the time she hung up the phone she knew she was going and, in the end, she went.

She climbed onto the plane in Houston with the temperature outside hovering at eighty-five. The weather channel in the airport bar said snow for most of Alaska.

The landing in Anchorage was calm after a perfect flight over the mountains. The city was blanketed in white, surrounded by an ice-blue wilderness that looked as though an entire continent of malcontents could vanish into it and never be heard from again. The gray waters of Cook Inlet wove through the feet of the peaks. Beyond the outskirts of the city, there was little to prove the hand of man had ever touched the land.

When she stepped outside the airport, the below-zero temperature instantly burned her throat and stole her breath away. A friendly check-in agent had told her that there were no roads into McRay or anywhere remotely near it. He directed her to a local flying service, where she met Zeke Rasmussen.

Yes, Zeke told her, he could fly her into McRay. What in the devil's name did she want to do in McRay?

"Visit a friend."

Zeke laughed. Another crazy from outside. *Outside*, Micky quickly learned, was anywhere but Alaska. The other states—excluding Hawaii, which Alaskans considered more or less a half sister—were referred to condescendingly as the Lower Forty-Eight.

Zeke flew her into McRay in a big twin-engined Cessna. He informed her that the pink glow on the horizon was a snowstorm blowing in. A lot of snow. Micky couldn't understand how there could be much more. The ground below them looked like it would buckle under the weight of the towering drifts. If it snowed again, she was convinced the razor peaks would disappear and the entire state would become one soft white blanket. They roared over the Kuskokwim range, the arctic wind whipping the plane like dust in front of a broom.

Dropping through the high mountain pass, Zeke pointed below at a tiny puff of smoke and said, "That's McRay."

Beneath the plane, small clearings dotted the thick forest, which grew almost to the edge of the river. Tin roofs and tiny smoking chimneys betrayed the presence of cabins hidden in the woods. Suddenly they were over the impossibly short dirt strip.

But Zeke put the plane down on the runway with only a single bump. They coasted to a halt at the end of the strip and Zeke jumped out while the props were still spinning. He tossed wooden chocks under the wheels and unceremoniously pitched Micky's trunk and backpack onto the ground. Micky tightened the wolf-ruff parka around her face and pulled on her heavy mittens.

"Where's the terminal?"

"The what?" Zeke laughed.

"Where do I go?" she asked. The light was fading and the mountains seemed like something out of the remote, savage past. Zeke glanced anxiously over his shoulder toward the approaching storm.

"Where's your friend?" he shouted, over the plane's engines and the buffeting wind.

"I have no idea!" She stamped her feet, already chilled despite her winter boots.

Zeke nodded toward a track that twisted through the spruce trees at the end of the short runway. "Look for smoke."

He had to go, he told her. He couldn't get caught in the storm. He had only an hour of daylight left. She watched his plane disappear into the darkening clouds, listening as the wind drowned out the retreating engines

And just like that, she was alone.

It occurred to her then that she might die here on this landing strip and for all she knew it would be months before anyone found her. Maybe that was the one good thing that she had accomplished with this fool's errand. Maybe she was just going to freeze to death.

Where the hell is Damon?

Tire tracks that seemed too narrow for a Jeep or truck, meandered away into the trees.

She squared her shoulders and scooped up her backpack. There was nothing she could do about the trunk. She glanced up at the mountains already buried in cloud and started hiking.

Thirty yards into the trees a growling noise caught her attention and she froze. The Glock was stored away in the pack. But Zeke had informed her that the pistol was pretty much worthless where she was going, anyway. Nothing smaller than a .357 magnum had any chance of stopping a bear.

The Honda four-wheeler cleared the cusp of the hill before

she realized that what she was hearing wasn't in the least bear-like. It didn't dawn on her until later that no self-respecting, hibernating bear would be stupid enough to be out on a frigid day like this. The little vehicle looked like a cross between a motorcycle and a riding lawn mower but it bounced down the rough trail with the confidence of a mountain goat. The driver was going so fast that he couldn't stop and wheeled around Micky, coming to a halt facing back up the trail. Micky had a bewildered expression on her face when the driver flipped back his parka hood and offered a gloved hand. Micky reached across the handlebars and felt a small but powerful grip. She stared into the face and was surprised to discover the driver was a woman.

"Rita Cabel," said the driver, in a voice like steel wool. She had thick gray hair and bright blue eyes. Micky guessed her age at fifty but she might have been ten years older. When she climbed off the four-wheeler and tossed Micky's pack into the rear basket, she seemed closer to thirty. She moved with the easy grace of a younger woman.

"Get on," said Rita. "Unless you want to stay out here and freeze to death. Damon mentioned you'd be coming. I knew he'd forget."

"He forgot me?"

Rita laughed. "You must know how he gets if he's onto something. He and Marty cooked up some scheme to boil water in barrels and heat the ground around their claims by driving pipes into the ground and running steam through them."

Micky gave the woman a baffled look.

"They're digging up gravel that way so they can have it ready to run through the sluices when the creek thaws in the spring," said Rita.

Rita drove Micky up to the cabin Damon had rented for her from Aaron McRay. The place was small but tidy. Rita's husband, Clive, had a fire going in the stove and coffee in the pot. Rita educated Micky in the intricacies of wood heat and how to tuck pieces of old blankets on all the windowsills and under the doors to keep as much of the draft out as possible. Then Rita and Clive said their good-byes with the promise of a tour of the town the next day.

Micky locked the door behind them with the simple sliding latch. She listened to the giant hands of the wind, clawing at the eaves, trying to rip the roof off the cabin. She stared out into darkness so black that it was like being inside the middle of a giant squid and she shivered.

But the cabin was snug, the kerosene lamplight reassuring, and the roof didn't sound as though it had any intention of losing its battle with the wind. She climbed up into the loft and found that the old feather bed, though smelling of dust, was clean and quite comfortable.

She dug out the Glock, checked the chamber, and placed it beside her on the bed.

And she wondered, yawning, just how much farther from anything she could possibly be. She fell asleep thinking of Wade.

All the lanterns in the cabin burned brightly throughout that long arctic night.

MCRAY, FOUR YEARS LATER
MAY 2, 11:30 A.M.

MICKY LEANED OVER THE rough-hewn table that was the centerpiece of her log cabin, concentration furrowing her brow. She wore heavy gloves. The custom-made soldering iron, even with its thick ash handle, was hot and she'd been burned before. She molded the lead strip around the irregular-shaped pieces of glass, delicately fitting the soft metal into the space between the panes and stopping to slip in a piece of local quartz, polished by hand.

Her trademark.

The piece had been commissioned by a buyer in Anchorage. Micky wasn't expected to turn out an exact replica of what the owner wanted—an overhead view of salmon spawning—but an artist's rendition, and that was what the owner was getting.

She put the finishing touches to her soldering and studied the shards of glass remaining on the table. Several were cut to fit but never used. Others lay farther from her hand, different shades and variations of the swirling interior colors, uncut, in case she chose to replace one of the pieces. One lay by itself, exiled. Its hue and the distinct coloration had been exactly what she wanted.

It irritated her that she had not been paying attention when she cut it.

Usually a piece of glass broke along the fault lines created with the scribe or allowed itself to be nibbled with her special cutting pliers. But sometimes, for myriad reasons—pressure of the tool, inconsistent force from her hands, or just the unpredictable obstinacy of an inanimate object—the glass would not break cleanly. Instead, it fractured through the layer of glass itself, creating microthin, jagged edges that were sharper than razors.

She called pieces like that scalpel glass.

She'd recut it and use it somewhere else.

The spring light through her windows was perfect for stained-glass work. In early May the sun hung over the Kuskokwim Mountains like a light peeking over the top of a miner's helmet, shining golden onto her table. Although at this time of year the sun came up officially sometime after five in the morning and didn't set until ten at night, the high, snowcapped mountains on three sides bathed McRay in almost perpetual twilight.

In the bush, the light and the weather were king.

Although spring was capable of flooding the narrow valley with verdant life, it was just as likely to bury it under a sudden snow squall or flood the plains below with weeks of torrential rain that turned the wide, placid, Kuskokwim River into a snarling deluge of ferocious power. Snow could bury the mountains in a night and then the next day the sun and warm Chinook winds could melt it all. Or send it roaring downhill in deadly destructive avalanches that ripped gaping wounds in the forest.

Outside, jays screeched at the ravens, fighting over the leavings of last night's dinner. Micky knew she shouldn't be throwing food so close to the cabin. But the birds were so thick this time of year that they'd clean up every scrap before a grizzly could get wind of it. Besides, the big bruisers were just starting to come out.

There was a scratching cry as one of the birds chased another away from its food, and then silence.

It was as though the entire world had taken a deep breath.

She rested both hands on the table and waited for the birds to begin squabbling again.

It had taken her a long time to become accustomed to the

silence in McRay. There was a world of difference between hearing the traffic outside your bedroom window and listening to the low soughing of a night wind under your eave. Of being accustomed to the wail of sirens and hearing nothing more for hours on end than a willow ptarmigan flapping through the brush.

Was it even quieter than usual?

It was four years since Houston. The temperature range was an average of sixty degrees lower and the population was a few million less.

But it was the quiet that had taken the most getting used to.

Micky finished fitting the stone and set the iron back down in the coals of the woodstove. The window was finished. Of course there were always areas to improve. She would keep retouching and polishing forever if she didn't force herself to say enough. Over the past weeks she had removed and replaced dozens of pieces of glass, searching for just the right balance of color and light. Chasing the perfection she saw only in her head.

But Cary at the Mendenhall Gallery was getting antsy. Clive Cabel had stopped by yesterday with a phone message from her. The gallery owner wanted the piece on the next mail plane and that would be coming in around five o'clock. But occasionally Rich was early.

She walked around the table, studying the stained-glass window.

It wasn't perfect.

But they never were.

She could almost see something good in the piece.

Something magical.

If she removed this piece of glass and replaced that one. If she reshaped that corner. If she made the work less a depiction of fish and more a study of light and shade . . .

She pulled her hand away.

She glanced at the crate in the corner and made up her mind. Time to pack it up.

You can't hold on to your babies forever.

By the time she had the window safely stored in the wooden crate it was almost lunchtime and her stomach was starting to grumble. She pulled a can of milk down from the shelf over the woodstove and poured a bowl of granola. She opened a can of butter—one of those odd, long-shelf-life foodstuffs that bush villagers accepted as standard fare—smeared a generous helping on the biscuits left over from last night's dinner, and carried the meal over to the table, pulling up a three-legged stool.

Her cabin was comfortable, with one large living area downstairs and an open sleeping loft above, without being too big for her to take care of. When she moved in, it had three large fixed windows and she had spent much of her first summer creating and installing three more stained-glass ones. The window in the loft opened to allow cross ventilation between it and the front and rear doors. The doors themselves were massive affairs with black, hand-wrought iron hinges and locks and hand-carved spruce planks with X-braced interiors.

She glanced around the cabin and thought of Houston.

Has it really been four years already?

McRay was home to her now. It seemed as though she had stepped out of Zeke's plane that day and found not a strange, unfamiliar land, but a refuge.

Outside, the jays were screaming their heads off again.

12:00

Dawn Glorianus stared at their wet clothing, laid out on grass still brown from winter. The clearing on this side of their cabin was covered with a patchwork lawn. Her mother insisted that the washing smelled better if it dried that way rather than on a line.

Snow circled the spruce trees around the cabin where the bases of the big conifers were shaded from the sun. The temperature was barely in the fifties. But it was warm enough for Dawn's mother, Terry, to decide that it was time for spring cleaning. Every item of winter gear, every blanket, every pair of long johns, every sock was washed clean by hand in the big galvanized tub that doubled as their bath.

Terry knelt over the frothy water, sliding a sheet up and down the washboard, her shoulders heaving. Dawn glanced at the handkerchief in her own right hand. Terry had finished washing it but Dawn didn't know where to put it yet. And she was more concerned with her mother's anger. When Terry got in one her moods, there was no sense talking to her. Dawn knew that she had incited Terry's wrath even if Dawn didn't think it was her fault.

Dawn hated McRay.

In McRay, people lived like animals. They did dumb things like washing their clothes in a tub. Stupid things, like putting them on the lawn to dry. Even though the temperature would drop to freezing the second the sun dipped over the mountains. Even though the clothes would all be frozen solid in the morning, anyway. In McRay you got your schooling through the mail. And if you ever had any notion of meeting a boy, you could just forget it.

Dawn didn't know much about how her counterparts lived, Outside. But she was pretty sure from her voluminous reading that they met people of the opposite sex, had things called dates, and did other wonderful things that she was still two long years away from getting to experience.

As soon as she turned eighteen, on that very day, McRay, Alaska, would be history.

But all Dawn had said, this time, was that she was old enough to fly into Anchorage by herself. She didn't need to be chaperoned on a yearly shopping trip. She could stay with her pen pal, Judith.

That was all Terry needed to hear. She blew up. Just as Dawn was afraid that she would.

But for Terry a blowup wasn't like a temper tantrum for the normal parent. Terry didn't scream or throw things. She didn't stomp around their cabin and slap her hands against her sides or sit and slowly heat up like a tea kettle.

Terry *cleaned*.

She swept the floor until bristles snapped off the broom. Then she mopped.

She slopped scalding water onto the bare floorboards and swung the mop like it was a hockey stick until soap suds clung to the walls.

She pulled every plate and pot out of the cupboards and dusted them *and* the cabinets.

She polished the inside of their two windows until Dawn was sure she'd wipe the glass right out of the frames. Then she went outside and scrubbed the other side of the windows.

And then she started washing clothes.

She hauled bucket after bucket up from the North Fork, heating them over the glowing woodstove that made it too uncomfortable to stay inside the cabin. She kept two buckets heating on the stove as she beat piece after piece of clothing and linens to death against the washboard.

But Dawn knew that Terry was cooling off now. Pretty soon the spring inside her that was all wound up would wind down, and then she'd be able to talk almost like a normal human being again.

Terry wiped her forehead with the damp sleeve of her calico shirt. Her shoulders sagged. When she dropped back onto her haunches and rested her hands on the tub, Dawn approached her quietly.

"I'm sorry, Mom," she said.

Terry turned slowly and looked up into her daughter's dark eyes. Dawn stood motionless under her mother's inspection. There was love on Terry's face.

Love.

Anguish.

Fear.

And something else.

Something too terrifying for Dawn to want to try to understand.

Terry stood and wiped her hands on her jeans. They were chapped, worn hands. But the fingers were long and delicate. She was still a beautiful woman and Dawn had inherited her good looks from both sides of the family. A winning smile and lanky build from her father. High cheekbones and dark hair from her mother.

"You don't know what it's like out there, honey," said Terry. "They killed your father."

Dawn didn't want to fight the same old battle. There was no argument that would convince her mother that there was no *they*. That her father had been killed by a crazy act of violence. He'd been an innocent bystander, shot in a holdup. It could have happened to anyone.

"When I'm eighteen I'm going to leave," said Dawn.

"I can't stop you."

"But you won't come," said Dawn. She didn't want to leave her mother. She just wanted to get the hell out of McRay.

"No," said Terry, looking around the small clearing, at the high peaks, at the azure sky that had no match anywhere else in the world. "No. This is where I live."

"You can't hide from the world, Mom," said Dawn.

"Yes, you can." Terry bent to heave the soapy water out

onto the ground. Dawn watched it form a rivulet then seep into the soggy soil, like blood into a bandage.

"People die out here, too," said Dawn. But she had no proof of that. No one had died in McRay in her lifetime.

A jay leaped from its perch in a dead spruce and screamed away, angry. Terry and Dawn watched it go. Boots crunched on the trail that led along the creek and Dawn knew immediately who it was. El Hoskins.

She turned away, acting as though she hadn't heard, and slipped behind the cabin. She didn't like El and didn't want to have to be polite to him. Terry had told her on numerous occasions that she needed to act friendlier. El was their neighbor and he had always treated both of them with respect. But there was just something about El that always gave Dawn the creeps. The way he insisted on being called *Eldred* for one thing even though everyone in town called him El behind his back. Everyone except for Dawn's mother.

She heard her mother say hi and, to Dawn's dismay, El replied. He wasn't continuing down the trail. He was stopping to talk.

Great.

Dawn slumped against the logs of the cabin, twisting the wet handkerchief in her hands. The rough bark jabbed her back and she scrunched around, getting comfortable.

"Going to the store?" asked Terry.

"Mmm," said El. Dawn could hear his boots, closer now, crunching in the gravel outside the cabin door.

"Nice day for it," said Terry.

"Mmm," said El. That was another one of the things that drove Dawn crazy, the way he talked. You had to drag words out of him. That and those stupid sunglasses he wore all the time. He looked like a janitor trying to look like a movie star. He was skinny and tall and his shirts were always pulling out of the back of his pants.

Dawn knew without sneaking a peek that he had that big .44 magnum pistol on his hip. The gun looked like it would weigh him down enough to flip him over. He always walked with his hand on it as though he was ready to do a quick draw.

Dawn had overheard Stan Herbst and Marty Kiley making fun of El one day down at Cabels' Store. But her mother had shaken her head and pulled her away from the conversation.

"He's a nice man," Terry had said. "But I wish he wouldn't carry that gun. It makes me nervous."

"All guns make you nervous," Dawn replied.

"You're right," said Terry. "But I guess people need them here. Not like in the city."

But Dawn didn't think El carried the gun for protection. She figured he carried it for show. She'd seen him down at the store, watching himself in the window when he didn't know anyone else was looking.

"Could I have a cup of coffee?"

El's question shook Dawn out of her reverie.

Coffee?

El had never been in their house before. Never been invited.

Now he's inviting himself in?

Terry took a minute answering.

"Sure, Eldred," she said. "You all right?"

"Mmm," said El.

Dawn peeked around the corner. Her mother peered at El curiously but he just stared through her with those stupid mirror glasses. Terry headed into the house. El glanced around and almost spotted Dawn, but she jerked back.

"Where's your daughter?" he said.

Terry's answer was muffled by the thick, bark-sided logs. A pot clanged on the stove. There was another stretch of silence and then the bang of another pot hitting the floor.

What the hell?

Terry's scream sliced the air like scissors slashing thick cloth. At the sound, Dawn raced around the corner of the house toward the door. It was darker inside and the figures seemed more silhouettes than real people.

Her mother screamed again.

Another pot hit the floor. Then another.

But they weren't falling from the cabinets.

They were being ripped out of them.

A terrible clamor erupted as Terry clawed the last of the pots and dishware out of the cupboards. She wasn't screaming now. The noise that made its way out of her mouth was a throaty gurgle that terrified Dawn.

Terry must have turned to get the coffee from the canister and El had pulled the big hunting knife that he wore in the sheath on his boot.

As Dawn watched, paralyzed, El brought the knife up again, and then again, plunging it down so deep between Terry's shoulder blades the hilt hit her bloody shirt. Each time he had to lean his elbow against her back to lever it out of her flesh.

Terry's head sagged forward and she slumped over the counter as he continued to stab her limp body, following it down until he was on his knees above her. The blood pooled so wide and thick on the floor that Dawn thought it would never stop. That it would run in a river past her feet and turn the Fork itself crimson.

Terry's face was twisted toward the door. Dawn was riveted by her mother's eyes and her strangely calm expression. Dawn had anticipated surprise. Something like this was surely the last thing her mother expected to happen in McRay.

No one ever died here.

El fumbled, trying to wrench the knife out again. Another horrible guttural noise bubbled from Terry's lips, and Dawn gasped. El spun. He was an alien, with a humanoid face and giant glassine eyes.

Dawn couldn't comprehend what was happening. Couldn't figure out how to get her body to listen to her mind. Her mind kept screaming for her to run. But she couldn't move.

El struggled to his feet, leaving the giant knife pinning her mother to the floor.

He whipped the huge black Ruger out of its holster and pointed it at her.

She backed away two steps but she was still looking down the barrel of the gun that seemed large enough for her to crawl into.

She wondered if she would see the huge gray bullet coming at her eyes.

12:10

MICKY STOOD ON HER front stoop, staring at the trail that forked in her front yard. One path led directly through the woods to Cabels' Store. The other followed the creek, from the store all the way up the valley to Aaron McRay's cabin.

Creek or woods?

She was in a hurry. Clive might be busy and she wanted to be certain he could make time to pick up the crate.

She chose the woods.

But she had hardly started down the trail when a high-pitched screech stopped her. It sounded for all the world like a woman screaming. Micky listened for a moment but heard nothing more. She wrote the sound off to the crying of a jay.

Then the *pop pop* of two muted gunshots stopped her again. The shots had come from across the creek. She turned in that direction.

Either Stan or Marty had hit a find. They always fired their rifles when they did.

Their claims and Damon's ran along three hundred yards of the South Fork and they had four different sluices set up there, long washboard affairs where they had diverted part of the stream.

Damon's claim was just this side of Marty and Stan's. But it wasn't Damon shooting. He hadn't worked on his claim since the year before. And Damon hated guns. His experience with violence was mostly secondhand. But it had scared him, nonetheless.

In the four years since she'd moved to McRay, Damon had spoken less and less of the experiences that had driven him to leave his profession. But she understood the internal pressures that had forced him into the life change. And she understood why he didn't want to have anything to do with guns. Vegler had killed his victims with a .22 rifle.

Micky had spent a day with Damon and Marty and Stan the past summer. Marty tried to teach her the intricacies of placer mining. He looked like a Tolkien dwarf, with his tangled beard and bushy gray brows. His shoulders were broad from years of hard work. Stan always said that Marty should smoke a long thin pipe, like Gandalf. But Marty was strong as a horse.

"You shovel it up and you dump it in," Marty had said, doing just that. "Why don't you show the lady?" He gave Stan a look that said maybe Stan could do more with his shovel than lean on it.

Stan stalked off toward the other sluice box.

The gravel skittered down the washboard bottom of the sluice. The heaviest rocks and debris dropped between the ridges.

"Gold is heavier than anything," Marty told her, picking out the larger pebbles and tossing them aside. She leaned over to see. Bright specks of gold gleamed through the icy water.

Damon was across the stream, fiddling with a hose on Marty's old diesel-powered pump.

"What's he doing?" she'd asked Marty.

"We use that to wash the gravel down off the slopes and into that sluice box over there." Marty pointed to a spot along the stream below Damon. "But the damn pump breaks down all the time. Not worth the effort."

"Damon will get it running."

Marty laughed, running a hand across his bald scalp. "He would. But he don't put in the time up here he used to."

"Why not?"

"Damon's getting the bug."

"The bug?"

"Starting to look for *The Mine*."

"Not Aaron's mine?"

"The same."

"Damon told me it was a myth."

"He don't believe that anymore. He thinks it's real."

"You're kidding."

"You know Damon."

"Oh, Jesus," she muttered.

"He'll get over it," said Marty.

"You haven't known him long enough."

"Maybe you're right," agreed Marty, grinning.

Suddenly a loud cursing rattled out from beneath Stan's sluice. Micky and Marty rushed over and leaned under the support braces to give Stan a hand. He'd slipped on the loose gravel and slid down the slope and managed to snap the shovel handle at the same time. Marty shook his head as Stan dusted himself off.

"Damn shovels are made in Taiwan," muttered Stan.

"I never seen anyone break more tools than you," said Marty, spitting.

"I think I got another one in my shed," said Stan.

"Like hell you do. You're just going to go sit on your ass."

"You got no call to talk to me like that."

"Stan, you're the laziest bastard I know," said Marty, winking at Micky, who had begun to get a little nervous. "You stay here and try to make yourself useful if that's possible. I have another shovel in the cache down by the Fork."

Marty hiked off downtrail and Stan made a ceremony of filling his pipe. When he finally got it lit great puffs of smoke billowed around him.

"You like it here?" asked Stan.

"Yes," said Micky.

Stan chewed the pipe and nodded knowingly. "Nice place to ruminate."

"Ruminate?"

"That means to cogitate. Or muse."

"I knew that," said Micky.

"Nice place to do it."

"I suppose it is." Unlike Marty, who was a what you see is what you get type, Stan bewildered her. Was he trying to impress her with his vocabulary? Or was he serious?

"Sometimes I can stand for hours and stare at the mountains," he said.

"They're pretty."

"Drives Marty crazy."

"I guess it would."

"That's part of the beauty," said Stan.

Damon had laid the hose parts down between his thighs and was staring up into the mountains himself. He had his hands on his hips. Silhouetted by the sun, he looked like a bronze statue.

"Damon told me that hard-rock mining wasn't worth a person's time," she said.

Stan picked up Marty's shovel and tossed a half spadeful of gravel into the sluice. "It ain't, mostly. Not unless you're a big company. Takes a lot of heavy equipment."

"Then why waste your time looking for a gold mine?"

"Well, if you find the mother lode, it's worth a fortune. I've seen a slice of gold as thick as your little finger wedged between two pieces of quartz. A man finds a vein like that, the equipment cost don't really matter. But it isn't the gold."

"What do you mean?"

"People like Damon. And Aaron. When they get it into their head to find that vein, it isn't the money. It's the *finding*."

Micky stared at Damon's back, his body set against the mountains, every bit as unyielding. And she knew exactly what Stan meant.

"Jesus," she muttered again.

She smiled, remembering Stan's pleasure when he'd pulled a dime-sized nugget out of Marty's sluice.

He wouldn't admit it.

But it was the finding with him and Marty too.

She hiked on. Away from the sound of the gun.

12:15

"COME ON, DAWN," SAID EL.

He was standing on Terry's clean laundry. Blood splotched his shirt and his pants and there was enough on his boots that he left partial red footprints on the damp sheets.

"You can't run through the bushes. There's nowhere to go."

He strode across the laundry, kicking it away as a towel stuck to his foot. He stood in the center of the path, staring down into the alders on both sides of the stream. There was just enough of an opening in the trees there to allow Terry and Dawn to gather water.

Dawn had raced straightaway from the cabin door and instinctively dived into the thick foliage. Now she peeked out at El, not daring to move or breathe. Her thoughts raced. The rough gravel bit into her knees and elbows.

"There's nowhere for you to go!" he repeated, nodding to his right. "That way's my house." He looked down the other direction, around the cabin and across the bridge. "And that way you have to go through me. You can't get away, Dawn."

He calmly flipped open the side port of the single-action pistol and ejected two spent shells, replacing them with cartridges in his bulging pants pocket.

Dawn crouched farther down the slope, trembling like a leaf. She couldn't get the horrible images—Terry's frail body quivering on the floor as El stabbed her, the empty darkness of the big pistol barrel pointing in her own face—out of her brain.

But El had slipped in her mother's blood and his shots had gone wild. Even in death, her mother was looking out for her. In the end she had saved her daughter from one of the very creatures that inhabited her worst nightmares.

"You all have to die," said El. "You can't stay here anymore."

The most terrifying thing to Dawn was the casual way in which he said it. Like he was saying "We have to get ready in case it rains."

What's wrong with him?

And what does he mean by all?

Was he talking about her and her mother?

He took a step closer to the slope and she could no longer see his face. But now she could see the pistol again, hanging beside his bloody pants leg. That and one boot.

She held her breath and tried to stop shaking.

He was whispering now, as though he knew exactly where she was. How close he stood to her.

"You can't live. You have to understand that, Dawn. Your mother knew. She turned her back for me so it wouldn't hurt. I don't want to hurt you either. But you can't stay here."

She wanted to scream at him to go away and leave them alone. But the instant he heard her he'd shoot her dead. Her only hope was that he didn't really know where she was.

The trouble was that she couldn't hold her breath any longer. It all wanted to come out in a gigantic burst. There was sweat on her hands, on her face, trickling down into her eyes and the back of her neck. She exhaled so slowly that it was just a silent hiss of air across her lips and a fierce stinging in her lungs.

She breathed back in the same way. But it wasn't fast enough or powerful enough to fulfill her body's need for oxygen. She did it over and over, the ache intensifying, praying that El would give up and go away.

When he leaped forward and crushed through the branches, she nearly screamed. He stumbled around, grunting and stamping like a wounded grizzly. The alders jerked and slapped her face. She was tangled in them like a fly in a web.

"Come out of there!" shouted El.

She could see both his boots now, inches away from her, and a razor of fear sliced up her spine.

He was standing on the handkerchief.

She'd still had it in her hand as she scrambled over the side of the bank, down to the Fork, and she must have dropped it as she dived into the alders. Until El stepped on it, the scrap of cloth had been forgotten. Now it seemed to point to her hiding place like a neon sign.

Had El noticed it yet?

Dawn glanced slowly around to see if there was any escape. But she knew there was none. El would never miss at this range.

She was screwed.

But his big black boot covered all but the corner of the handkerchief. If he didn't look directly down at it, he might not notice . . .

"Come on out, you little bitch," said El. He kicked at the brush. But there was no anger in his movements. His voice never rose, although he had been shouting before. He sounded almost as though he was bored. As though he was talking to himself.

Curling up tightly, she held her breath until she knew her lungs would burst.

12:20

MICKY WAS A THIRD of the way to Cabels' Store, her mind on the letter she had just completed to Jim, explaining once more that yes, she was fine but no, she had no intention of leaving McRay. And no, there was nothing between her and Damon. They were just friends. Jim had hoped for more out of their relationship, but he'd have to live with that. She and Damon had never been destined to be anything but friends. Damon didn't need a woman the way some men did. Damon needed a direction. A focus. Something he could lock on to the way he had once locked on to his practice.

A pair of squirrels chittered overhead, playing hide-and-seek with her along the trail and she thought of Aaron McRay. The old man was feisty and bright-eyed as one of those small animals. Micky never knew when Aaron was kidding or how he could say some of the wild things that he did.

His dark eyes would flicker as he spit out some crude remark. Testing or teasing.

Micky had been in town only three weeks—two longer than she'd intended—when Aaron had pounded on her door.

"Buy the place or get out," he'd said.

"Excuse me?" She didn't know whether to invite the old man in out of the cold or slam the door in his face.

"My cabin," he said, nodding at the wall, not her.

"You're Aaron McRay."

"No shit."

"I was invited here," she told him. "I thought you knew. I'm sorry."

"Did know. You want it or what?"

"Want what? The cabin? I'm only visiting."

"Don't give me that crap." He spit tobacco juice onto the snow beside the stoop. A brown trickle ran through the whiskers on his chin. "You aren't going anywhere."

"Who told you that?"

"They never do."

"They?"

"The assholes that move into McRay."

She couldn't help herself. She laughed in his face.

His scowl cracked a little. "Think that's funny?"

"I have an odd sense of humor."

"Good. You want the fucking place, or what?"

"I said I'm just visiting." Had Damon mentioned the old man was a little insane? She didn't remember.

"You crazy?"

Was he reading her mind? "Excuse me?"

"Heard you might be crazy."

Micky burst out laughing. "Just mildly psychotic."

"Cy what?"

"Yes," she said. "I'm crazy."

"Good. Women don't belong in the bush, though." But his scowl definitely cracked.

"Really."

"It's a fact."

"Says you."

"Says me."

He turned to leave.

"Like some coffee?" she asked impulsively.

He glanced back over his shoulder. "Any good?"

"No."

"Sure." He pushed past her and took a seat at the table. She couldn't help laughing at the absurd conversation.

After that she had decided that laughter was the key to Aaron.

He'd say something outlandish.

She'd laugh.

She'd laugh again.

He'd glare and say something more crude or politically incorrect.

He smiled. No teeth. Just a thin-lipped sneer.

But she'd also discovered that Aaron could be incredibly thoughtful.

That same winter, when Damon was off somewhere with Marty and Stan, Micky glanced out of her bedroom window one morning and saw snow halfway up the side of her outhouse. Her woodpile—purchased from Clive, who sold wood as one of his seemingly inexhaustible line of services—was covered in deep powder and a waist-high drift nearly blocked her front door.

The firewood was twenty feet away. She hadn't stacked it against the building yet and, with a sinking heart, she realized it would take her all day just to dig it out.

She was bundling up to do so when she heard the scrunch of a shovel out front. She glanced out of the loft window to see the back of Aaron's bright blue parka. He was digging out her woodpile. She zipped up her jacket and bulled her way through the drift, grabbed a shovel, and joined him.

She said hello.

He nodded.

Two hours of silent work later, they both leaned huffing over their shovels.

"You didn't have to do that." she said. It was early afternoon but already the sun was long gone and green-and-yellow tendrils of Aurora Borealis ribboned over the peaks.

"Gonna have fun getting your wood free, now," said the old man, nodding toward the pile that was frozen together with thick ice. "*Cheechako* thing to do." *Cheechako* was what all the old-timers called greenhorns.

"I should have stacked it under the eave," she agreed.

"Too fucking late now."

"Never too late," she laughed, watching him stomp off back up the trail to his cabin. "Thank you!"

Aaron lifted one gauntleted hand over his shoulder but didn't look back.

"I'll take it!" she shouted without thinking.

"Take what?" He kept walking.

"The cabin."

He turned.

"You never asked my price."

"I don't care," she said, thinking of the money from both her parents' and Wade's insurance policies, gathering dust in some dark bank vault.

"Take it," said Aaron, with a thin-lipped smile. "I give it to you."

Micky stood in the snow, shaking her head.

A month later the deed had arrived in her mail.

In a slash of blue, one of the jays whipped down through the trees and chattered at her and she thought how like a jay Aaron was. All chatter and no bite.

Another gunshot rang through the still air.

Just across the creek. Maybe it wasn't Marty or Stan. Maybe El had spotted a bear. They did come out this time of year and rummage around the cabins sometimes. Clive had told her to bang a spoon on a pot to frighten them away— noise bothered the big animals—but most people trusted gunfire better.

But the grizzlies weren't usually aggressive. Not unless you got between a sow and her cub.

Micky wondered idly if she should go back and get the Glock just for its noise value. But she was already halfway to the store. She began to whistle and snap her fingers as she walked, anything to let a wandering bear know that she was coming. Next to running from one of the giant beasts, the worst thing you could do was startle one.

The trail was narrow and twisting, strewn with boulders and still dotted here and there with tufts of crusty snow. Hares usually shot out of the woods as she traversed the path, but today they were strangely shy. She spotted only one, peeping around a grandfather spruce, off to her left, but he swiftly vanished.

"Nervous, old bunny?" she said. "You know I wouldn't hurt a fly."

Maybe the gunshots had the rabbits on edge. Howard MacArthur and most of the other men in the community hunted the big snowshoes for meat but no one hunted this close to her cabin. Still, the animals were savvy enough to know what the sound of gunfire meant to their species.

"Sorry," she whispered, speaking to the empty forest. A sudden burst of anxiety thickened the very air around her. She stared at the spot where the hare was hiding.

She knew exactly what it felt.

She could sense it quivering, feel its fear.

To the rabbit, the gunshot would be echoing like cannon fire, the ground beneath its soft pads vibrating with the terror of the explosion. Its tiny nose would be sniffing the air for the intruder, its ears twitching, eyes shifting desperately left and right, every shadow in the forest a portent of impending pain and death.

And suddenly she felt an intense hatred for the hunters.

It was an irrational and emotional response that she should be able to reason away with a good walk on this beautiful day. But the shots touched a bad place in her heart, and just as irrationally she felt the fear not dissipating but growing. She had the crazy thought that it wasn't the hare that was in danger.

It was her.

Her heart pounded and her breath quickened. Her palms were damp and her mouth was dry.

She glanced back down the trail behind her, then hurried on.

12:25

EL SPUN AND FIRED while he was still in mid-sentence, still coaxing Dawn to come out of hiding and give herself up. Now he had his back to her, searching the brush.

When he fired, she'd ducked instinctively. His sudden movement had disturbed the snarl of branches and now all he had to do was turn around and they would be face-to-face.

She felt like a rabbit.

The shot still rumbled in her ears and tears leaked from her cheeks into the rock-hard ground beneath her palms.

What set him off again?

A noise in the alders?

A puff of breeze?

The North Fork was only a few feet through the branches to her right, and once again she considered making a break for it.

He had missed with his first two shots when she ran from the cabin. But she didn't see how he could miss at this range if he spotted her. And the brush would slow her flight so much that he could unload the pistol at her before she even reached the creek. He'd probably reload before she made it to the safety of the far shore.

If he didn't just chase her down and stab her to death.

The handkerchief was still stuck to his right boot, glued on with blood and mud. She lowered her head and tried to make herself as tiny as possible. El flailed at the brush, peering this way and that.

"Come on out, now," he said, the calm in his voice even more terrifying than before.

How could anyone do what he had done, be doing what he was doing, and act so calm?

Suddenly she knew what it was about El that had always set her teeth on edge.

There was never any emotion in his voice. As though there were no life going on inside him, just the automatic actions of a machine, just chemicals boiling inside his body and his brain.

"Come on, Dawn. If you're hit, you're going to bleed to death in there and the little animals will pick your bones. You don't want to die like that. Come on out and you can be with your mother. I'll close up the cabin after you. That will be better. You'll be with your mom."

The mention of her mother made the tears sting again. Snot ran down her face, dripping like tears onto the ground, and it grossed her out but she was scared to wipe it away. She wanted desperately to blow her nose. She was afraid some weird instinct of El's would point her out to him and he would spin and fire a shot in her direction. She tried even harder to press herself into the ground.

It seemed only an instant before that she had witnessed the horrible scene in the cabin. But it also seemed as though she had been crouching in the alders for hours, for days. She felt certain the horror would continue forever. That she would be hiding here for eternity, holding her breath, stifling the shivers, terror paralyzing her, waiting for the death blow to fall.

El spun again and she stiffened, bracing for the killing shot. Her eyes were focused—her entire body was focused—on the scrap of bloody white cloth twisting beneath his boot.

Why doesn't it come off?

Is blood that sticky?

She felt the mirror glasses searching the welter of brush. Felt them on her. Her breath came in involuntary gasps, none large enough to fill her burning lungs. She couldn't quell the shaking of her hands in the dirt.

The boots finally turned away, upslope, and a tentacle of hope attached itself to her heart.

But the damned handkerchief chose that instant to dislodge, just as El was taking his first step away, back toward the cabin.

She saw him bend. His fingers plucked the bloodied square of cotton from the gravel. He lifted the handkerchief, inspecting it closely. Then he sniffed it, like a bloodhound might.

"Got you," he said in that same flat voice. "I knew I hit you. If you aren't dead, you need to come out, Dawn. You can't go up the trail without passing me. You're either going to bleed to death here or I can make it fast for you. Come on up to the cabin. I don't have all day."

He thinks the blood on the handkerchief is mine.

If he thinks I'm dead, will he just go away?

El tossed the handkerchief aside and vanished over the bank.

12:45

HOWARD MACARTHUR KEPT HIS ears open for another shot. He rubbed sweat off his brow with the sleeve of his blue-denim shirt. Blue-denim shirts were all Howard owned. He wore them summer and winter along with blue-denim pants.

Not blue jeans.

Trousers.

At eighty-five his hearing was amazingly acute, although his vision required the aid of bottle-thick glasses and he didn't get around near as well as he let on. Rheumatism stiffened nearly every joint in his tall body but only Clive Cabel knew how much aspirin and Advil he ordered. Howard despised old age almost as much as he hated sympathy or pity. He had accepted all of both he cared to when his wife Elizabeth died in '65. He'd been alone ever since her death and had given no one any excuse to feel sorry for him.

The shots had come from near the Glorianus place.

Howard was cleaning up around the outside of his tiny cabin, the smallest in town, even tinier than Marty Kiley's one-bedroom shack. Howard didn't need much room for frills. He'd spent most of his life living out of a pup tent in remote locations, working for Alaska Fish and Game. He was a silent, self-contained man and had been lucky early in life to meet a woman who didn't expect a man to be around every day. They'd had a wonderful marriage, although the Lord hadn't blessed them with children and Howard liked children.

He liked Dawn Glorianus and had since she and her mother moved in, six years before. But he felt a little sorry for the girl.

Not everyone was cut out for bush life.

When the first two shots rang out, Howard was lifting a black-plastic bag of garbage that had mysteriously ended up beside the back stoop and not in the bin where it belonged. The bag had gotten buried under the winter snow and now shrews had gotten into it. He was shoveling it into another bag so that he could dispose of it by burning the entire thing in his fifty-gallon barrel incinerator when he got around to his spring fire.

The shots were muffled, as though they were in very deep woods or the gun was covered somehow. He wondered if Terry had spotted a bear. But then it occurred to him that Terry didn't own a gun, wouldn't have one near the house. Howard understood why.

Everyone in McRay knew about Dawn's father. And everyone in town sort of looked out for the mother and daughter. The pair were like a couple of orphaned cubs that couldn't take care of themselves no matter how much they figured they could. Howard had been glad when they took the cabin vacated by Harry Townsend, since it gave him someone new to wave to on his daily walks and it placed them in a central location so that there was someone living pretty much all around them.

Of course their nearest neighbor was El Hoskins.

Howard didn't like the man. But at least he was a man. Howard was of the firm opinion that women alone didn't have any business living out in the bush. But lately it seemed the town was filling up with them.

He set the shovel down and moseyed around to face the bridge that led to Terry and Dawn's cabin. The sun was in his eyes but he wasn't really looking.

He was listening.

After a couple of minutes, when no more shots were fired

and no one came screaming down the path, he decided that it was El, shooting at a hare, and went in the house to get a cup of coffee.

He had no sooner poured one and sat down when the third shot rang out.

That didn't sound like anyone rabbit hunting.

For one thing this shot was too near. He knew that Terry wouldn't put up with anyone shooting around her house like that. Not unless it was an emergency. And if someone was having that much trouble with a grizzly, then Howard needed to get over there. No one in town had half as much experience as he did with the big bears and if it was El using that damned hogleg he carried on his hip, then the fool was probably getting ready to wound the animal and get himself and maybe someone else killed too.

Howard set his coffee on the table and pulled himself painfully to his feet. He reached behind the door and grabbed a short-barreled Mossberg shotgun. The tubular magazine was loaded with alternating rounds of double-aught buckshot and solid lead slugs. It was a bear killer. Unlike his hunting guns, this was strictly a survival weapon, only good for short distances, the range at which bears attacked. It had enough power, in the right hands, to stop one of the nasty fellows dead in his tracks.

He hurried down the trail to the bridge, not bothering to close the door behind him, feeling his old bones ratcheting in their sockets. It seemed like his whole body needed a good lube job. Before he even reached the bridge, he was panting. He forced himself to slow down a little. It wouldn't do anyone any good, his falling and breaking a leg or hurrying himself into a coronary.

Wouldn't that just be something?

El chases off a grizzly, then comes to tell him and finds him dead as a coffin nail in the middle of the bridge.

He leaned on the rough-hewn railing of the bridge he had built. It was wide enough for two people to cross at once, or for Clive to drive his four-wheeler across, though most times, when the water wasn't too high, Clive made his way right across the Fork. Howard stared down into the crystal-clear water and thought for the millionth time how beautiful it was. Like liquid crystal. The melted glacier water had a blue cast that gleamed in the sun. It was a product of the erosion of solid stone, the eating away of the mountains that would one day be flat as the Texas prairies. But Howard didn't expect to live to see that and didn't want to.

What the hell are you thinking, old man?

He caught his breath and moved on at a fast walk, the shotgun cradled in the crook of his left arm. He wondered if Micky had heard the shots. Micky didn't like shooting around her place either and for about the same reason as Terry. Howard had mulled over the strange coincidence that brought two wounded women to live in such close proximity in so remote an area. He knew what had driven both of them to come but he sometimes wondered if it wasn't the beginning of a flood.

Was McRay going to turn into some kind of haven for survivors of urban tragedy?

He hoped not.

Alaskan towns had always offered a kind of refuge. But until recent years, most of the people seeking solace in the remote villages had been men like himself, people who didn't fit anywhere else. Some came because of a hurt that had befallen them, others just couldn't stand civilization trying to press their round spirits into square holes. In places like McRay that didn't happen. In McRay a man could be himself. There were no time clocks or factory whistles. Nobody was under- or over-dressed. You came and went as you pleased and no one stuck his nose into your business.

But, unlike Micky Ascherfeld, Terry Glorianus didn't seem better for her move to McRay. Terry was friendly enough, said hi, even visited on occasion. But the woman was a closed book. She explained about her husband's murder and why she was in town. But she let it be known that as far as she was concerned his murder wasn't an isolated event. Terry hadn't moved with her daughter to McRay to get over their grief. She was here to bury herself and her daughter. She was besieged, making her stand by surrounding herself and her only surviving family with as much distance, as much wilderness as she could put between the two of them and the rest of the world.

Howard felt sorry for her and especially sorry for Dawn. But he never tried to argue with Terry. People had their own ideas and their own lives to live. He didn't believe in saving folks from themselves. Maybe Terry would eventually come out of it or maybe she'd spend the rest of her life in the purgatory she had built for herself. Howard wasn't a psychiatrist and he didn't believe that one of those damned head doctors could have helped her either.

We all create our own private hells.

Micky, on the other hand, was more Howard's kind of woman. She made him wish he was forty years younger every time he talked to her. Howard had heard Micky's story from Damon. Micky had faced more terror and more heartbreak than Terry Glorianus could even imagine.

Micky had been a part of the terror. Lived it firsthand. Maybe that was the real difference between the two women. Maybe it was harder for Terry because the horror for her was all in her mind. She hadn't seen her husband killed and maybe somehow that made it all the worse.

Micky had come out the other side of her trauma and straightened out her life. Howard had come to accept Micky as a part of McRay in a way that he had never accepted Terry. Terry he thought of more the way a man thinks of an old stray animal he's caring for. He'd take care of it. But it was never really going to be his.

Terry was a stray. And strays got hurt again and again. Even in places like McRay.

Micky was more like a wolf. You could hurt one once, maybe twice. But the critters learned. They licked their wounds and they got cagey. Micky could take care of herself pretty much.

But Howard also knew something that he wasn't sure Micky was aware of. He knew that El had a crush on her. Howard had caught El staring at her one day when El didn't realize anyone else was around, and the intensity of the look El gave her made Howard nervous. Since that day, Howard had made it a habit to watch El.

The trail wound up a short slope with a ninety-degree turn through the trees and alder bushes, so that Terry's cabin was obscured by the brow of a small knoll. Howard kept his eyes on the underbrush. A bear startled by gunshots might likely eschew the easy track and move into the protection of the trees.

More than once in his life Howard had been surprised by a grizzly. The big bastards could explode out of thick alders like runaway trains if they were startled. And fear turned a grizzly into a murderous machine that might weigh nearly a ton, with claws as long as a grown man's fingers and sharp as ice picks.

Howard's best friend had died outside of Cordova when a big sow charged out of the woods. The man didn't have time to lift his shotgun before the beast was on top of him. Her claws hadn't killed him, although his chest and shoulders looked like shredded beef. He'd died when the bear took his entire head in her mouth and buried her huge canines in both temples.

Every time Howard thought about it he couldn't help but imagine the sickening crunch as the animal's teeth sank in. Couldn't help but wonder if that had been the last sound his friend had heard.

Howard whistled and clicked his tongue loudly to let any creature in the area know he was coming.

Better a wary monster than a surprised one.

12:50

THE CLEARING AT CABELS' Store was the largest open area in the valley. The big log structure sat in the center facing the path to Micky's place. Micky glanced across the clearing to her right, past the round telephone antenna toward the airstrip. To her left, the bridge crossed the Sgagamash and the trail led to Howard MacArthur's cabin.

Clive's workshop was attached to the airstrip side of the store and covered with a low tin roof. The sliding door to the workshop was closed. Micky didn't see Clive's four-wheeler and she wondered if he was around. He might be out on a delivery. She reprimanded herself for procrastinating. If Clive couldn't get her glass to the runway today she was screwed.

Micky climbed the steps onto the broad front deck. The heavy doors bore twin carvings of eagles, soaring over jagged mountains. Foot-tall letters, sculpted of the same native spruce, proclaimed that this was the site of the Cabel General Store. A painted handset from a telephone sign to her right announced the official AT&T Telephone Site for the area.

The store was heated with wood and lighted with kerosene mantel lamps. But the telephone took power. On the roof, solar collectors fed a bank of marine batteries. A small windmill on the ridge helped too. The phone was McRay's only instant communication with outside and Clive maintained it zealously. He had explained to Micky that McRay had the last radiophone system in the state. All the other villages had gone cellular. But Clive was proud of being low-tech.

Few people used the service. Anyone making a call was as likely to be one of the Inuits or Athabaskan natives, going to or from their traditional fishing camps. Clive also called in regular weather reports to Anchorage. Otherwise, the little glassed-in room in the store sat mostly empty.

When Micky opened the door she was blanketed by the sweet, thick smell of fresh-roasted coffee and cinnamon, tobacco, and the salty, tangy aroma of the chunks of moose jerky and smoked salmon that hung on chains over the counter. The salmon reminded Micky of her glass piece awaiting shipment. The dried fish was ruby red and had soft rounded contours along flesh that was leather hard and bled light in crimson rays. It was so salty that it was impossible to chew a piece without a beer to wash it down. Clive frequently used that as an excuse to get her to have a drink with him.

Rita leaned on the counter. She looked up from the book she was reading, staring at Micky over the top of her glasses.

"Hi, hon. Shopping?"

Micky nodded. She sauntered over to the counter and turned the book around.

"A romance novel?" she said.

"I have my dreams," Rita replied, laughing and shrugging. "How you been? Haven't seen you in a coupla weeks."

"I had to finish that last piece before Rich got in today or my agent is going to wring my neck."

"You done?"

"I need Clive to come up and get it. I have it all packed up. I thought I could get him to haul some supplies up to my place and take the crate back. Is he around?"

"Probably asleep in the back room," said Rita. "Lazy bastard."

Clive's laziness was a standing joke in McRay. The Cabels'

store and their sleeping quarters upstairs were always spotless, the logs oiled and gleaming, the interior as Bristol-fashion as the exterior. Everyone knew that if they needed a hand, Clive would be ready to lay down whatever he was doing and help. Micky always insisted on paying him but she knew that most of the things she asked him to do, Clive would have been happy to do for free.

Now he strode out of the room behind the counter with an oily piece of mechanical equipment in his hands, swabbing it with a rag, and tweaking something with a pair of needle-nosed pliers. He smiled when he saw Micky.

"Thought you were asleep," said Micky.

"I do this in my sleep," said Clive, nudging his wife.

"Must have heard us and jumped," said Rita.

"Did I hear you say you needed a crate picked up?" said Clive, sliding in next to Rita at the counter. Rita went back to her reading but Micky knew that she was listening to every word.

"Yeah," said Micky. "I need it to go out with Rich today."

"You picking up supplies, too?"

"Coffee, tea, milk, sugar, flour, crackers. You got any of those big boxes of potato chips in?"

"Couldn't get them last time. But we have the large cans of mixed nuts you like."

"I like the chips," Micky said.

Clive laughed. "I'll get some in as soon as a shipment comes into Anchorage. I guess we bought them out."

Micky laughed too. A large order of chips for the Cabel General Store was five boxes.

"Haven't seen you in a while," said Clive.

"I'll get out more now with the weather like it is. I had to finish that piece."

"You been up to see Aaron?"

"No," she said, feeling instantly guilty. "Maybe I'll go up this afternoon and see how he's doing."

"He's doing fine," said Rita.

"How do you know that?"

"How would he be doing?" replied Rita. "The old coot's meaner than Satan and twice as ancient. He'll outlive all of us and then claim he owns the land and resell it."

"He's really not like that," said Micky.

"So you two say," said Rita, pretending that she was way too busy with her book to continue the conversation.

"You got a list?" asked Clive, winking at Micky.

"What?" she said, suddenly far away. She was picturing Aaron all by himself up in his cabin and she had the strangest sensation of terrible loneliness, although she knew that the old man didn't care for visitors.

"A list?" repeated Clive, smiling.

Micky shook her head.

"Here." Clive slid a small pad of paper and a pencil toward her across the counter. "Write down everything you need. Rita will ring it up and I'll bring it by as soon as I get this carburetor back on the four-wheeler."

Micky looked dubiously at the piece of aluminum-colored metal in his hands. "Are you going to be able to do it today?"

"Won't take but a minute to put this back on," Clyde assured her. "I'll probably have it done before you're through shopping. Where's the crate, in case I beat you home? I won't have room on the wheeler for you and the supplies."

"Right inside the door," said Micky, unable to get the picture of Aaron, all alone, out of her mind. She had no idea why it bothered her so. It was as though he were calling to her and she had the most overpowering instinct to go to him. "I'll write it all down. You sure you won't mind if I'm not there? It isn't that heavy."

"No problem."

Micky was suddenly unable to breathe. Her mouth dropped open and she stared stupidly at Clive.

Why did he say that?

Why had he used that expression?

"Are you all right, Micky?" said Clive, cocking his head and giving her a sympathetic look.

She managed to close her mouth and nod, trying to focus, trying to get the irrational worry over Aaron out of the front of her head and pull herself back into the warmth of the store. Into the safe here and now.

"I don't know what came over me," she said, shaking her head.

But Clive had already rounded the counter. He led her to

a rocker in front of the stove that he and Rita used for both heat and cooking.

Rita quit pretending to read and came to sit on the other side of Micky. "You're white as a sheet, honey. What happened? You have a flash or something?"

Micky let out a slow deep breath, trying to relax.

"I don't know," she said. "All at once I felt terribly worried about Aaron. Isn't that silly?"

Clive and Rita exchanged glances.

"I'll say," said Rita. "That old goat is tougher than you and me and Clive put together."

"Silly," Micky repeated.

"The mind plays tricks on you sometimes," Rita told her. "What you need is a nice hot cup of tea." She hurried off into the back room. When she returned she put a platter beside the stove. She poured Micky a steaming cup and handed her a chocolate chip cookie.

I'm being silly, Micky thought.

The gunshots and the rabbit spooked me.

And those damned jays.

Warm golden rays of sun gleamed through the front glass, etching long shadows across the dark-wood interior of the store. The walls were lined with high shelves, crowded to the ceiling with cans, glass jars, and cardboard boxes. There were blankets and sleeping bags and the omnipresent rubber boots. The store sold sweaters and long johns, shovels and picks, rifles and pistols and ammo, and it smelled of lantern fuel and the fine sweet odor of dried foods, crackers and chips and flour.

If Cabels' didn't have it, you really didn't need it.

Rita claimed that Clive didn't buy inventory, he bought the things he needed and now and then someone else purchased some. And they were always open. Clive joked that closing time was fifteen minutes after everyone was gone.

"Did you hear shots a little while ago?" asked Micky. "Over by the Glorianus cabin?"

Clive and Rita exchanged glances again, both shaking their heads.

"I been in and out of the shed," said Clive. "Working on

that carburetor, and Rita's had her head in that trashy novel. We wouldn't have heard a shot probably. By Terry's place, you say?"

"That's what it sounded like."

"Maybe it was Damon," said Rita.

"Damon doesn't own a gun," Clive reminded her.

"I thought at first it was Marty or Stan," said Micky. "But then there was a third shot, right across the Fork, and it sounded more like a pistol. I was wondering if maybe El had run into a bear." She thought of the high-pitched screech she'd heard. But she was certain it was just a jay or maybe her imagination. For some reason she was jumpy today. Her mind might very well be playing tricks on her.

"I hope not," Clive said. "Bears would do well to stay away from El Hoskins."

"That boy's crazier than a shithouse bear," agreed Rita. "One of these days he'll hurt someone with that damned gun."

"He's just a jerk," said Clive. "One day he'll get *himself* killed with that damned leg cannon of his."

"He's not just a jerk," argued Rita. "You talk to Marty or Stan. They've crossed El a couple of times when he's in one of his funks. They both steer clear of him. Sooner or later he's going to be trouble."

"Damon says he probably isn't a danger to anyone," said Micky, not believing it.

"Damon's a shrink," said Rita, making a face. "They think the devil just needs a good talking to."

"If El was shooting at a bear, you can bet he didn't hit it," said Clive. "But that would be a good thing. If he did hit it, he'd only wound it, and then there'd really be hell to pay."

"More than likely he was just shooting, period," said Rita. "He makes me nervous."

Micky didn't say that nervous wasn't near what El made her. She'd been terrified of him since the first time they met.

It was early in her first summer in McRay and Micky was just becoming accustomed to the idea of actually living there. Accustomed to the new rhythms, new sounds, and new smells. Accustomed to waking when she chose. Working when she chose.

She was heading back to her cabin after a visit with Aaron. Taking her time. Tossing stones into the creek; picking wildflowers like a schoolgirl.

She rounded a curve in the trail and there stood El. Unmoving.

Staring at her through those damn glasses.

The part of her brain that had nothing to do with logic or reason screamed at her to run. Her subconscious kept telling her that El was the same man who had followed her through room after room of her family's shop. Hunted her like a wounded animal. The same man who had trundled on fifty pounds of Kevlar body armor and pursued her down that terrible narrow corridor.

The same man who haunted her dreams.

He had stalked her from her youth, from her past, from the flatlands and burning heat of south Texas to the high passes and frigid cold of rural Alaska and now, here he was, wearing those same damned glasses.

She wanted to scream at him to take them off.

Instead she had bitten her lip that day and stared El down.

"I'm Micky Ascherfeld," she said. She stepped up to him, holding out her hand, wishing she had the Glock in it.

"Mm," said El, unmoving.

"I'm your neighbor. Across the creek."

"Mm," said El.

What the hell was wrong with the man?

They stared at each other. The day was silent as death. Micky glanced at El's hand, still resting on his gun butt. El followed her eyes.

"I have to be going," she said, dropping the flowers beside the trail and sidling around him.

She could feel his eyes that day, burning into her back, all the way to the first turn in the path.

"I hope he didn't scare Terry," said Clive, glancing at Micky. "You know how she is."

"Terry needs to live in a gated community," said Rita, shaking her head.

"Maybe I'll run over there after I bring back your crate," Clive said. "Make sure everything's all right."

"Take your rifle," said Rita.

12:55

D
AWN'S ENTIRE BODY ACHED. She couldn't remain in the same position much longer. But she was afraid that any tiny movement would rustle the alders and El would see them moving from his perch in her backyard. The damp ground was icy and the cold pierced her shirt and jeans like needles.

If I stay here, I'll freeze to death.

With a shaking hand she reached out and gripped the branch directly in front of her eyes. The alders rustled in the freshening wind. Though it was getting colder, at least the breeze would camouflage her escape.

It occurred to Dawn that El might have been lying.

He might not be waiting at their cabin at all.

He might have gone on down the trail and only said he was going to wait so that she would stay where she was and not go for help.

Or, then again, he might be sitting right up on the bank, just waiting for her to stick her head out.

She prayed for the wind to pick up.

The rush of the water, bouncing around the rocky bottom of the North Fork, sounded like angry voices as she strained to catch any hint of El's presence. Her mind was cluttered with grief and fear and disbelief. She had to pull herself together and get to help.

She thought of Micky Ascherfeld. Micky was closest. Just across the shallow creek a fork in the trail ran up the hill to her cabin.

But Micky was a woman. At that moment Dawn wanted a man. A big man. Her best bet was to cross the stream, then head down the trail directly to Cabels' Store. Clive had guns and there was the phone. They could call the State Troopers and get real help.

But she had to get out of these alders before she could cross the Fork.

She crawled, one fearful inch at a time, expecting a shot to ring out, wondering if she would hear it or if she would be dead before the sound reached her ears. The ground was rough and frigid. Her fingernails were torn from her crashing slide down the slope and her hands were raw. Her clothes kept getting snagged in the branches and she had to feel out each impediment, dislodge herself before edging forward again, glancing upward in case an opening in the branches appeared and suddenly left her vulnerable.

When she emerged at the spot at which El had first trod upon her handkerchief, she caught her breath. Her eyes locked on the lip of the trail, where it disappeared over the top of the creek bank. The stream was closer here and there was no intervening brush to deaden the sound of rushing water. She would never hear El approaching now. Her only hope was to slip across the stream to the far bank before he came back.

If he was coming.

Why would he wait for me up by our cabin when he knows I'm in the alders?

Wouldn't he just move farther downstream and wait for me to cross?

He'd have a perfect shot up and down the straight run of the Fork.

She lay there for a moment, undecided.

But she had to do something.

Her mother was dead.

And El was going to kill someone else soon. She was certain of it.

She wriggled out of the last of the protecting branches into the center of the trail. She had never felt so exposed, so alone and vulnerable, in her entire life. She lay flattened down against the path, waiting, listening, watching, her heart thudding in her ears.

She couldn't cross the creek without knowing where El was. She had to see over the lip of that bank. But her body refused to obey her commands to crawl upward. She pictured El, just over the top, tall as a spruce tree. With that deadly gun in one hand and the bloody knife in the other. Leering down at her.

How long can I wait here like this?

She shivered so hard her jaw ached.

El's call sounded over the chatter of the creek like the dull droning of a giant bee.

"Come on out, Dawn. You can't stay down there forever. You're hurt. You must be cold. Come on out."

His voice made her want to throw up.

But, at the same time, it reassured her.

He wasn't just over the lip of the bank. His voice was coming from up near their cabin.

She began to slide backwards on her stomach, down toward the water, pushing off with her hands, trying to keep the gravel from making noise as it created tiny avalanches beside and beneath her. When she felt the icy stream pushing her feet and slippery rocks crunching beneath the toes of her boots, she stopped.

My feet'll be soaked in seconds.

Like that matters.

She clawed at the frozen dirt like a frightened animal.

I'll be dead in a few minutes.

Decide.

1 : 00

HOWARD REACHED THE EDGE of the Glorianus property, where the alders ended and the trail cut across the open grass that led up to Terry and Dawn's stoop. The cabin seemed dark and, although smoke was rising from the stovepipe, he didn't see any movement through the windows.

It was more than possible, knowing Terry, that she had grabbed young Dawn at the first sound of gunfire and was holed up inside. Howard didn't want to frighten the woman by showing up at her door with a loaded shotgun and, there was no reason to. If El was shooting at a bear, it sure wasn't going to be inside Terry's house.

The climb from the bridge had winded him again. He set the shotgun on its stock and gripped the short barrel for support. If this expedition turned out to have been for nothing, he was going to hit Terry up for a cup of coffee and a piece of one of the cakes she was always baking.

The wind gusted and he tugged at the collar of his shirt, thankful that he was wearing his goose-down vest. When his wind had come back a little, he hefted the gun over his elbow, but tucked his left hand in the vest pocket to warm it. He was making his way toward the cabin when he heard El, calling to Dawn.

Now, why had Dawn run off?

She was always arguing with her mother, of course. The girl was at that age and Howard knew that she hated living in the bush.

But why was El here looking for Dawn and what had the shots been about?

Did he fire them to get the girl's attention?

Where's Terry?

It occurred to Howard that Terry, being the way she was, might have panicked and gone to El for help if Dawn had run off. Or, maybe something far worse had happened. Maybe the girl had run afoul of a bear and now El and Terry were trying to find her.

Howard picked up his pace.

He rounded the cabin and the sun hit him directly in the eyes. He could barely make out El's silhouette. He did see the gun hanging in El's right hand and a slight quiver of doubt rose in his heart. But, at that instant, Howard was far more worried about Dawn.

"What's the matter, Eldred?" he said, in as conversational a tone as he could muster, still winded. "Where's Dawn?"

El turned to face him.

Howard pulled his left hand out of his vest and tried to shield his eyes from the blinding sunlight.

El raised the pistol and Howard's mouth dropped open as he realized the terrible mistake he had made.

The boom of the pistol wasn't nearly as much of a shock as the powerful ripping sensation of the heavy-gauge bullet tearing through his breastbone. The ground came up fast, driving the wind from his lungs, knocking the glasses from his face.

Howard's mind functioned at lightning speed.

Have to get the shotgun up.

Got to shoot the bastard.

He's like a wounded grizzly. But cold and calculating. Not mad with rage.

El had cracked.

It happened to people in the bush.

Howard had seen it before.

Folks got cabin fever during the impossibly long dark winters. Went completely batty.

Howard struggled to lift the heavy shotgun with just his right arm but all he could do was scrape it along the ground. He heard another blast and dirt blinded him where the bullet cratered the gravel inches from his right eye. He jerked and the shotgun fired into the ground beside his feet.

That was his only shot.

He didn't have the strength to pump another round into the cylinder now and it didn't matter anyway.

El straddled him and Howard stared up into sunglasses that masked the face of a demon. He watched the pistol rising to point directly into his eyes and knew that he would do no more fishing along Sgagamash Creek.

"Go to hell," Howard said.

The big gun bucked again.

1:05

RITA TOTALED THE BILL and Micky paid cash for it.

"Carburetor's almost in," said Clive. He leaned out of the door to his workshop, wiping his hands on a rag. "I'll be right behind you. I need to catch Damon about his last order. Some of the stuff he needs isn't coming in for a couple of weeks."

"I think he's up the valley with Stan or Marty today. But you never know with Damon; he could be off prospecting."

"I'll catch him later then."

"If I see him I'll tell him you're looking for him. I picked up a couple of things for Aaron. I'm going to hike up and see him."

Rita grimaced and Micky laughed.

"He really isn't so bad," she protested.

"Have it your way," said Rita.

Micky opened the heavy door and stepped out onto the porch. The breeze blowing down the valley buffeted her and she was surprised by the chill in it. The clouds were still high cirrus and the sun shone beneath them. But by the time she reached the edge of the clearing and headed back up the trail toward home, she realized that she had better stop and grab a heavier jacket and gloves and maybe a hat. One of the things that Aaron had taught her was that only *Cheechakos* went out unprepared for bad weather. If the weather changed abruptly and took you unawares, it was no one's fault but your own.

Aaron had taught her a lot things.

How to bank a fire so it would burn all night.

How to bake bread in a pressure cooker on top of a woodstove.

How to walk in snowshoes.

How to live today and not yesterday.

That was the most important thing that she had learned from Aaron. The hardest for him to teach. The most difficult for her to learn.

Four months after the incident at her woodpile, she and Aaron were sitting on his porch, watching the mountains turn a thousand shades of blue in the distance. A pair of ravens played aerial tag over the needle tops of the spruces and Micky was feeling almost at ease.

"Quit living with dead people," said Aaron.

She glared at him as though he had two heads. How dare he say something like that to her? How dare he intrude on her grief in that manner?

And how did he know I was thinking of Wade?

"Now you're going to stomp off and say what an old shithead I am. But you know I'm right."

"I'm getting better," she said.

"No, you're not." His grizzled gray beard jarred with blue eyes that seemed far too young for his wrinkled brow and gnarly old hands.

"Are you just trying to start something today?" she asked, prepared to do just what he said, stomp right off.

"Look around." He waved his hand around the valley. The sun was high overhead, fireweed burned blue in the grass, and the Kuskokwim was wide and gray with spring runoff. "This whole damned planet is filled with life. Think about it. Think how much more life there is than death."

She turned away from him.

"And yet you waste your time on the dead side," he said. "You know what happens then?"

She waited.

"Wonderful people like me, that you could have been thinking about, by the time you get around to doing it, are dead."

She laughed, knowing that that was exactly what he had aimed for. He laughed too.

But it had been a serious lesson and she knew it.

Whether it had been well taught, or whether she had been about ready to step over the threshold of recovery anyway, she never knew. But McRay started to feel more like home after that, and, though she still thought of Wade often, they were fond memories. The image of him in the cruiser, the memory of her parents, facedown in pools of their own blood, were mercifully blurred and seldom recalled.

That was Aaron's gift to her.

She was almost to her cabin when she thought of the hare again. She slipped silently off the trail and with a stealthy tread, crept around to the far side of the huge spruce. But the snowshoe rabbit was gone. She glanced through the deep woods; the sunlight filtered amber and gold down into the thick carpet of pine needles. Aaron might have been able to figure out where the animal had wandered off to, but tracking a rabbit across soft forest bottom was still beyond Micky's abilities.

She thought she heard something splash in the creek and immediately turned downslope. But the forest between the trail and the Fork was dense. She couldn't see the creek and no further sounds came from that direction.

But something about the noise set her nerves back on edge.

The shots.

The nervous rabbit.

Her intuition about Aaron.

Now the splash.

Singly, they were all easily explained and nothing to worry about. Put them all together and they added up to a huge mass of feminine neurosis. Aaron would have a fit.

She was sweaty from the brisk walk and chilled by the rising wind. She hurried into the cabin to get her heavier jacket, stopping to give the crate a once-over, jiggling it from side to side, although she knew that it was perfectly boxed.

She replaced her Thinsulate jacket with the goose-down one, making sure her gloves were in the pockets. She grabbed a wool cap from a peg beside the door and pulled it on. Her hair barely showed beneath it. She kept it close-cropped now. Easier to take care of. There weren't any hairdressers in McRay. Every few months she paid Rita to cut it and she didn't spend any time admiring it in her one mirror. Rita wasn't a butcher. But she'd better not give up her day job, either.

Micky thought again of the shots and the possibility that a bear was moving around, then fetched the Glock from the table beside her bed. She checked the chamber, then set the gun down on the worktable, trying to remember where she'd put her holster. She hadn't worn it since leaving Houston. She finally found it on the shelf beneath the kitchen washbasin. She held it in both hands, staring at it. The feel, the weight, the smoothness of the jet-black leather instantly bringing back the ugly memories she had rigorously exorcised under Aaron's tutelage.

She placed the holster on the table beside the Glock and backed away. Suddenly she didn't want to handle it. She glanced at her wristwatch, hanging on a nail on the wall, and thought how the gun and watch were symbols of life past.

Time.

And violence.

Time meant little in McRay.

A day could last forever or she might glance up from her worktable and wonder where it had gone.

And violence, the violence of the gun, was a thing of her past.

She grabbed a couple of paperbacks she had ordered for Aaron and stepped back out into the sun, closing the door behind her.

Better without the gun.

Aaron always said the Glock was a girly pistol fit for nothing but target shooting anyway.

If there was a bear in the vicinity, she'd stick to whistling and snapping her fingers.

When she reached the creek, she glanced up- and down-stream. She could see fifty yards in either direction before the creek meandered around a bend. But there was nothing unusual to be seen. No bear. No one cavorting in the creek. It was a normal spring day and the stream was running just as it had run for a million years before she got here. No one was shouting on the far shore. No one running through the brush.

But a terrible sense of foreboding gnawed at her.

The wind died for an instant and the forest grew utterly still.

She considered hollering across to Terry. But a hand seemed wrapped around her vocal cords and she remained silent.

Her shout might frighten Terry. Micky had spoken to Terry and Dawn on numerous occasions and Micky knew their story. Terry was afraid of the air around her. The woman was like a small bird that was so frightened it could die of a heart attack before any hunter got it. Micky would have loved to help Terry but couldn't figure out just how to do it. She sensed that the brusque technique that Aaron had used on her would be a decided failure against Terry's fears. She'd broached the subject with Aaron and he'd agreed.

"You can't fix someone like Terry," he said. "She isn't damaged. She's broken."

"She's just afraid," said Micky, shaking her head. "I know about being afraid."

"Like you were in Houston?" Aaron was the only one in town, other than Damon, who knew the whole story.

"The fear comes back," she said.

"But that afraid? So afraid that you can't move? That you piss your pants?"

"No."

"Well, that's how afraid Terry will be for the rest of her life. Afraid that if she leaves the protection she thinks she and Dawn have here, even for an instant, it will cost them their lives. She spends her entire time trying to find a way to keep Dawn here after she reaches legal age and it's killing her because she knows she can't."

"How in the hell do you know all this?"

"The difference between you and Terry," said Aaron, "is that deep down you want to be better. Terry doesn't. She doesn't want to be not afraid because to not be afraid would mean that she's wrong. It would mean that the world wasn't an evil place. That it hadn't singled out her husband for a sacrifice. That his death was just a fucking meaningless tragedy. The worst thing is, if her kid don't get out of here pretty soon, she's going to start catching her mother's fear and be too scared to."

Micky knew exactly what he meant.

To accept the fact that the men who had callously murdered her parents and her lover and the girl in the strip joint were simply criminals who had just happened to cross their path denigrated their memories. She wanted there to be reasons for their deaths where she knew there were none. And once she finally accepted that there were no reasons, she'd reached the road to recovery.

And what Aaron said about Dawn was true, too.

Terry would never recover. The best thing that Dawn could do was get away before her mother's sickness infected her as well.

Still burdened by foreboding, Micky turned uphill. Aaron's cabin was a mile and a half up the winding valley, but just around the bend ahead she would be able to see El's place. His cabin sat down close to the water, and she'd passed it countless times but never without wondering how anyone could live there.

Even El's property was forbidding somehow. It seemed as though the cabin itself would have liked to get out of that clearing as fast as possible. And Micky was already edgy.

Passing by El's cabin would be bad enough.

The last person she wanted to see that afternoon was El.

1 : 10

IF MICKY HAD TURNED and walked toward the store when she reached the creek at the foot of her cabin, she would have found Dawn, cringing in the alders. Dawn had finally steeled herself and made the dash across the North Fork, while Micky stood in her cabin, looking down at the gun she could not force herself to carry.

Dawn had made more noise than she expected, splashing across the narrow creek. When she clawed her way up the shallower slope on the far side, she had instantly burrowed down deep into the brush again. Now, all she could make out was a few feet of trail out in front of her and scattered glimpses of the far shore.

It had been almost impossible to get the nerve to stand up and sprint across the stream.

Then she heard Howard MacArthur's voice and something snapped in her brain.

Without thinking she'd scrabbled her way upward, mouthing words that made no sound. Trying to scream without success. She wanted to run to Howard, to throw herself in his arms, to tell him to save her. At the same time, another part of her brain kept asking who was saving whom.

She had to warn Howard that El was killing people. Her

fingers ripped at the loose gravel and her head was just over the top of the bank when she saw the surprised look on old Howard's face, just a few feet ahead of her.

El's gun roared and a bright splash of blood plumed on the front of Howard's crisp blue shirt. He dropped hard onto his back, his head twisting from left to right as though he was telling himself that this wasn't happening.

But Dawn could have told him that it was.

She hung there, her hands gripping the lip of the bank like a man clinging to the edge of a cliff, as El leaned slowly over Howard and pointed the long black barrel down into his face. Mesmerized, she watched El cock the hammer with his thumb, but twisted her head to the side just as he pulled the trigger again.

The gunshot thundered down the valley.

Dawn whimpered. She let her hands slip and her body slid halfway back down the bank. She hung there, motionless, unable to move, her face buried in the rich-smelling soil, her body trembling, waiting.

Is he coming now?

It seemed two eternities before she gathered the courage to claw her way upward once more. She raised her head and looked quickly all around the clearing, fighting down the sobs that choked her.

Howard lay sprawled in the sun. There was something odd about his left eye but at that distance she couldn't make it out.

He wasn't moving.

And El was nowhere to be seen.

Which way did he go?

Has he crossed the bridge to Howard's place?

She would have heard him if he'd gone back up the path to his own cabin, and more than likely he would have taken one last look down into the creek and discovered her.

Or is he in our cabin again?

The idea that El was inside their house again, with her mother's body, sent a shudder of revulsion up her spine.

She slid back down to the creek, squeezed her eyes shut.

But she knew in her heart she couldn't stay there. At any minute he was going to come back looking for her.

So she ran.

The icy runoff caught at her pant legs, slowing her down, splashing noisily. She gasped as jagged tendrils of pain shot from the tips of her toes to her knees. Slipping on the rocks she threw frightened glances back over her shoulder, expecting to see El come charging down the bank after her at any moment.

But she made the far shore and clawed her way up, across the narrow trail and into the waiting alders, digging in like a wolverine. Her face was scratched, her hands and arms were raw and bleeding, and she was soaked through to the skin over most of her lower body. The wind picked up, chilling her. She had to get someplace warm and soon, or she would die of exposure.

What did El mean by "You all have to die?" *All* didn't sound like he was talking about her and her mother.

He was crazy.

Could he be crazy enough to kill everyone in town?

Suddenly she had a premonition. She saw El striding across the clearing toward the store. Saw Rita and Clive standing innocently on the front steps. Watching him come . . .

If El was headed for the bridge that led across to the store she had to hurry. She was already across the creek. She could beat him to the Cabels'.

She wrapped her arms around her, gripping her shoulders tightly, trying to gain any warmth she could against the increasingly icy breeze.

She edged out into the exposed trail, glancing up and down like a terrified bunny.

Then she ran.

1:25

"YOU GONNA GET THAT thing fixed or not?" Rita leaned on the doorjamb, her book dangling in her hand.

Clive glanced across the top of the four-wheeler. "Something wrong?"

"Micky needs that crate picked up."

He set his pliers on the seat and stood up, wiping his hands on his pants.

"So?"

"You told her you'd go get it. That's all."

Clyde frowned, glancing at his watch. "Rich won't be here for three, maybe four hours. I'm almost done. What's the hurry?"

Rita tapped the book against her leg before she replied.

"I don't like what Micky said about those shots."

"You want me to go check it out?"

"On foot?"

Clive made a face, gestured at the carburetorless four-wheeler. "Well, what do you want?"

"I don't know," said Rita, glancing nervously back into the store. "Just hurry up. Okay?"

Clive shook his head and went back to work. All he had to do was put it on the new gasket on the Honda and tighten the bolts. He wiped it clean and put his tools away. Then he stuck his head through the doorway.

"I'm done," he said. "I'll run to Micky's now."

"Be careful," said Rita.

"Jesus, Rita," he said, taking a half step into the store. "What's the matter with you today?"

"It's stupid," she said, tossing the book onto the counter. "Micky's got me itchy. Take your rifle. All right?"

"Sure."

He opened the sliding door and pushed the Honda out onto the grass. The wind was picking up, the high clouds lowering. He zipped his jacket and slipped on a pair of gloves. He punched the starter button on the four-wheeler and revved the motor with the thumb throttle. Rita stepped out onto the porch and waved at him and he shot her an okay sign, rocking off down the trail toward Micky's cabin.

He drove fast, wondering if he'd catch Micky before she reached her cabin. Not that it mattered, he was just having a race with himself, giving his mind something to do on a track that he had driven dozens of times. The Honda bounced and bucked and he let the handlebars slip between his fingers, balancing expertly on the balls of his feet on the pegs.

The engine had a throaty but high-pitched whine that echoed through the trees and could be heard for a mile or more up and down the valley. Aaron never failed to bitch about the noise when Clive delivered supplies up to his cabin. But the old man always ordered more and Clive had noticed that with each passing year Aaron seemed to load fewer of his necessities into his backpack.

Micky, on the other hand, never commented about the noise. Clive got the feeling that she kind of liked to hear it. He suspected that the four-wheeler represented civilization to her and to others like Terry Glorianus, reassuring them that they hadn't exactly fallen off the edge of the earth by moving to McRay.

He pulled up close to Micky's cabin stoop and turned off the machine.

The sudden silence seemed ominous, as though the surrounding forest had been deadly quiet before he arrived. He glanced around the clearing and then down the trail to the

Fork. The wind stirred the trees and he had the strangest feeling that he was being watched. It gave him the creeps, but he shook it off.

There was nothing to be afraid of in McRay. Even the bears shied away from the noise of the four-wheeler. It was better than barking dogs for driving bears away.

The thought of barking dogs reminded him of Scooter.

In the entire village, Scooter had been the only four-legged inhabitant.

Unlike most Alaskan towns, McRay was not overrun with stray dogs. Aaron had never gotten into the habit of raising them, never been a dog sledder, and the people who moved in later had come either to hunt or to mine. They weren't interested in keeping pack or sled animals since they used either snow machines or their feet for conveyance and it wasn't that far from the airstrip to anywhere in McRay. So, there had always been a more or less unspoken agreement between all inhabitants that the town didn't need any dogs.

Except for Scooter.

Scooter had appeared one day on the front porch of the store.

He was a rat thin, Siberian husky with scars on his haunches and muzzle that were fresh from fighting and a limp on his right front leg that never quite healed. He had a unique white slash of fur down the middle of his back, between his shoulder blades. Clive knew right away that wherever the dog had come from he had traveled a great distance to find humans. And it didn't take Aaron to tell him that the scars were from the wolves that routinely ate huskies stupid enough to wander away from the safety of hearth and home.

Scooter moved into the store and Rita slowly nursed him back to health.

He became a fixture on the front porch during the summer and in the winter he claimed a special place by the woodstove, where he was certain to find any scrap that happened to drop from anyone sitting in the rockers. He grew fat and sassy, though his scars never completely covered with fur. All in all, Scooter looked like the perfect mascot for McRay. Old, tough, and worn, but not worn-out.

Scooter had the habit, about five o'clock every day, of going for a tour of the valley. Even in the winter, people would find his tracks, on a regular route, up to Micky's, past Damon's place, then nearly up to Aaron's. But the dog always turned around before completing the trip to Aaron's cabin, as though he were checking on the old man but knew better than to disturb him.

Then the dog would head back down the trail to Terry's place looking for a handout, crossing the creek below El's cabin, so as not to have to pass across El's property.

Everyone in town loved Scooter.

Everyone but El.

From that day four years ago, when the two first laid eyes on each other, there'd been unmistakable enmity.

El hadn't been in town two days before he sauntered into the store with the big gun on his hip and the mirror glasses covering his eyes. That day, standing in the doorway with the sun at his back, he looked like a man trying to look like a cop. El's left hip was cocked, his right hand rested on the pistol butt, his head back, staring down that beak of a nose at the interior of Clive's store.

Clive had met El the day before, but this was Rita's first exposure to him, and when Clive glanced over at her he saw something he had never seen in her eyes before.

Fear.

Scooter rose from his perch beside the stove and Clive noticed that his hackles were vertical. The dog's eyes were slitted and focused tightly on the silhouette in the doorway. A low, guttural growl rumbled from his throat. Clive was afraid the dog was about to leap on top of El and he hurried to place himself between them.

El was a few inches shorter than Clive, thinner and wirier. He glanced around Clive, staring at the dog, and Clive knew instantly that for whatever reason, there was a natural hatred between the two.

"Rita," he'd said, sharply, "put Scooter in the back room."

She shooed the dog ahead of her around the counter. But Scooter fought the maneuver all the way, backing up but trying to see around her pant legs, his head weaving and bobbing like a boxer trying to get around a referee, the low growl almost but not quite turning into a bark. When Rita had Scooter in the shed she closed the door and returned to the counter.

"Sorry," said Clive. "I don't know what got into him."

"I don't like dogs," said El.

"Scooter's never done anything like that before," said Clive.

"Mmm," said El, his hand still on the pistol.

The man definitely made Clive nervous.

After that, whenever either Clive or Rita saw El approaching they locked Scooter in the shed and there was no trouble.

A year ago Scooter hadn't returned from his walk. Clive went searching for him the next morning.

He discovered that the dog had made it as far as Micky's place. She told Clive she'd given the dog some biscuits and bacon and watched him head off up the trail on his appointed rounds.

Damon wasn't home, so Clive stopped at Aaron's, but the old man hadn't seen the dog. That left the downhill side of Scooter's route. The side that took the dog past El's place. The closer Clive got to the little ford across the Fork near El's cabin, the more apprehensive he grew. Clive was certain that with Scooter's feelings for El and El's hatred for the dog, Scooter must have shied around El's cabin like a skulker in order to get down to Terry's place.

That day Clive stood staring at the inch-deep water in the creek where the runoff was almost gone. It had been a dry spring and the snow had melted early. He knew instinctively that the dog had gotten at least that far. There was no sign of Scooter in the woods and he didn't believe wolves had gotten him.

Wolves did come into the valley and Scooter often went out on the front porch on bright moonlit nights to listen to them howling. The dog would shiver beneath Clive's hand but Clive sensed that there was more to Scooter's anxiety than just fear of old enemies. There was an eerie attraction for Scooter in the sound. Scooter realized that the wolves were dangerous, but they exerted a powerful fascination as well.

Still, Scooter was a damned smart dog. If he hadn't come home, something far more insidious than wolves was at work and Clive was pretty sure what it was.

He waded across the shallow stream and scrabbled his way up to the trail, turning back toward El's cabin. He was angry already, though he had no proof of any wrongdoing.

As he came out of the woods, into the clearing around El's place he wasn't surprised by the mess. He'd seen it before, but it did touch something inside.

This was wrong.

People lived pretty much anyway they wanted in the woods.

But most of the people in McRay were neat. They kept the inside of their small cabins clean and tidy because they were in them for hours or days on end. And come spring, they raked around the house, picked up the winter garbage, pushed fallen limbs back out into the brush and made repairs.

El's cabin had sat abandoned for years, moldering and uncared for, and at first Clive had been happy to know that a new owner was taking up residence. Rather than having the place rot away to the ground and the forest reclaim it, someone would be taking care of the house.

Only El never did.

There was a broken pane in one window that El had stuffed with rags. The stovepipe, hit by a high wind one winter, still hung half-busted, the smoke rising not from the top, but through a twisted opening in the lower joint. And, though firewood was stacked neatly enough against one wall, bags of garbage were piled beside it and one was torn open. Paper and cans and trash littered the clearing and Clive could see clearly enough that bears would be back to take care of the rest.

Maybe El thinks the big animals are his disposal service. Is he that stupid?

Clive wondered then if the bastard was baiting the bears. If the animals were rummaging around his cabin, it would give El a perfect excuse for shooting one of them.

Suddenly Clive wished that he had brought along a gun himself.

Standing there in the trash-covered clearing, Clive had the terrible fear that inside the shadowy darkness of the house, El was pointing that big .44 magnum right at his chest. He could feel the sights centered on his breastbone and suddenly he felt naked. Exposed. He pictured Scooter, sauntering down the trail across the creek, his nose in the air, eyes alert. Sensing the same thing that Clive did.

Eyes.

Clive strode on out into the clearing and El stepped out of the cabin, closing the door quickly behind him.

Just as Clive had suspected, El had been watching him all along.

El stopped on the top step and Clive walked up as casually as he could.

El had on the pistol and those glasses. He looked down his nose as Clive approached.

"Have you seen Scooter?" said Clive, stopping at the foot of the stoop, knowing that El had. He suspected that El had watched the dog, just as he had been watching Clive, from the cavelike protection of his darkened cabin.

El shook his head.

Clive looked around the clearing and then up and down the trail.

"He got to Micky's place," he said, trying not to sound accusing.

"Didn't come by here," said El. "I don't like dogs. I told you before."

El's hands rested on either side of the porch rail, as if he half expected Clive to come charging up the stoop at him and try to get into his house. Clive wondered what El would do if he did. Suddenly he wondered just how dangerous El really was.

He could tell that El was afraid of him, though he couldn't figure out why. Clive had never been anything but perfectly polite to the man. But he sensed real fear behind the glasses, masquerading as bravado, and he wondered if it hadn't been there all along.

Is that why El always wears the big gun and the glasses, to hide his fear?

Suddenly a lot of things made sense.

And just as suddenly Clive knew that the fear in the man could turn equally quickly to violence if El thought that he was being pressed.

Clive had taken a step back away from the stoop. He noticed

that El's hands were gripping the porch rail so tightly that his knuckles had turned white. The man was like a coiled snake and Clive realized that he had come within a hairbreadth of finding out just what El was capable of.

"Don't know where he got off to," Clive had said, still backing away.

El watched him, his lenses glinting in the sun.

"Mmm," he'd said.

As he wound his way along the path that led to Terry and Dawn's cabin that day, Clive knew in his heart that El had killed Scooter. And everyone else in town came to believe El had done it. It was just one more reason to exclude him, although El did a pretty good job of excluding himself.

Clive shook off the memory. But the old anger returned as he stared down at the Fork, knowing that the bastard was right across the creek. He unstrapped the bungee cords on the back basket of the four-wheeler and tossed them onto the ground beside it. He was thinking about El as he opened Micky's door.

1:30

THE SOUND OF CLIVE'S four-wheeler blasted through the trees above Dawn. It sounded like he was heading toward Micky's place. Dawn was closer to the store now than to Micky's and the engine noise faded fast into the forest.

Her intuition told her that El was right across the creek. Though he had said he was going to wait for her at the cabin, she thought he was lying. Maybe he just wanted to frighten her into staying in one place while he killed everyone else.

She couldn't get his words out of her head.

"You all have to die. You can't stay here anymore."

El wasn't talking about her and her mother. He'd killed Howard, too. When he said *all*, he meant everybody.

She could beat him to the store if that was where he was headed next but she knew she had wasted valuable time in hiding. While she'd crouched, paralyzed with fear, he was making his way past Howard's place and down to the bridge. He might well be there already.

She forced herself up out of her new hiding place and stood shivering in the trail.

She hated the thought that her fear had given El time to beat her to the store. She needed to warn Rita.

She raced down the gravel path until her lungs burned like fire.

Ahead, the trail widened, sunlight streaming through the trees. She was almost to the clearing. When she reached it she stopped.

The store lay to her right, thirty yards ahead, the windows brilliant in the sun.

To her left she could just see the sun-bleached wood of the bridge.

What if El is already inside the store?

What if he's on the trail just across the Fork?

She stood there for long moments, undecided, prepared to race back up the trail and into the woods at the slightest provocation. But a pair of ravens exploded out of the trees on the other side of the creek, screeching and complaining. The big black birds flittered above the spruce trees and alders on the far bank.

El's on the trail.

Dawn threw caution aside and ran.

1:45

THE TRAIL SLOPED EVER upward, barely wide enough in some places for Micky to squeeze through the alder branches. Then it would suddenly widen again and open into a small mountain dell or a deadfall run where an avalanche had cut a swath through the brush and trees. Shrews skittered under pine needles and squirrels chattered angrily at her when she disturbed them.

The clouds were lowering. No longer high cirrus, they grazed the peaks overhead and the temperature dropped with her every step. She began to wonder if a trip to Aaron's was such a good idea.

Getting snowed in with the old man wasn't Micky's idea of fun. But the thought of turning back filled her with dread too. She couldn't banish the irrational anxiety she felt for Aaron's safety. The darkening day seemed ominous.

Where the trail ran beside the North Fork, the rush of the creek obscured all other sound. But whenever she moved back into the trees, the gathering wind *whoofed* and gusted.

Where the Fork neared Aaron's cabin, it was no wider than a yard and barely four inches deep. The glacier water ran clear as glass, between polished gray-green stones. Any day now trout would appear in the narrow waterway.

The fish would wriggle crazily upstream, their shiny silver backs—glistening like sequined silk—exposed to the air.

The tundra beside the Kuskokwim was mostly muskeg, that strange symbiosis of water and mosses and low-level plants. But here in the high valley, the ground was rock hard and covered with grass, brown from the long winter. Soon this grass would turn green and blue seas of fireweed and purple monk's hoods would dazzle the senses.

A hundred yards higher and Micky was able to look back down the valley and see the roof of the Cabels' store below. Beyond that, the river wound like a giant gray snake, on its way to the Bering Sea. A pair of eagles, pinpoints in the blue blanket of the sky, swooped and twirled over the shallows two miles away.

Aaron had the best view of any homestead in McRay and that was fitting. After all, McRay was Aaron's town. From his front porch he could look down on the metal roofs of all the other cabins, except for Marty's, which was too deep in the woods. Aaron could sit in his rocker with his coffee any afternoon and survey his domain.

The rising wind jostled Micky toward Aaron's and the diminished creek gurgled alongside. The path grew steeper as she neared the spot where the cabin would come into sight.

The wind whipped around suddenly, rushing back down the valley. Micky caught the sweet-sour smell of woodsmoke and burning garbage.

So, Aaron was home, anyway. She'd been worried that he might be out prospecting.

She smiled, imagining what the old man would say when she showed up.

"Grab a shovel."

Or something equally pleasant.

He no longer tried to offend her. And he wouldn't force her to work. But he didn't waste much time on conversation. She could either help him with what he was doing or sit and watch.

She shifted the books under her arm and hurried up the final yards to the clearing.

The smoke was thicker here.

But it was already dissipating. The gusting wind held it close to the ground and buffeted it away in gray puffs, up the ravine.

The paperbacks thumped to the ground at Micky's feet.

What was left of Aaron's cabin—charred beams, soot-stained glass, and the dark-metal mass of his big old cook-stove—had collapsed in upon itself. The smell was more pronounced here.

Not garbage.

What she smelled was Aaron's world, vanishing.

"Aaron!" she screamed.

This was high valley. A notch in the jagged mountains. Aaron's clearing consisted of a half-acre shelf of flat land. Beyond the house, the valley narrowed to a steep ravine. The outhouse and toolshed still stood, pressed back against the rocky slope, behind the remains of the ruined cabin. The rest of the clearing was covered in dry grass as tall as Micky's knees. Luckily it was still damp with dew from the cool night before or the fire might have become a conflagration.

"Aaron!"

She rushed across the clearing but the timbers were still so hot she couldn't get within twenty feet of the giant embers.

She glanced beyond the cabin toward the ravine. A half mile ahead, the narrow gulch opened into a high pass. Micky squinted, searching for movement.

But the smoke was carrying that direction.

If Aaron had gone that way, he would have smelled the fire and hurried back.

He wasn't in the clearing. And she hadn't passed him on the way up.

"Aaron!" she screamed again, staring at the unholy pile of rubble.

Think.

If he isn't up the trail and you didn't pass him, maybe you missed him.

That was possible.

Aaron came and went as he pleased and the valley was spiderwebbed with trails.

On a day like today he'd most likely have gotten up early.
He was probably out looking for that damned mine.

But what if he isn't?

How long did it take for a fire to burn a log cabin to the
ground?

One hour?

Four?

Flames barely flickered on wood turned to ash and hot
charcoal.

Did the fire start in the night?

Was Aaron overcome by smoke?

She paced the edges of the cabin, approaching as close as
she dared to the heat. On the downwind side she had to
cover her nose and mouth with her jacket. The smoke stung
her eyes and scratched her lungs.

Nothing in the debris looked like human remains. But
the beams and logs and melted metal roofing were heaped
like broken PickUp Sticks. Anyone inside the cabin would
have been cremated or crushed.

"Aaron!" she screamed, glancing feverishly around the
edge of the clearing.

Did he make it out of the blaze but succumb to the
smoke?

He was a tough old bastard but not nearly as tough as he
pretended.

Through the thin gray wisps over the embers, she noticed
an area where the dead grass had been crushed flat, as
though something heavy had been dragged across it.

She had barely reached the ominous track when she saw
crimson spatters on the grass.

Drying in the wind.

Blood.

The track veered sharply and vanished into the grass. But
if she looked carefully across the top of the field, she could
just make out the thin zigzag line that broke the rippling
brown blanket. She cut across to the point at which the flattened grass met the far slope.

"Aaron!" She was running now.

Panting.

Covered in sweat.

What the hell am I going to do when I find him?
The vastness of the land below seemed hostile now.
Empty.
A cold, savage wilderness.
There were no ambulances.
No 911.
Aaron kept a big first-aid kit, beside his front door.
Gone.
Remember your training.
She slowed to a trot. Searching the rocks and trees.

The stunted spruce that grew at this higher elevation looked even shorter under the gray light of the overcast sky.

Aaron leaned against a boulder. His feet were splayed. Head lowered on his chest.

His hands lay in his lap and he was staring toward the ravine.

He looked as though he was searching for something up there and couldn't quite make it out.

But there was a small hole in the center of his left breast pocket.

Blood soaked his pants and the belly of his flannel shirt.

"Oh, Aaron," Micky gasped, dropping down beside him.

She lifted his arm and it was cool and slightly stiff in her hands. Rigor mortis occurs from four to six hours after death. But exertion speeded up rigor and cold slowed it. There was no way of telling how long he'd been dead. She eyed the fire again.

Two, maybe four hours to burn to the ground like that?

But that was only a guess.

She sniffled, breathing loudly through tight lips. Aaron would be ashamed of her if she broke down like a sobbing child.

She set his hand back down gently, and fingered the hole in his shirt, peeking inside at the neat round wound in his chest. There were burns on the flannel and tiny black specks of powder tattooing around the wound.

The gun had been close.

She let the shirt fall back into place and glanced over her shoulder again at the remains of the cabin. She followed Aaron's bloody trail with her eyes.

The bullet must have just missed his heart. He'd been strong enough to drag himself out of the burning house, but of course he was in shock, disoriented. He couldn't find the path that would take him down the valley to help. Or maybe he wasn't looking for the trail. Maybe he was just trying to get away from his killer.

It was amazing that he'd made it as far as he had.

"Who did this, Aaron?" she said. "Why?"

Suicide was not an option. For one thing the typical suicide chose the head as a target. But, even if Aaron had shot himself in the chest, the wound itself would have exhibited a burn ring. If he had pressed the gun against his body, the entry hole would have been a star-shaped tear, from the burst of hot gases beneath the skin.

The shot had been close.

But not that close.

And besides, why shoot yourself and then crawl outside to die?

An image entered her head.

El.

El and that damned huge pistol.

She bit her lip and fought a sob.

Aaron didn't like El. Nobody liked El.

But, of course, Aaron couldn't keep his mouth shut.

There been an angry scene between El and him the summer before.

Micky had been inside the store that day, talking to Rita.

"You wouldn't know what to do with that fucking hogleg if you needed it, boy." Aaron was sitting in the rocker, drinking a soda and resting his feet on the cold stove.

Rita's eyes slitted and Micky turned toward the door.

El had his hand on the pistol butt as usual, and he was glaring down at Aaron.

Everything stopped.

Everything but Aaron's mouth.

"Why don't you skeedaddle your *Cheechako* ass on out of town and play Marshal Dillon somewhere else?"

"I'm not bothering you," said El. He looked wound real tight but his voice was flat.

"Tell Aaron to shut up." Rita leaned close to Micky's ear but Micky could barely hear her.

"You bother me by being here," said Aaron, rising. "You bother my sense of propriety, my sense of common decency. You just fucking bother me, period."

"Aaron," said Micky, sliding over beside the old man, grabbing his arm. "Cool it."

He shook off her hand, never taking his eyes away from El.

"What do you say to that, Hot Shot?"

"I never did anything to you." There was finally something almost human in El's speech. A whine. The sound of a spoiled child. El had already said more than Micky had heard him say since she'd known him. But always before he had spoken in that lifeless singsong.

"No. You never did. And I, for one, don't intend to give you the chance. Pack up and get out."

"Aaron!" said Micky.

"I'm not going anywhere," said El.

"Get!" shouted Aaron, flapping his hands.

To Micky's surprise, El did just that. He backed out the door and disappeared.

"That was rude," she said.

He'd laughed. "I'm way too old not to be rude to people."

"Sometimes you aren't funny."

His smile faded. "Sometimes I don't mean to be."

He threw his pack over his shoulder and left. Micky didn't offer to walk with him that day. She didn't like El, either. But she had no excuse to be abusive to him and neither did Aaron.

"Do you believe that?" she'd said, catching Rita's eye.

"Believe what?" asked Rita. "That Aaron was crude? Or that El was getting about ready to shoot all of us?"

Micky winced. "Are you serious?"

"You telling me you didn't see what I saw?"

"El was tense."

"Tense? Honey, tense is when you need a damn good

bowel movement and your old man wants to use the shower. El Hoskins isn't tense. He's cranked up like an overcharged battery. He scares the shit out of me. Always has. To tell you the truth, seeing what I just saw, it was like déjà vu. Aaron had his back up just the way Scooter did the first time El came in here. You telling me, with your background, you don't think anything's wrong with El?"

"Yes," Micky admitted. "There's something wrong with him. He's a loner. An introvert. Doesn't talk to anyone or socialize. And he makes up for feelings of inadequacy with that big pistol and that bowie knife he wears on his boot."

"And?" Rita demanded.

"And he scares me."

"Bingo."

"But he hasn't done anything wrong."

"Maybe he hasn't. Maybe he has."

"You mean Scooter? You have no proof."

"Proof, shmoof. El did it."

Micky said nothing.

She too believed that El had killed Clive's dog.

Who else would have done it?

But that was no reason for Aaron intentionally to try to set El off.

When Micky left the store that day, Rita had stopped her at the front door.

"You be careful going home," said Rita.

"Are you serious?" said Micky. The fear in Rita's voice chilled her. Micky had never realized that El affected Rita the same way he did her.

"I'm serious. One of these days El is going to explode. You mark my words."

"Proof, shmoof," said Micky, trying to make light of the moment.

"You just take care," said Rita, turning back into the store.

Micky gently closed Aaron's eyes with her fingertips.

Proof. Shmoof.

She backed away from Aaron, careful not to disturb the scene anymore than she already had. When she stepped out of the grass near the cabin once more, she noticed small, over-turned stones and scratches in the dirt near the stoop, leading toward her.

Aaron had been in the house or near it when he was shot.

But what had caused the fire?

Maybe Aaron accidentally set the blaze himself, getting out. Or maybe the killer torched the cabin trying to cover up the murder, not realizing Aaron was still alive.

That was for the State Troopers to figure out.

But before she ran the three miles to the store to call them, Micky intended to break protocol. Procedure was to leave a body just as it was found until the CSU had a chance to go over it. But Micky couldn't stand the thought of Aaron out in the open like that, unprotected.

Snow clouds scudded overhead, obscuring the tops of the tallest trees. It was getting colder.

She trotted around the smoldering cabin to Aaron's stor-age shed. There had to be something in there, a tarp, an old dropcloth, even a sheet of plywood, with which to cover him.

Aaron had built the shed tight against the rock wall so he only had to construct three sides. But a heavy padlock hung from the hasp. She rattled the lock in frustra-tion.

She hurried back to Aaron and, removing her gloves from her pockets, covered his face and chest with her jacket. She had on long johns beneath her flannel shirt. She'd be all right until she got back down to the valley.

She could hear Aaron's voice in her head telling her not to be a damned fool.

"I'm sorry I wasn't here for you, Aaron," she said.

"Not your fault," said the voice.

But she knew that it was her fault.

It had always been her fault.

One of the old man's hands remained exposed and she thought of Wade.

I couldn't do anything for him either.

I have to get to Cabels' and call the troopers.

"I'll be back, Aaron," she said, tucking his hand beneath the jacket.

She turned and ran.

1:50

DAWN MADE IT UP the stoop, wheezing, holding her sides. She glanced back over her shoulder but El hadn't broken out of the trees near the bridge yet.

She burst in as Rita balanced precariously on a stepladder, putting boxes on a shelf. Rita rushed to Dawn, who leaned against the comforting solidity of the thick double doors, gasping for breath, trying to talk through a throat as raw as torn flesh.

"Honey! What the devil's wrong? Talk to me, now!"

Dawn couldn't think what to say first. It all came out in a jumble.

"El! Came and . . . my mother . . . Howard . . . dead!"

"Shit," whispered Rita.

She hurried to a hook on the wall, grabbed an oil spattered, fleece-lined jacket and returned to wrap it around Dawn's shoulders.

"Put this on," said Rita. "You're trembling."

Dawn shoved Rita away. "El! He's coming. He's killing everybody."

Rita nodded.

She hurried around the counter again and grabbed an ancient-looking bolt-action shotgun that looked two sizes too big for her. But she checked the chamber as though she had done so a hundred times before and clicked off the safety without looking.

"Clive will be back real soon," she said. "He'll know what to do."

"Shouldn't we call somebody?" Dawn whispered.

"I don't think we have time," said Rita, looking through the front window.

1:52

EL SAUNTERED ACROSS THE clearing as though he didn't have a care in the world.

"The son of a bitch looks like he owns the place," muttered Rita. There was anger and fear in her voice.

"He'll kill us," whispered Dawn.

"The hell he will," said Rita.

She strode out onto the porch. Dawn stayed inside. Through the light filling the window, she could see El, walking up the trail, twenty yards away. His right hand rested on the butt of his pistol. Dawn could see Rita's back through the crack between the door and the jamb. Rita's head was up, the shotgun held across her body.

Dawn stayed behind the door. She wanted to scream at Rita to shoot El. But fear had robbed her of speech.

"That's far enough, El!" shouted Rita. No fear in her voice now.

El stopped mid-stride.

Dawn peeked around the window jamb. She could just make out El's face. The mirror shades looked like the eyes of a praying mantis and suddenly that was how Dawn saw him. He was some kind of deadly carnivorous insect. He stood in the worn track that led up to the stoop, silent, waiting, staring at his prey.

Rita raised the shotgun once and lowered it again on her elbow.

Shoot him!

"What have you been doing, El?" Rita asked. "You got blood all over you."

He cocked his head, giving her a *who me?* look.

"Just need a few things, Rita," he said.

"Not today. Been a lot of shooting today." She eased the gun around to point it at his feet.

"Don't aim that thing at me," said El.

"Then don't you be coming up here," said Rita.

El shook his head. There was something wrong with the movement. As though El weren't flesh and blood inside but some kind of robot that didn't quite fit beneath his skin.

"You don't belong here, Rita," he said.

You can't stay here anymore.

El wanted McRay to himself and he was going to kill everybody in order to get it.

Dawn knew at that instant that El had reached the exploding point again. She opened her mouth to scream at Rita to get back inside before it was too late.

But it was already too late.

El sidestepped, pulling the big pistol from its holster. Rita jerked the shotgun in disbelief and Dawn lunged into the doorway as the two explosions shattered the stillness. Rita's shotgun clattered away over the railing and El's .44 caliber bullet drove her back into the doorframe and then into Dawn.

Wet, warm blood gushed onto Dawn's chest from the gaping wound in Rita's back. Rita dropped like a sack of concrete, sliding away from Dawn onto the floor.

He's coming.

He's coming up the steps, I know it.

Dawn didn't wait to see if Rita was dead.

She didn't think that El had seen her yet. Rita had fallen back through the door so fast that El was still off to one side and below the level of the porch. Staying low, Dawn raced around the counter. She half ran, half crawled through the open door to the storage shed.

One tiny four-paned window threw a dirty golden light into the room. A gas-powered generator sat alongside a rough workbench, beneath which were a row of batteries. Wires were stapled along the round log walls, leading outside. Oil stained the floorboards and tools hung on pegs on the wall.

But there were no guns. All of those were safely locked in glass cases or stored away where Dawn had no time to search for them.

She had to get out and away before El discovered she was inside.

"Where's Clive?" said El, in that dead singsong.

Dawn froze in the middle of the storage room, knowing that there was no possible place here for her to hide. Terror crackled along her skin like electrical bolts.

"Where's Clive?"

Dawn suddenly realized that El wasn't talking to her.

He's talking to Rita.

Does he really think Rita's going to answer?

But the bullet that blew the huge hole in the back of Rita's body had to have killed her.

She tiptoed ever so slowly, ever so silently over to the big sliding door that was the only exit from the workshop.

A large hook-and-eye latch secured the door.

The latch looked well oiled and shiny with use. But opening the door would be noisy. El was certain to hear and come around the counter before she could escape. It was thirty yards to the nearest brush, on the airstrip side of the store.

She'd never make it.

She left her hand on the latch, praying that El would go away.

Outside, Clive's four-wheeler sounded and Dawn jerked, clenching her teeth.

Clive was coming back.

And El was waiting.

She considered yanking the door open and racing out into the clearing to warn Clive.

As the engine noise increased, Dawn eased the latch upward, catching her finger painfully between it and the door, but biting down her gasp of pain. She wedged her hand inside the frame, surprised at how silently the heavy door slid on the runners overhead.

Even the scattered sunlight outside blinded her and she hurried into its welcome warmth. She was shielded from the front of the store by ten feet of log wall with no window. Around the corner, the four-wheeler crossed the clearing.

She stepped away from the building.

Clive was climbing off of the Honda. Surprise filled his friendly face as he spotted her. He raised his hand in her direction just as she opened her mouth to scream at him to run.

She wondered in that instant if Clive felt the shotgun, centered on his chest.

Dawn could almost see the thick lead pellets as they flew through the air like metal wasps. The bullets struck Clive so hard in the breast that his feet lifted off the ground and he fell back across the seat of the Honda in a heap.

1 : 5 4

MARTY REACHED UP OVER his head and gave the nail another whack. The sharp echo rapped down the ravine, reminding him of the gunshots he'd heard earlier. He wondered if that was what his construction sounded like to people down below.

But anyone with half a brain could tell the difference between a gunshot and the sound of a hammer.

He gave the support posts for the sluice another good shake to see if his makeshift bracing was going to work. Seemed sturdy enough, but the force of the water bouncing off the sides and down over the rough bottom vibrated the sluices so that they constantly required new braces. Along its thirty-foot length Marty had installed ropes and wires and trimmed saplings to shore the contraption up.

But his mind remained on the shots.

Someone potting a rabbit.

Then the third rattled up the valley and he'd stopped, cocking his head to give a listen.

A man might miss a rabbit twice. But it was unlikely that the creature would hang around for a third shot.

Maybe he'd wounded it and was finishing it off.

Pretty damned lousy shooting.

Marty had gone back to work. And he wouldn't even have heard the next shot if he hadn't stopped to give the sluice another shake.

That was a shotgun. More of a booming sound. And farther away.

What the hell were they shooting at?

Had to be a bear.

People shooting grizzlies made Marty nervous. The only reason for shooting the big bastards out of season was to protect yourself and that was always a dicey affair. By the time you decided you were in trouble it took a cannon to kill a damned Griz. Marty had plenty of experience with bears. They were always hanging around the valley, looking for garbage or foraging for berries. But in twenty years in the bush he'd never had to shoot one.

He tried to remember exactly where he'd heard the first shots coming from. But sound was funny in the valley. The ravines and canyons created weird echoes and dead spots. The thick forest muffled some areas and the rock walls amplified sound in others.

The shots sounded like they came from Howard's. Or maybe Terry Glorianus or even Micky's cabin. But it might have been over at El Hoskins's place.

Marty frowned.

Some of them had sounded like pistol shots. Like the roar a big .44 might make.

The thought of El shooting at a bear with his pistol left Marty with mixed emotions.

He felt sorry for anyone who had to face a grizzly with a pistol. But the picture of El doing it was humorous.

El, his mirror glasses glinting, his legs splayed, shoulders back like Gary Cooper, facing off on Main Street with Yogi the Bear.

"Dumb-ass," muttered Marty, spitting into the creek.

He tossed the hammer back into his plastic bucket and wrapped a piece of tarp over the top, tying it with a bungee cord. He climbed back up to the top of the sluice and picked up his shovel. A couple of snowflakes fluttered against his face.

Another shotgun sounded and he stopped.

What the hell was going on?

1:56

ONCE AGAIN DAWN CROUCHED in the alders. The airstrip was a couple of hundred yards behind her. But there was no help there.

Clive lay across his four-wheeler, ten feet from the front stoop.

And, although she couldn't see Rita, Dawn knew by the way El was sidling in and out of the door that he was stepping over her body.

At first Dawn thought that El was intent on stealing everything in the store. He'd made trip after trip, his arms full of boxes and bags, piling them a few yards away from Clive and the four-wheeler. Then he started putting rifles on top, stacking them in a neat pyramid.

She couldn't figure out how he intended to get away with all of the goods he was taking, but it occurred to her that he couldn't haul them all off at once. He'd have to leave some of them where they were and she might get a chance to grab a gun. Even if he didn't leave any guns, she could sneak back into the store and use the phone to call Anchorage for help. That thought brought her her first real ray of hope.

This time, when El came back out, he carried a red Jerry can and he began to soak down the heap of weapons with the contents of the can. He reached into his pocket and pulled out a butane lighter. Then he grabbed one of the gleaming wet rifles and touched the flame to it. The gunstock burst into flame and he tossed it into the pile.

The heap erupted with a fierce *whoomp*. The heat surged and shells popped like firecrackers. El backed toward Dawn's hiding place and she crouched tensely, prepared to dash for deeper cover at the slightest sign that he had spotted her.

He was so close that she could hear him muttering to himself.

"You can't stay here," he kept saying. "None of you can stay here."

He seemed to be having an inner quarrel with someone. Dawn had no idea who was winning or whether or not it was that kind of argument. After a minute, El ambled back down to the store and disappeared through the door into the storage shed.

2:00

MICKY DIDN'T RUN.

She *threw* her legs out in front of her, down the slope, and then followed them. It was a lurching gait. A controlled fall. But it used less energy.

Let the mountain do the work.

It's still a long way down.

Don't want to wear out before I get there.

She was almost to the turnoff to Damon's place.

She had to stop and at least see if Damon was home, to warn him. Damon would walk right up to El and say hi. Never knowing. Damon insisted on being friendly to El. Damon was friendly to everyone.

More than anything she wanted to reach her cabin and hold the Glock in her hands. Suddenly the gun didn't seem so evil to her. She could feel its comforting heft. She wanted its power.

Because right now, if she raced around a corner and El was standing in the trail with that big Ruger, she wouldn't have as much chance as one of the timid bunnies.

It's El.

Each crunch of her boot in the gravel pounded his name into her brain.

He's finally snapped.

She could picture him at the moment he slid into that dark abyss in his mind. His face deadly calm, just a slight tremor in his hands. His body tight as a drum. Graceful as a dancer, yet tense. Like the shooter in the padded suit. Like the killer in her parents' shop.

That had been the last chance to stop him before someone got killed. Right then, when his brain was boiling but before he exploded like a stick of dynamite.

But how could I have foreseen that moment?

How could I have stopped him before this happened?

Shoot him?

For what? Because maybe he'd killed Clive's dog? Because he *looked* crazy? Because both she and Rita were scared of him and Aaron hated his guts? Because he reminded her every time she saw him of the murders in her past?

She reached the fork in the trail and trotted through the alders toward Damon's place. The cabin was buried in the deep woods, the clearing barely extant, trees almost touching above his roof. She couldn't understand why he liked it that way. He hated being cooped up even worse than she. He'd torn all the interior walls out of the house so that the downstairs was just one large open area. Even his outhouse had no door.

But he'd refused to cut down one tree on his property.

She knocked on the door but the hollow echo told her all she needed to know.

It looked like Damon was gone as usual.

Out in the woods somewhere. Looking for that damned mythical mine.

She pushed open the door and stepped inside.

"Damon?"

Sunlight through the windows turned the interior to gold. Every surface inside was polished and pampered. The dish towel was folded neatly on the sink. The two chairs stood at attention beside the table. Books on the shelf beside Damon's recliner were arranged in alphabetical order. Wherever El was, it looked like he hadn't been here.

She stepped back onto the porch and started to close the door.

A firecracker rattle coming from the direction of Cabels' Store startled her.

2:02

STAN HELD THE SHOVEL at shoulder height. The blade rested upside down on the edge of the two-by-twelve side of the sluice chute. He barely heard the gravel sloshing down the washboard bottom or the sound of South Fork above his head. He was trying to place the popping noise coming from far off down the valley.

He wondered if it had anything to do with the earlier gunshots.

Gunfire wasn't unusual in the valley. People were always potting rabbits. Calibrating their gunsights. And, of course, this time of year, there was the possibility of someone trying to scare off a bear. Gunfire didn't trouble Stan. Hell, if no one in the valley complained about his dynamiting, who was he to bitch about a little target shooting? But the popping Stan kept hearing wasn't someone hunting rabbits.

It sounded like a celebration. Stan was always up for a party.

He shoveled another spadeful of gravel into the sluice, then picked up what remained in the bucket and dumped it in. Hooking the bucket onto the end of the shovel and the shovel over his shoulder, he climbed to the creek bank, balancing on the narrow path. The wind whipped down the narrow defile and low clouds ran like an upside-down river, flowing through the ravine.

Scattered flakes danced in the wind.

Marty would give him a hard time for quitting early. But he headed down the trail anyway.

Stan worked the easier pickings in the gravel of the high South Fork, where the stream disappeared into the mountain. Marty eked out a living on the lower run of the creek, just above Damon's claim. Rolling boulders with a seven-foot steel pry bar, to find his nuggets. But both shared the wealth, having pooled their claims from the first week they met, years before. Marty bitched about Stan's laziness. But he knew that Stan found the gold easier and faster than he did. It was a fair partnership.

Stan tugged his sweatshirt hood down tight and his gloves out of his back pocket, tossing the shovel and bucket onto the trailside, where he could pick them up later. If it snowed a few inches, the tools would be buried. And since he'd conveniently broken all his other shovels in the past three weeks, he wouldn't be able to work again until the snow melted.

Too bad.

He crossed the narrow stream and picked up the trail again on the other side, heading downhill. The creek cut a deep jagged swath through the mountainside, and retreating glaciers had, over the eons, left rugged boulders and gravel strewn along the walls and floor of the tiny canyon.

The farther downstream he went, the more popping he heard. Where the canyon widened into a tree-lined clearing, Stan found Marty leaning on his shovel, facing downstream. Marty never wore a cap, his sunburned bald head shone like a welcome beacon.

"Get to work!" shouted Stan, startling Marty. When Marty swung around there was a curious look on his face. He nodded back downstream.

"What's that, you think?" he asked, with just the slightest trace of a Scandinavian accent.

Stan shook his head, frowning in the direction of the noise. "Can't figure it." He moved up alongside Marty. "Sounds like Clive is celebrating something."

"Celebrating?"

Stan shrugged. "You know. Fireworks?"

Marty gave him that look that said *what are you, a dunce?*

Stan hated that look.

"That isn't firecrackers," insisted Marty. "Listen."

For the first time Stan really considered what he was hearing. Marty was right. It didn't sound like firecrackers. It sounded like gunfire. Only there was something different about it.

"Sounds like shells going off. Raw shells. Like someone threw them in a fire," said Marty.

That was it. The explosions had that odd *pop* to them. They didn't sound compressed like the explosion inside a gun. And there were no accompanying cracking noises that bullets made tearing through the trees.

"That's not right," said Marty and Stan had to agree. Someone was trying to tell them something.

"I think we better get down to the store," said Stan.

Marty nodded, dropping his shovel.

"Better grab a couple of rifles," said Stan, following the smaller man down the trail to Marty's cabin.

2:04

THE CLICK OF THE latch on Damon's door mixed with the machine-gun chatter coming from the direction of the store. Micky froze on Damon's stoop, listening.

What the hell is that?

It sounded like ten strings of firecrackers going off at once.

But Clive didn't sell fireworks. Too much fire risk in McRay. And Alaskans celebrated with guns, not firecrackers.

On any other day Micky might have been just curious.

But after discovering Aaron's body—and having had the time on her run down the mountain to percolate some of the possibilities—she was increasingly apprehensive.

Ravens and jays screeched overhead, scattering. The noise was driving them up the valley.

Her own animal instincts told her to flee.

To hide.

She walked slowly back toward the main trail, listening, trying to understand the sound.

It sounded like fireworks. Only it wasn't.

What then?

Bullets.

But not the staccato, regular rhythm of a machine gun. Not the compact noise bullets made exiting a gun.

Bullets exploding.

Someone had put a lot of them into a fire. It sounded like cases of them.

Clive would never do anything like that. Like anyone else, he'd fire his rifle if he was in distress and keep firing. But he wouldn't set off a case of shells like that.

Aaron had been dead for hours.

El had had plenty of time to hike back down the trail and get to the store. If he was on a killing spree and Clive wasn't prepared, he could easily have murdered both Clive and Rita.

But that didn't explain the bursting bullets.

Or maybe she had it all wrong.

Maybe there was another explanation for the noise and El had already vanished up into the mountains to hide.

She hoped that he had.

Let the troopers find him and deal with him.

The popping noise died away just as she turned along the creek toward her cabin.

Toward El's.

El's place appeared through the trees, across the stream and she stopped.

The place looked deserted. But it always had that feel to it. The door was closed. She could see the padlock on its hasp. El was the only one in town who locked his door. But at least he couldn't be inside.

She breathed a little easier.

The one front window was very dark.

A drape?

The stream here was narrow and no deeper than her calves. She thought about crossing to investigate. But she had no time and she still wasn't armed.

That was the most important priority.

To get a gun.

There was no telling where El was right now.

For all she knew he could be behind the next bend in the trail.

2:05

D AWN WATCHED AS THE last of the rounds exploded in the flames. The fire was dying down. The rifle stocks and pistol grips were blackened fiery embers, the barrels red-hot. El had disappeared inside the store.

It was growing colder by the minute. The winds were out of the north, blowing frigid air down right off the Pole.

When El returned, he had a rifle in his hands and his pistol was back in its holster. He leaned the rifle on the porch rail and strode to Clive's four-wheeler. He was talking and gesturing with his hands and once again Dawn had the queer sense that he believed he could communicate with the dead. She wondered if he was explaining to Clive just why Clive couldn't live in McRay any longer.

Grabbing Clive by the cuffs of his pants, El dragged his body toward the porch. Dawn looked away as Clive's head struck the ground.

When Dawn turned back, El had Clive halfway to the front steps. But it seemed to be more of a job than he had planned on. He leaned on his knees, huffing and puffing and still talking. Then he straightened, hands on his hips, breathing deeply, and surveyed the scene. Dawn remembered what he had said to her when she was hiding by the creek, about putting her inside with her mother to protect her from the animals. She wondered if he had stopped to put Howard inside their cabin.

El took another deep breath and grabbed Clive's legs again. Eventually he disappeared inside with the body.

Dawn seized that opportunity to crawl a little deeper into the alders. She wanted to be farther from the airstrip trail, should El decide to explore in that direction. But she also needed a good view of the store through the branches.

As long as El was inside the store she couldn't summon help. Her mother and Howard were dead and the mail plane wouldn't be coming for hours. El knew the plane was coming and Dawn figured that he had that contingency all planned for too. It seemed to Dawn that he'd been master-minding this for a long time. That thought stirred a fire of rage in her stomach that didn't burn the fear out of her, but did give her a little strength.

El had murdered everybody he came into contact with and he had been planning on doing it since who knew when. Planning on murdering people who had never been anything but kind to him.

He came back out on the porch and took a long time peering around the clearing. Dawn was pretty sure that El had no idea that she had run from her hiding place by the creek up to the store. He hadn't seen her when he shot Rita.

That was about the only advantage she had.

El took another long look around, then shouldered the rifle, tapping the butt of the pistol with the palm of his right hand, as though tamping it into place. He stepped down onto the trail beside the four-wheeler and seemed to be ad-miring it. Then, he climbed on the machine and cranked the motor, whipping the Honda into a tight 180-degree turn.

He shot off up the trail toward Micky Ascherfeld's place.

Micky was alone.

And she didn't know El was coming or what he'd been doing.

But there was nothing that she could do for Micky now.

Dawn had her own troubles.

2:10

MICKY HURRIED DOWN THE trail to her cabin when she heard the reassuring sound of Clive's four-wheeler, but she was still a quarter mile from the cabin and from the sound, he was just reaching it from the other side.

Why was he returning?

He might have forgotten something simple like closing the door. Or he might have forgotten bringing something on her list. Clive was good about things like that.

She thought about the bursting shells.

Was it a warning?

Or something worse?

She hurried down the path, careful not to twist her ankle or rush through a turn and bust her ass.

The day was darkening, the frigid wind ripping through the trees.

It was starting to snow like a bastard.

2:12

DAWN COULDN'T LIE IN the alders and wait until the mail plane came in. She'd freeze to death and if El was planning on murdering the pilot—and Dawn was certain now that he was—then she wouldn't be able to stop him. Her only chance was to get a message to the outside and to do that she had to go back into the store.

She wasn't afraid so much of crossing the thirty yards of open ground. She had heard the four-wheeler shutting off clear over at Micky's place. It would take El at least three or four minutes to get back. As soon as she heard the motor crank up again she could be back in the woods before he showed up.

But she didn't want to go back into the store.

She stood in the middle of the trail, gathering her courage and at the same time bracing against the shots that she expected to hear from Micky's place any second. The bullets would crack through the woods like whips snapping. She could feel them in the middle of her back even though they'd be aimed at Micky and not her. Guilt had stung her as she stood watching El murder her mother. The frustration at not being able to help Micky was like a knife in her chest.

She shuffled hesitantly down the trail.

When she reached the center of the clearing, she felt completely exposed. Then she ran. The faster she ran, the more exposed she felt, until she hit the side of the log building hard, stopping herself with spread arms, her heart pounding madly. Sweat was icy on her forehead and her legs quivered. She stared at the sliding door, then shook her head.

Instead she walked up the front stoop, tossing frightened glances over her shoulder in the direction that El had gone, but there was no sound of the four-wheeler and no shot. It occurred to her then that he might just leave the four-wheeler at Micky's and hike back. Then she'd have no way of hearing him. But at least it would take him longer to return. Dawn estimated five or six minutes. She didn't have much time. She needed to get in and get out.

She opened the front door and stood staring into the gloom.

El had put out all but one of the mantel lamps. It sat in the middle of the counter, throwing weird shadows around the crowded store, mixing them with the shadows cast by the last of the light from outside. The sun wasn't due to set for another four hours. But it looked as though it already had. The wind made eerie whistling noises through the eaves and Dawn found it harder and harder to take that first step into the interior of the building where two corpses waited.

She stepped silently inside and put her back against the door.

The store was a mess.

Boxes had been pulled from all the shelves and lay in scattered heaps along the walls and on top of the counter. The glass cases had been smashed and the items inside were thrown here and there.

Even the woodstove had not escaped El's rampage. The cast-iron door was off its hinges, lying on the floor. Dawn couldn't decide whether El had been looking for something inside the stove or if he was trying to cover up something on the floor.

Rita's body was gone.

Dawn noticed that there were ashes around her feet and she was making tracks in them.

Her footprints were a death warrant if El returned. She glanced around and saw Rita's broom, leaning behind the counter. She brushed away her tracks, careful now where she stood.

The trail of ashes led from the door, along the far wall and into the glassed-in phone room. It looked as though El had taken a shovel and scooped ashes from the stove and then shaken them in a wide path through the store. Dawn knew then what the ashes were for. El was soaking up the blood. He'd dragged Rita's body into the phone room and then covered the bloody trail of her body with ashes.

Dawn stared at the little room.

It was about six feet square, sitting in the rear corner of the store, there was no ceiling in the phone room, and the walls didn't reach the high-beamed roof; they gave privacy to whoever was on the phone, but the bottom of the walls were pine-sided only as high as Dawn's waist. The rest was glass. The telephone rested in its cradle on the table. There was nothing else in the cubicle but a couple of chairs.

Dawn had used the phone a couple of times. She'd spoken to her aunt in California and to her best friend in Anchorage. It suddenly occurred to Dawn that she had made a stupid mistake because she had no idea how the radio connection was made. Clive had always done that from the back room.

But she knew that that just was an excuse.

She had to at least *try* to contact someone.

How hard can it be to make a connection on the phone? It's probably just a switch.

She glanced around the counter at the door to the work-shed, remembering El dragging Clive in through the side door. But the outside door was closed now and it looked even darker in there than before.

She eased around the counter, then stopped. There was cardboard and broken glass on the floor, covered with what appeared to be flour, and El had scattered the contents of a large can of coffee over the mess. One of the shelves had broken in half. It looked as though El might have tried to climb it. Big jars that had been on the shelf lay shattered. One lid was overturned with a jagged crown of glass still centered in it. It sat in the middle of the floor like some kind of deadly trap.

She stepped gingerly, careful not to tread on coffee or flour and leave footprints. She reached the door to the workshed and peered into the room. The tiny window admitted almost no light. Somewhere in that darkness lay Clive's body and she had the weirdest sensation that he was watching her with dead, empty eyes.

She backed up to the counter and picked up the lantern, holding it in front of her with both hands. It threw a steady golden glow but it also lightened the things in front of her and blinded her completely to things on the periphery. The room closed in around her. Whenever she glanced to the right or left there was only lurking, silent darkness. Now she had a corpse behind her in the gloom and one somewhere ahead, yet to be discovered.

She knew that she had nothing to fear from either Rita's or Clive's bodies. They had been friends in life. Surely they wouldn't harm her in death. But a childish, unreasoning part of her mind questioned that assumption.

Who knew what happened to people after they died?

What if they were controlled by El now?

What if they were like zombies, under El's spell?

Or some kind of vampires?

She wanted to scream at her own mind to stop, to leave her alone and quit coming up with bullshit horror stories. But the more she denied them, the more they tormented her, the more her palms grew clammy and her skin crawled. The more the wind creaked and the building squeaked and shifted, as though people she could not see were moving about in the shadows.

She stepped into the shed, lantern first, and spotted Clive immediately.

She screamed.

The noise shattered the silence like glass and Dawn nearly dropped the lantern.

Clive was staring at her.

But he had no eyes.

Two gouged sockets oozed blood onto his cheeks.

Dawn spun away and vomited.

Did El do that to Rita too?

To Howard and her mother?

Dawn was suddenly terrified that Rita had sneaked up behind her and was about to grab her. Dawn jerked to the side and glanced back into the gloomy store. But there was no one there.

One way or the other she was doomed to have a corpse behind her. If she faced the store she would be terribly close to Clive and if she watched Clive then something could sneak up behind her from the store. She wiped her mouth on her shirtsleeve but the sickly-sweet taste would not go away.

Clive leaned against the far wall, sitting upright, his hands resting on the floor between his legs. A small puddle of blood pooled around his butt. Dawn slipped past him and set the lantern on the worktable, lifting the big latch again and pushing the sliding door half-open. A dull gray light seeped in and so did frigid air and fluttering flakes. It felt more like February than early May. But the weather was funny in the mountains. It could thaw in December and Dawn had seen a freak snowstorm in late June. This might be just a cold front blowing in for a day or so or they might soon be buried.

Now, with more light, she studied the telephone-equipment room. There was a heavy handmade door, like all the doors in McRay, with a smaller AT&T logo on it and a doormat in front of it. Clive had always wiped his feet before going in. That struck Dawn as stupid, since no one else ever went in the room. But then, maybe the AT&T people came down to work on the equipment now and then and Clive was the type of person to run a neat place.

There was a heavy padlock on a big steel hasp. The lock was nearly the size of her fist and there were no exposed hinges on the door. The door swung inward. She thought about finding a pry bar or some other tool but when she glanced around the room, the only tools she could see were saws and wrenches. So she grabbed a large crescent wrench off the worktable, sidling around Clive and glancing once more into the dark store, but all the wrench did was twist the lock around. The bolt of the lock was almost as thick as the steel handle of the wrench. No way she was breaking in.

Where would the key be?

Suddenly her anger at El and the world in general mixed with her frustration at not being able to get into the radio room. Without thinking, she flung the wrench across the shed, praying even as it left her grasp that she didn't hit Clive.

The wrench clattered along the concrete floor and out the door.

Where was the damn key?

There were only three places Dawn could think of that Clive would have put the key.

She crept back out into the store.

She searched the money box beneath the counter, surprised that El didn't seem to have disturbed it. But then he wasn't after money. He was after the whole town.

There was no key.

The other place would be on a key ring attached to the four-wheeler. She tried to remember if she'd ever seen other keys hanging from the starter on Clive's Honda, but couldn't.

That left only one place. She stood in the doorway, trying not to look at Clive's empty sockets and chewing her lower lip.

2:20

CLIVE'S FOUR-WHEELER WAS parked in front of Micky's stoop and her front door was open. The wind stung her face and whipped noisily through the trees. Large white flakes gusted in thickening flurries.

As soon as she reached the end of the trail and saw the Honda she had wanted to shout at Clive.

But why was he here now?

No way it had taken him this long to come by for the glass piece.

She thought of the popping noises she'd heard and the gunsmoke she could now smell coming from the direction of the store and fear gripped her.

Micky slid quickly behind a big spruce just as El stepped out onto her porch. Her heart pounded and her throat tightened. El had Clive's short carbine in his left hand. He glanced around the clearing, as though he had heard or seen her, but of course that was impossible.

But Micky knew from experience that in situations such as this senses were heightened. She remembered *knowing* what the gunman was doing on the other side of the door in the bar.

Did El sense that she was here?

After a moment he turned and went back into the cabin and, thankfully, he closed the door behind him.

But what is he doing in there and how did he get Clive's four-wheeler and gun?

Clive wouldn't have given either of them up willingly.

El might have taken it at gunpoint and left. But what were the popping noises?

Was El destroying all the ammunition at the store?

Or was the store itself on fire?

Could the shells exploding sound that loud, inside the store?

Micky didn't think so.

But none of that proved that Clive and Rita were dead. Micky clutched at that straw of hope. The last thing she wanted to consider was that she was going to be left alone and weaponless in McRay with an armed madman.

If El was destroying guns and ammo, he would have found the Glock in her cabin immediately. But he had to be certain that it was her only gun. He was probably ransacking her house.

She glanced at the four-wheeler and considered making a getaway. She was pretty sure she could start the machine, but driving it was another matter. And anyway, by the time she got the motor kicked over and figured out how to get it into gear, El would have come outside and blown her brains out.

But the Honda still held her attention.

She studied the small VHF radio strapped under the gas tank.

There was a matching radio beneath the counter in the store. Clive kept both of them charged and Rita turned on the radio whenever Clive left, so that if he needed to get a message to her he could. That radio was the quickest way that Micky could think of to find out if everyone was okay at the store, and to let them know what had happened to Aaron.

The only problem was getting it.

The four-wheeler was fifteen yards away and completely exposed. The cabin door was closed but she would be seen easily through the window if El happened to glance in her direction. He could shoot her right through the glass. She'd never even hear the bullet that killed her. She stared at the little black box in its leather holster and gauged her need against her chances.

She had to find out if anyone was alive at the store but the presence of the four-wheeler here at her cabin argued against that. Realistically she didn't see Clive giving it up or, alternatively, El overpowering Clive and Rita and leaving them alive. Not after what she'd seen at Aaron's. El wasn't tying people up.

He was murdering them.

Still, the radio called to her. She didn't have access to a gun now. Communication with another sane human being might be her only means of saving her own life. And if she stayed low, El would have to be right up close to the window to see her.

Dropping to her hands and knees, she watched the door, trying to estimate how long he'd stay inside searching her house. He might come out at any second. But she had to chance it.

She did a fast low crawl to the four-wheeler, curling up tight behind the rear wheel. Her fingers fumbled at the snap of the radio holster. She was shaking from cold and fear but she managed to get the radio into the pocket of her jacket just as the door creaked.

She froze.

The door opened just a crack.

Did the wind do that?

Or was El peeking out through the slit, waiting?

The wind could open her door. The latch didn't always hold unless the sliding bolt was secured in place from inside.

But it was just as possible that El had heard it blow open and was now glancing through it at the clearing.

Which was it?

A million scattered snowflakes twisted and twirled in the wind.

But not enough to obscure the view from her door or the window.

A giant spruce behind the cabin grated against another tree.

She couldn't stay where she was.

She rolled over onto her side and skittered back down the way she had come, into the protection of the woods below. But she didn't stop there. She burrowed into the brush and found a spot where she could pull branches aside to afford a narrow view of her cabin and the clearing around it.

No gunfire erupted.

So El hadn't been watching.

But now the front door swayed back and forth, with the changing pressure of the wind.

Something tickled the back of her spine. Foreboding swept over her and she glanced in mounting horror at the four-wheeler.

She had forgotten to close the snap on the radio holster. It hung limply, advertising the missing radio.

Damn!

It seemed like hours, but in fact it was less than a minute before El came back out. He hurried down her steps and climbed back on the Honda. He fastened the carbine on the handlebars and was about to press the starter when he stopped. He leaned over and glanced down.

Micky knew that he was staring at the empty radio holder.

She stiffened.

El's hands dropped from the handlebars to his sides and he ever so slowly surveyed the entire clearing and cabin area. Three hundred and sixty degrees. When the reflective lenses of his glasses passed over her it was all that she could do not to leap up and start running. That old feeling of utter helplessness gripped her.

If she let it grow, it would overpower her. She had to do something to help herself or she was going to end up cowering here, waiting until El found her.

It occurred to her that that might not be such a bad idea. Hiding right here, until help arrived.

El had already murdered Aaron and probably Terry and Dawn, Rita and Clive.

Micky knew now that the shots she had heard earlier, across the creek, had been El. The scream she didn't want to think about. But it kept replaying itself in her head. The cry she had written off as the noise of a jay sounded exactly like her mother's death scream. Like Terry or Dawn Glorianus crying their lungs out. Why hadn't she recognized it for what it was?

She had ample excuse for finding a good hiding place and simply waiting for someone to rescue her.

That's what she'd done last time.

And the time before that.

And she'd survived.

She'd hidden and she'd lived.

The mail plane was due in a few hours. And of course Anchorage would start wondering why there was no weather report coming in, and if Clive didn't answer the phone, AT&T would send someone to investigate. Pretty soon the troopers would be on the scene.

But she knew in her heart that El would kill everyone else left alive in town if she didn't warn them. There were no Houston cops outside and El wasn't likely to give up and wander away the way the kid that murdered her parents had.

If she didn't do something, a lot more innocent people were going to die.

Nonchalantly, El reached down and resnapped the radio case. He cranked up the motor and made a wide circle across Micky's front lawn, coming within ten feet of her hiding place as he passed. She watched his face as he rode by and involuntarily, she sucked in her breath.

Her mind was playing tricks on her.

But in that instant, as she saw his hair whipping in the wind, and the dull light reflected in his glasses, she was certain that he was the same man who had murdered her parents, the same man who had returned years later to murder Wade. And now he was here, in McRay, still looking for her.

She crouched deeper into the shadows of the alders and shivered, clutching Clive's radio tightly in her hands and praying that the demons in her head would leave her alone, as the four-wheeler whined away down the trail.

2:25

CLIVE WAS STILL WARM and his flesh was soft beneath his clothing. Dawn patted the cloth and discovered the keys instantly. But getting them out was another matter.

His bloody face was only inches from hers and she was terrified that, just as she slipped her hand into his pocket, he would reach up and grab her in his dead embrace and pull her tightly to him. Goose bumps covered her entire body.

She fought her fingers down into his pants pocket and weaseled at his keys with her fingertips until she snagged the ring and jerked and worried it out, backing hastily away from Clive's corpse.

Clive never moved.

But all the keys were much too large to fit the lock. She flung them across the room in disgust and went to find a hammer. But now it, too, had proven ineffectual. She dropped it back into the toolbox and stared at the hasp.

Behind her, through the sliding door, she heard the distant sound of the four-wheeler and her breathing quickened. She had to get away. If she wasn't out of the clearing before El came down the trail again, she was dead. A gust of wind slapped her hard in the face as she started to step outside.

A tiny voice came from inside the store and she nearly peed her pants.

It was a nasal whisper and her first panicked thought was that it was Rita, that she was still alive and calling for help. Dawn stepped back into the shed and listened.

"Rita? Clive?"

The voice was scratchy and low, but it sounded like Micky Ascherfeld.

Dawn stared into the store. The growl of the four-wheeler was getting nearer. She made a decision. Closing the big sliding door but not latching it, she slipped back into the store.

The voice returned. "Rita? Clive?"

This time Dawn recognized it as coming from a radio. She glanced under the counter and there, beside the cash drawer, found a small handheld transceiver. She picked it up and fumbled for the transmit button.

2:27

HOLDING THE RADIO AGAINST her cheek, Micky closed her eyes and tried to compose herself.

Dawn chattered into the radio and Micky struggled to make sense of what the girl was saying.

The teenager was hysterical. She wouldn't let go of the transmit button. But Micky understood enough to know that El had been very busy and that she had been incredibly lucky in her movements. If she had stayed home and not gone to visit Aaron, she would no doubt be dead. It appeared that just about everyone else was.

Not only dead either.

Not according to Dawn.

The way Micky figured it, El had killed Aaron first. Then there must have been a very brief cooling-off period. El probably went back down the trail as far as Damon's place before crossing back over the creek.

And if Damon hadn't been off in the woods with Marty or Stan, he'd be dead now too.

That close.

Then maybe, instead of crossing over to the Glorianus place, El might have gone straight after her. If he had walked up the path to greet her, she'd have been frightened by his sudden appearance. But not frightened enough to run for her pistol. He'd have killed her just as he had the others.

It sounded as if Howard had just happened to show up at the wrong place at the wrong time. Then El continued down the far side of the trail to the store. There he murdered Clive and Rita.

"Dawn!" Micky shouted into the radio. "You have to get out of there. He's coming back. He's coming back right now."

There was an unwelcome stretch of silence. "He's already here."

Micky squeezed the radio even tighter.

"Hide," she said. "Hide *now*. I'm coming."

"Don't leave me."

The sound of the girl's plaintive voice cut Micky like a knife. She knew what Dawn was feeling. She knew exactly what she was feeling.

"I won't," Micky promised. "But you have to tell me before he gets close. I don't want him to hear me talking. And you don't talk, either. You understand?"

"Do you have a gun?"

Should she lie? The girl might hear that in her voice if she did.

"No," she said.

"Then what are you going to do?" said Dawn.

What the hell are we going to do?

"We have radios. That's a start. Now we know where he is and what he's doing. Dawn, you need to hide."

Micky thought that she heard the throaty growl of the four-wheeler over the radio but it was probably just static as Dawn clicked off. Micky glanced up at her cabin and noticed a flickering light through the front window.

Was there any chance at all that El had missed the Glock?

She raced up the front steps and through the door. The stench of smoke and melting plastic assailed her. The light had not been a lantern as she had thought, but flames trickling down the table leg.

Melted plastic created a violet liquid fire that dripped off the tabletop and puddled on the floor. Acrid smoke stung Micky's eyes. The smell was coming from her pistol, set in the center of her worktable. She pulled the collar of her shirt up over her nose and, squinting, rushed to the gun.

What El had done to her pistol was bizarre.

He had removed the gun's magazine. Then he'd used her propane torch, melting plastic glasses and bottles into and over the pistol, melting the gun itself—the Glock being mostly plastic resin—turning it into some kind of weird statuette. Micky's first instinct was to claw the misshapen pistol out of its plastic tomb but, even if the slight touch hadn't singed her fingertips, the gun was obviously useless.

She grabbed her dishpan and slopped the soapy water over the table, stomping out the flames that remained on the floor.

"He's coming in."

Dawn's staticky voice cut through the smoke. Micky wanted to claw her way through the radio to the girl.

She knew the layout of the store. She'd had dinner often enough with Clive and Rita. She'd helped Rita ransack her one clothes closet, trying to decide what to wear, the day of her and Clive's twenty-fifth wedding anniversary. There weren't many places for a sixteen-year-old girl to hide in the building. Under the bed. In that one narrow closet. Under the counter in the store or back in the workroom. If El made any kind of search, he was certain to find her.

It was a miracle that she and Dawn had survived this long. If Aaron was dead and Terry and Howard, then El would surely have made certain of Marty and Stan before crossing the creek to the store. And he was destroying the weapons. That was what the popping had been about. He'd been destroying all of the ammo at the store.

She threw on a jacket and slipped the radio into one of the pockets.

But she needed a gun.

And there was only one place she could think of where she might find one now.

But the thought of going there chilled her to the bone.

2:30

MARTY AND STAN WERE arguing as they always did, standing in the middle of the trail with snowflakes the size of silver dollars whipping around them, facing one another with rifles across their arms. Neither smiled and both stood spraddle-legged across the narrow path.

"If you want to go back and get your pack, then go get it," said Marty, glowering.

"So then I bring back all the supplies," said Stan, his face reddening.

"I wasn't going for supplies. I thought we were going down to see if there was trouble."

"We might as well make the trip worthwhile," said Stan. That made perfect sense to him. Why waste all that energy, then come back empty-handed? The gunfire and the explosions were probably just El blowing off steam. They'd get down to the store, have a good laugh, then pick up enough supplies so that they wouldn't have to hike back down for a couple of weeks. That seemed easy enough for even Marty to understand.

"The trip will be worthwhile if we get there and everyone is all right," said Marty.

"Why wouldn't everyone be all right?"

Marty shook his head. "Are you an idiot?"

"Don't call me an idiot," said Stan.

"I was just asking," said Marty. "You want to go back, go back. I'm going down to see what the shooting was about."

Stan glared at him like a frustrated twelve-year-old. Marty turned around and started down the trail without looking back. Before he'd gone ten yards, Stan hurried to catch up.

"Goddammit, Marty!" said Stan, huffing up behind.

Marty shook his head and kept on walking.

2:32

EL KNELT ON THE floor inside the front door of Cabels' Store. He had Clive's lever-action carbine in his left hand and his right was on the butt of the pistol. He glanced over at the boxes that he had tossed on top of Rita's shotgun. He'd taken a liking to the gun. Something about the age and wear. All his other weapons were shiny and new.

But he hadn't wanted to leave it out in the open.

What if Rita or Clive started moving around and found it?

Meager sunlight filtered through the snow outside, gleaming silver across the ash on the wood floor. El studied the neat, half-moon form of the tip of a bootheel, in the very edge of the ash trail.

He held his fingertips over it and it disappeared. It occurred to him that it might not be a print at all but something that had fallen into the ash. A jar lid perhaps.

But there was nothing like that around and if there had been, then where was it now? The wind couldn't have carried it away and not disturbed the bed of ash.

He glanced around the inside of the store and tried to remember exactly how he had left it. But when he had last been inside he had been in one of his cold funks and when one of them came over him he remembered little about them later. They were just collages of sound and light and violent heat that seemed to be inside and outside of him at the same time. Sometimes when he was in a state like that he seemed to experience things beyond the perceptive ability of normal human beings.

But that didn't surprise him.

He knew he wasn't like other people.

He occasionally heard odors, for instance, or felt as though he was seeing sound. The touch of a rough-hewn tabletop could elicit long-forgotten tastes and smells, just as it always did when he was inside Micky Ascherfeld's cabin.

Now, resting on his left knee, the front door nearly closed but wafting cold air across his face, he ran a finger along the edge of the imprint, and the soft dusty feel of the ash sent a shiver up his spine.

It was only wood ash.

Not soft and flaky and littered with bits of bone like the ashes of a human being. But it was so sensual to him that he lifted his fingertips to his lips and licked the ash off of them, savoring the dry, dusty grit against his teeth.

He squinted at the impression in the ash and wondered what had caused it.

His original plan was already half-completed.

Although it had started suddenly and not exactly as planned, long before nightfall it would be done.

Everyone who had to go would be gone and the valley would be purified. When the killing was complete he would return to each and every homesite and torch each of them to the ground. Only his cabin would be left standing. Of course, before he set fire to the store, he intended to strip it of everything that might be of value to him, since he had no intention of ever having contact with the outside world again.

But now the print in the ash revealed a new facet that he hadn't given a lot of thought to.

What if the original inhabitants of McRay could not be induced to leave, once they were dead?

That might be worse than having them alive.

Would he be forced to live in a valley surrounded by malevolent ghosts?

El knew what ghosts could be like.

He brushed the print away brusquely with his fingertips and stood, still holding the rifle by the barrel. He followed the trail of ash with his eyes, right up to the door of the phone room.

He knew whose print it was in the ash. He just couldn't figure out how it had gotten there. A tiny tendril of fear ran from his gut to his groin. He leaned the rifle against the windowsill and pushed the door closed without taking his eyes from the telephone room.

A thought flickered across his mind and he retrieved the shotgun and placed it beside the carbine.

He stepped over the ash and edged around the woodstove, drawing the pistol and cocking it as he did so. There were six fresh shells in the gun. If he had to, he could cut Rita Cabel in half with it. But now he didn't know if that would be sufficient.

She was already dead.

If she was up and walking around, would a gun stop her? And if Rita was moving, then what about Clive?

El glanced into the darkness of the workshop. And although he could not see anything in the gloom, he knew that Clive knew he was there.

A whistling noise caused El to jerk to his left and sweat trickled down the back of his neck. But it was only the wind outside. He ran his tongue along his upper lip and tasted the salt and ash. The gun was heavy in his hand and he brought his left hand up to steady it.

The fear, as it grew, excited him.

He savored fear in a way that he knew other men could not. That was just one of the things that made him different. That and the fact that he knew—in a clinical way—that other men felt something when they killed.

Pity.

Sorrow.

Elation.

Release.

El felt none of those things. What he did feel was sensory perceptions as acute as those of any wild animal. When he killed he smelled the blood. He tasted fear in the air. He had the same sensation that a hawk has when its prey quivers and then grows motionless in its talons.

It wasn't emotion.

It was a more feral sense. An animal feeling of security. Of domination.

The only real human emotion that El had ever experienced was fear. And so he came to cherish fear the way other people cherished love or exaltation. He sometimes confused fear with these.

El didn't long for fear, or place himself in situations where it would come. He wasn't a thrill addict. He was devoid of the need for any emotion. But when fear did come he didn't react the way a normal person would. He let the fear ride over him, enjoying the quivering of the skin in the middle of his back. Pleased by the pleasant dampness in his palms, the slight quickening of his heart and lungs.

He let it build until he was full to bursting with it.

The he began to draw strength from it.

His hands shook. He was inside and outside of his own body at the same time, watching his fear the way a scientist observes the actions of a rat trapped in a maze.

He walked slowly around the stove, keeping his eyes on the door to the phone room but his ears peeled for any movement behind him. He was still licking his lips but there was no moisture on his tongue.

Rita lay on her side, against one leg of the table. There was ash around her on the floor and a thin dusting of ash on her pants, shirt, and face. Her eyes were gone. They had bothered him before. So he'd cut them out.

He had to. He hated the thought of them looking at him. Mocking him. Following him. Hunting him. The first eyes El had ever taken had been his mother's.

His mother had come back to haunt him too.

Nasty slut.

El had killed her in Texas. In the living room of the trailer they shared.

But she'd kept staring at him. When he cut her eyes out he'd been able to end her tyranny forever. Because he left her in Texas. But he wasn't planning on leaving McRay and he couldn't allow Rita and the others to haunt him.

He knew what to do about it.

He pushed open the door and walked boldly across the ash. The fear was thick on him now and he reveled in it. He put the pistol back in its holster, reached out with shaking fingers and grabbed the sleeve of Rita's blouse.

Why did she have to keep moving around?

Did she and Clive know the store so well they could walk around blind?

Could they find him and kill him in his sleep?

There was only one way to be certain that no one would be able to come back and haunt him.

Of course now he knew that he had to go back and finish the job on the others.

2:40

DAWN SLID ON HER belly along floorboards polished by years of abuse from booted feet. She knew she was crazy to leave her hiding place beneath the bed. But curiosity was driving her wild.

After the motor of the four-wheeler died she lay there on her back trying to breathe naturally, gripping the bed frame to still the tremors that wracked her body. She watched the bedroom door like a hawk, waiting for El to return.

She heard the front door open. Felt a draft stir the spread where it hung just barely covering the frame. She waited and waited but there was no sound from below.

Finally, she heard him.

He was talking to himself again but his voice sounded weird and amplified. She knew from the direction and the sound that he was inside the phone room with Rita. The small ceilingless cubicle acted as a megaphone, sending his voice up the stairs.

He was talking to Rita again. "You're not going to follow me around."

Dawn stared at the dusty metal bedsprings inches from her face, listening.

"My mother followed me. The bitch. But I stopped her. Now I'm going to stop you."

Dawn could hear him grunting and something scratching.

"I should have known," said El. "But you won't follow me now."

Dawn slid slowly out from under the bed, careful not to snag her clothes or make a sound. She crawled silently out the door onto the landing, dreading the open space. She felt like a mouse, crossing a wide kitchen floor.

"That's one."

There was a nasty sucking sound and Dawn didn't really want to know what was happening. But a macabre hand pushed her forward. She slid along until she could just see the back of El's head over the balcony, between the raw spruce limbs that Clive had barked and then varnished and bolted along the landing as a railing. El was moving his head this way and that and Dawn bravely lifted her own head to see better.

El straddled Rita's body and all that Dawn could see of Rita was her blue jeans. El was working at something near her head and the ugly sucking sound continued. A bolt of nausea engulfed Dawn and she bit her lip until she tasted blood in order to keep from throwing up.

"There," said El.

As always, his voice sounded dead. No satisfaction. No thrill. Just a flat reminder that a task had been completed. As he shifted position Dawn saw the big knife, dripping blood.

What was he doing to Rita?

What had Rita done to him that had singled her out for special treatment?

Something caught El's attention and he turned.

Had he heard something?

Or were her eyes on him enough to alert him to the presence of another living person in the room?

If she moved a fraction of an inch, he would spot her in his peripheral vision.

He pushed himself to his feet and, as he stepped over Rita's corpse, toward the open door to the phone room, Rita's upper body came into view and Dawn fought down a scream.

Her imagination had conjured horrors, visions of madness. But this was real. And the reality of it stunned. Rita's empty sockets stared up at her just as Clive's had, and at that instant, Dawn was certain that Rita was about to speak. That she would say something to draw El's attention.

But it wasn't Rita's missing eyes that left Dawn paralyzed. It was Rita's arms.

One of them hung from El's hand.

The other was missing.

Dawn knew she was losing it. Soon she would be as insane as El. Terror would drive the last vestiges of sanity from her mind and she would give herself up to him gladly to have this horror over and ended forever.

El stretched, the bloody knife swinging from his right hand. He twisted his head slowly back and forth like a hawk after a kill. It occurred to her that that was what he was. An animal. He wasn't killing everyone out of anger or hatred or fear.

He was killing them because that was what he did.

He felt no pity or satisfaction.

And that made it all the more terrifying. But something deep inside told her that, just then, she was as close to understanding El as she would ever be.

El took a deep breath and tossed Rita's arm onto the floor, pausing briefly to study his handiwork. He cocked his head to one side, then dropped back down onto Rita's body, facing her feet this time.

He lifted the bloody knife high overhead and plunged it down into Rita's thigh, just above the knee.

Dawn's nausea was wiped away by solid terror once more. This time she wasn't going to gag. She was going to pass out.

But not yet.

Not while he's here.

He'll see me or hear my head hit the floor.

And then he'll come for me.

He'll do to me what he's doing to Rita.

And then another realization struck like a physical blow.

I know where he's going next.

Rita wasn't singled out.

She was just the first.

El hacked and sawed, wiping sweat out of his eyes, smearing blood from the back of his hand across his face.

Mercifully, as the crying of the wind increased, Dawn could barely hear the awful sucking noises.

2:42

MICKY SPLASHED ACROSS THE icy creek. The water stung like needles where it soaked into her boots and nipped at her ankles. The rocks were slippery and the snow—now beginning to whiten the ground and cling to the branches—turned the trees on the far shore flat and featureless.

She searched for and finally found the opening in the brush, the one Terry Glorianus used when she went down to the Fork for water. Micky clawed her way up the bank. She was staring at the closed door of Terry's cabin when a staticky warning shocked her. She snatched the radio from her jacket pocket and was about to click the transmit button.

"Don't call back," said Dawn.

Micky turned the volume up and pressed the radio close to her ear. The wind was moaning through the trees and the girl was whispering. It occurred to Micky that had she pressed the send button there was the possibility that Dawn's radio might have squealed. If Dawn was still inside the store and El was in there with her, then that would have been a very dangerous mistake.

"He's cutting Rita up now."

Micky knew that there were numerous cases of serial killers who removed their victims' body parts for various reasons. Chickatillo in Russia had done so under the mistaken idea that his image would remain in his victim's eyes and he might be identified in that way. Others just seemed to get satisfaction from the mutilation.

But something told her that it was neither fear of discovery nor satisfaction that motivated El.

El was acting methodically.

Why was he doing this?

"He keeps saying 'You're not going to follow me around,'" whispered Dawn. *"He cut off Rita's arms and legs."*

Jesus Christ.

You're not going to follow me around?

Did he think the dead could get up and walk?

Micky wanted desperately to reply to Dawn, to ask how she was doing, to find out how close El was, to urge the girl to hide and wait. But she didn't dare call back until she was certain that El was out of hearing range of the radio. Now she kept the volume turned up full blast and headed back up the trail toward El's cabin.

The snow settled into a satiny layer of white beneath her feet. It reminded her of the silk lining of Wade's casket. Of the sheen of her father's blood against the clean tile floor. To Micky, white would always be the color of death.

2:43

MARTY AND STAN STOOD on Howard's porch, peering inside the empty cabin. They were still arguing. The door was wide-open and snow had begun to stick to the cabin floor.

"Shut up, Stan," said Marty.

Stan started to reply but Marty had already stepped into the cabin.

"Maybe you shouldn't go in there," murmured Stan.

Marty scowled.

Normally he would have considered it the height of effrontery to enter someone else's home without their permission. A man's home was his castle. Of course, if a man was caught out in the weather and needed shelter, that was a different matter. Go on in, use what you need, replace it when you can. Everyone in the Alaskan bush knew that was okay. But this wasn't a blizzard and they were just passing by.

"Something's not right," said Marty, glancing around the cabin.

"Looks all right to me," insisted Stan, still refusing to cross the threshold.

Marty tested the stove with a bare hand. "Warm."

"Probably gone hunting."

Marty glanced at the gun case beside the bed. "Must be planning a long trip," he said, walking over to it.

"What do you mean?" said Stan, taking a tentative step inside.

"He took all four guns."

Stan shook his head. "That doesn't make sense. Why would Howard pack all those guns?"

"Yeah. And the lock on the case is broken." Marty pointed to chipped wood where the door had been jimmied.

"Maybe he lost his key," said Stan.

"This stinks," Marty said, giving Stan another of those looks.

"Come on," said Stan, no longer interested in arguing. "Let's go find Clive and see what the hell is going on."

But Marty didn't move. He glanced slowly around the cabin, then back at the empty gun case.

"I can't figure it," he said. "Unless there was a bear and everyone came here to grab a gun."

But that made no sense. Unless everyone just happened to be meeting at Howard's at the time.

Marty looked out at the snow, wishing it had started earlier so whoever had been at the cabin would have left tracks.

"Come on," said Stan, turning away.

Marty started to follow. Then he spotted Howard's coffee cup.

"Stan." Marty felt the cup. It was cool to the touch but filled to the brim.

Stan moseyed over and touched the cup himself. But it was clear that he didn't get the significance.

"Why would he pour himself a full cup of coffee and leave it sitting here?" asked Marty, glancing over again at the busted gun case. "Howard left in one hell of a hurry. And he didn't haul four or five rifles out of here all by himself."

"Probably a bear."

"I don't think this has anything to do with a bear."

"Well, what *do* you think?"

Marty shook his head. "I think we better go find out."

2:45

MICKY COULDN'T BELIEVE IT.

She stood at the edge of the trail and stared at El's cabin.

On the front porch, taking up nearly the entire stoop, sat a fat old grizzly.

The bear was tearing into a large black garbage bag with gusto. Her huge claws raked the soft plastic, her nose buried deep in the delicious-smelling refuse. She emitted that peculiar snuffling noise that grizzlies make, a sound between a belch and a snore. And each time she pulled her black nose out of the bag she had paper hanging between her teeth as she gnawed greedily on the odds and ends.

She had her huge butt pressed against the only door into El's cabin and Micky considered giving up her quest as a bad idea. But the bear stood between her and her only hope of finding a weapon with which to even up the odds. Somehow she had to get the bear to move.

The animal was clearly past her prime, mangy from years of wilderness living and a hard winter. But old bears got that way by being tough and Micky didn't underestimate this one. She probably weighed in at well over eight hundred pounds and her claws could slash through skin and flesh and cartilage like paper.

Aaron said that bears were smarter than people.

You shouldn't just shoot them. You had to learn how to negotiate with them.

There were still eight or ten garbage bags the bear had not yet gotten around to scattering about the clearing. Evidently the grizzly had spent the past hour or so opening one after the other, and then tired of the game and dragged a bag up onto the porch to sample at her leisure. Micky stepped out into the clearing where the snow was starting to cover the debris with a pure blanket of white.

The bear looked up curiously.

"I'm going to go over there and open you up another TV dinner," Micky said, pointing toward the unopened bags. She didn't want to appear threatening. Her intention was to open a bag and toss the garbage onto the snow to entice the old sow off the porch. The animal's cold black eyes pierced the veil of thickening snowflakes, following Micky's every movement.

For all their bulk, the big bears were deceptively agile and swift. A grizzly could easily outrun a sprinter for a short distance and Micky didn't care to find out just how short a distance that was.

Micky took three slow, deliberate steps toward the side of the cabin. The bear cocked her head, keeping the ravished bag tightly wedged between her hind legs. She didn't seem disturbed yet. She emitted a grunt. A question in bear language.

Micky took another couple of steps and the bear stiffened. Micky could see the animal's thick brain churning, her eyes narrowing.

"Just getting you some more food!" Micky shouted over the wind.

No problem.

Without warning the words echoed through her mind and she knew that her subconscious must have realized before she did that there was a problem.

She froze in mid-stride.

The bear was no longer grunting.

She was growling.

2:47

T HE STORE," SAID STAN.

The rifle hung in his right hand and his left was fisted on his hip. Marty itched to smack him. He stood on Howard's stoop, glaring down at Stan, who reminded him, as usual, of a spoiled teenager.

"Someone shouted across the Fork," insisted Marty, nodding toward the bridge to Terry Glorianus's cabin. They had both heard it. A woman's voice, distorted by the wind and the lowering snow. It had to be Terry or Dawn. But it was hard to tell how far away the voice came from. "The shots came from the Glorianus place first."

"What about all the shells we heard popping? That came from the store. We need to get down there." Stan glanced around, nervously. "You know what you're thinking. You know it."

"We don't know anything for sure," said Marty. "We heard shots."

"And a shout."

"Maybe it's a bear."

"Maybe. So then why did Clive blast off all those shells?"

"We don't know it was Clive," said Marty.

"Exactly."

"We won't find out standing here."

"Why don't you say it?"

"Say what?"

"It was El Hoskins."

Marty spit into the snow. "I don't know anything of the sort."

"You been saying for years El was going to go off like a stick of dynamite someday. Everybody knows it."

"This is silly. We're wasting time standing here."

"We ought to get down to the store and find Clive."

"Ten minutes ago you wanted to take off and go back to get packs. Now you want to get right over to the store," said Marty, disgusted. "Go. I'm going to find out what the shouting's about."

He clomped down the steps and past Stan, close enough to brush him with his shoulder. He had one foot on the bridge, expecting to hear Stan's footsteps behind him, but the only sound was the wind howling overhead and the barely audible murmur of the creek, tugging at the wood pilings of the bridge.

Marty waited, as though catching his breath. But still there was silence.

Finally, he turned.

Stan was standing right where he'd left him, hand still on his hip, pouting.

Marty sighed. It was like bringing up a kid.

He waited.

Stan looked away, ignoring him.

Marty tightened his grip on his rifle and hiked back up the trail.

"I'm not going to the store yet, Stan."

"We should go there first."

"Stan, do you have any idea how much time we waste arguing?"

"Then don't argue," said Stan. "Let's go."

But Marty shook his head.

"No. First I'm going to go see if Terry and Dawn are all right. Doesn't that make any sense to you at all? We hear shots. There are two unarmed women here. It's time for bears to come out of hibernation. Let's think now." He tapped the top of his head with one finger.

"So, who took Howard's guns?"

The only idea that Marty could come up with on short notice was that someone had broken into Howard's cabin and stolen them.

But where was Howard?

Stan was right. The whole thing stunk of El.

"I don't know," said Marty. "I'm just trying to figure this out."

"Who would do something like that?" said Stan, shaking his head. "Everybody here knows everybody else."

"Maybe an Indian."

"Yeah," said Stan. "Maybe."

But Indians didn't steal and the chances of one bothering to wander deeper into the valley than Cabels' Store were almost nonexistent.

"I don't want to go on alone, Stan," said Marty.

"Well, why didn't you say so?" said Stan.

Marty hiked back across the creek, listening to Stan's boots clocking on the wooden bridge.

2:49

MICKY STOOD HALFWAY TO the cabin, in the midst of the garbage that now bore an icing of thin wet snow. The old bear sat up on her haunches, ignoring the bag between her legs, watching Micky.

The bear looked like a fat old woman, with her bag of popcorn, waiting for a movie to begin. If there had been a sturdy fence between them, Micky might have found the image humorous.

She had again considered giving up her quest and backing down the trail. But she had to get her hands on a gun and if El was trashing them all as he had hers, the closest place to look for one was inside *his* cabin.

Somehow she had to get the bear off the stoop without provoking the animal. The problem was that her plan to scatter more garbage for the bear had a flaw.

To get to the bags Micky had to edge along the side of the cabin and eventually that would place her outside the bear's range of vision and the old sow wanted to know where Micky was at all times.

The closer Micky inched, the louder and more ominous the bear's growls became. She was lazily baring her teeth to let Micky know that she wasn't happy. Micky could see the dirty ivory color of the animal's claws and she knew how sharp they could be. There were bear trees all around the valley, favorite scratching posts where the big grizzlies would stand on their back legs and reach up and rake their talons down through the bark, leaving deep scars in the trees, often an inch deep and ten or twelve feet off the ground.

"I'm going to get you some more food!" Micky shouted. "Food!"

She felt silly, talking to a bear. Even if bears did communicate, would they speak English? She tried to remember if she knew the Athabaskan word for food or garbage.

Jesus.

She might just as well have been shouting *oogahbooga* for all the damn bear understood. But she kept talking, more for herself than the bear's sake.

"Not going to bother you! Just gonna get you some more food!"

With each syllable she eased another mincing step through the snow.

Now the bear had to lean her head out to see around the end of the cabin. The logs on each corner were stacked in a staggered pattern and Micky could see the bear's muzzle framed between two of the square-cut ends. When Micky reached the point that she could no longer see the bear's one cold eye, she bolted for the stack of bags.

She hadn't counted on how slippery the trash had become beneath the dusting of snow. Her second step landed on something that shot out from under her. She lurched forward, and before she could brace herself, the ground hit her solidly in the face. The wind blasted from her lungs and her diaphragm screamed for air.

No problem.

She forced herself through a mental inventory to see if she had damaged anything.

Her first concern was her back. She recalled the long weeks in agony, the pain shooting up her spine, the nights when she had to sleep in a recliner because there was no comfortable position to be found anywhere in bed.

But there was no back pain.

Thank God.

What there was, was a snuffling sound behind her and a

nasty rash of goose bumps creeping up where the pain should have been. She lifted her head ever so slowly and turned to the rear of the cabin, where she got a fleeting glimpse of another big black nose, poking around the logs.

She managed to catch her breath but let it out instantly as the sow's cub came sauntering around to see what all the excitement was about.

2:51

D AWN MADE CERTAIN THE volume on the radio was way
down before depressing the talk button. She wasn't sure
if Micky was hearing her anymore but she desperately
needed to communicate with someone.

El was still in Clive's workshed. She could hear his voice
but couldn't make out what he was saying.

She pressed the transmit button and whispered Micky's
name.

Nothing.

She experimented by turning up the volume. Just a hair.

Nothing.

Outside the wind whistled under the eaves, and the day
was gloomier than ever. Dawn thought of her mother, back
in their cabin, surrounded by cold and darkness, and tears
stung her eyes.

She was alone as she had never been in her life. Her
mother was the only family Dawn had known for years and
she felt deserted and betrayed even as she experienced a
deeper guilt than she had ever known could exist.

I didn't do anything to help her.

*When El was stabbing the knife into her back, I didn't
even scream.*

She had just stood there, motionless, sucking in her

breath, terrified, useless. When he'd murdered Howard she had been equally worthless. She knew that Terry or Howard would have sacrificed their own lives to save her and she had done absolutely nothing for them.

A tiny voice argued that there was nothing that she could have done. That anything she'd tried to do would only have gotten her killed too. But it was a small voice and ineffective against the massive guilt welling up inside her.

El began to take on new dimensions.

Dawn began to wonder if El had some kind of magical powers.

Look how easily he'd killed her mother and Howard and Rita.

How he knew to wait for Clive.

And what was he doing to them now? Why was he cutting them up like that?

It seemed like some kind of sick ritual.

"Micky?" she whispered into the radio. "Are you still there?"

From the store below came the eerie sound of El, humming a tune.

2:55

THE CUB EYED MICKY curiously. He snuffled through the garbage on the ground around her while, behind her, Micky heard the alarming sound of the steps creaking beneath the massive weight of the sow. Dawn's voice screeched from the radio in her pocket.

Micky couldn't reach for it. She was afraid to move or breathe.

She couldn't believe the situation.

She pictured Aaron coming upon the scene and laughing.

A bear behind her. A bear in front of her. And she was lying in a pile of garbage.

Add to that the fact that Aaron was lying dead up the trail.

Terry and Howard lying dead down the trail.

And Dawn calling on the radio to announce that El was mutilating his victims.

Micky didn't know whether to laugh or cry.

She wanted to jump up and scream at the two bears to get the fuck out of her way because she really didn't have time for this shit. A part of her mind told her to go ahead. That it just might work. Bears were known to back down when faced with a noisy, aggressive opponent.

But not a sow with a cub.

Micky knew that if she stood up right now, if she made any move that the mother took to be in any way threatening to her offspring, she would die.

She turned her head to watch the cub but she sensed the sow right behind her. The big bear was close enough that Micky could hear its rumbling breath. Close enough that she got a good whiff of the rancid smell of the animal. She had heard that bears stunk but she never expected to get close enough to one to actually experience it. The odor was a mixture of rotten garbage and feces and wet soil.

Aaron said that some bears were like dogs. They liked to roll in anything that stank. Now she had direct proof. The cub dropped down on all fours right in front of her face and rolled over in the snow, dredging up half-empty food cans and plastic bread bags. He rolled back over onto his stomach, his nose inches from hers. At that range, with his canines exposed, he didn't look at all cute and cuddly.

Something sharp nudged the nape of Micky's neck.

2:56

MARTY LIFTED A PILLOWCASE from the ground and dusted off the snow. The rest of the laundry sculpted odd white patterns on the Glorianus front lawn. Stan reached down and retrieved a sheet. When he shook the clinging wet snow from it, Marty let out a low gasp.

"Shit," said Stan.

They both stared at the bloody boot print that desecrated the perfect white of the cotton.

Both of them dropped the linens and lifted their rifles. They turned back to face the dark windows of the cabin, which suddenly seemed to have a much more foreboding stare. Marty lowered himself into a crouch and hurried closer to the wall, where he wouldn't be a good target. He waved impatiently at Stan, who was still looking left and right, peering inside. Stan nodded, then slipped over beside Marty.

"You want to get your ass shot off?" hissed Marty.

"I didn't see anything."

"Neither did they," said Marty, nodding back toward the laundry.

"Yeah," muttered Stan.

They glared at each other for a minute, Marty knowing that he had to take charge and also knowing that Stan was going to argue with him.

Marty tried to think where the voice had come from. It sounded like a woman and it had barely carried through the gathering storm.

"You think he's inside?" said Stan. Both of them knew who *he* was. That wasn't a bear track on the sheet. And Terry would never have left her linens out in the snow.

This had to be El's doing.

He was Dawn and Terry's closest neighbor.

The shots had come from this area.

And nobody else in the whole world was as fucking nuts as El.

Maybe Dawn or Terry had gotten away and El was after them or maybe he had taken one or both of them back to his cabin. But then whose blood was on the sheet?

Or maybe he was inside.

Maybe he was wounded.

Maybe it was El's blood.

Maybe a lot of things. He and Stan couldn't leave the cabin without finding out first if El was in there or if Terry or Dawn were in there and needed their help. But Marty didn't want to shout to find out. What if El wasn't inside but close by? They'd just be alerting him to their presence.

"We need to find out if anyone's inside," said Stan, loudly.

Marty cuffed him on the mouth.

"Hey!" Stan reared back, his face reddening.

"Shut up!" rasped Marty. "Do you want to let him know where we are?"

"You shouldn't have done that."

Marty skittered along the cabin to the door. He reached out and pushed it in. Stan hurried past the opening to the other side of the jamb.

At least he was smart enough not to deliberately make a target of himself.

The door creaked slowly open.

Marty listened.

The wind camouflaged any noises from the cabin's interior. But a wide smear of blood started at the threshold.

Stan's jaw dropped.

The shit had definitely hit the fan in McRay.

2:57

MICKY STRAINED TO HEAR.

But the snuffling of both bears, the pounding of her heart, and the crying of the wind was closer and more immediate than the voice that she thought she'd heard back down the trail.

It sounded like a man's voice.

Had El slipped out of the store when Dawn wasn't looking? Was he coming back to the cabin? She pictured herself caught between two grizzly bears and a serial killer.

But surely he hadn't had time.

She closed her eyes and started to count seconds between breaths, forcing her lungs to take in only enough oxygen to keep her body running, and willing her heart to slow. She relaxed her hands and wriggled her toes in her boots.

The snow chilled her left cheek and she focused on that rather than the stink of the two bears' breath, steaming in her nostrils.

Then she felt the sow licking the back of her neck.

She opened her eyes in time to see the cub's long black tongue slap her cheek.

It tickled.

She fought down laughter, feeling her tortured diaphragm wanting to howl.

Salt.

They liked her sweat. Like two giant puppies licking their master's face. The tickling sensation and the absurdity of her situation were almost more than she could stand.

2:58

WELL SOMEBODY MUST HAVE gone batshit crazy." Stan's face was white as a sheet but he had come back inside and at least Marty wasn't having to listen to him heaving into the snow anymore.

Marty knelt beside Terry's body. He had lit one of the mantel lamps and placed it on the counter but from that position it threw jagged black shadows that made the ugly scene even more macabre. Terry's torso looked as though someone had decided to make sushi out of it and the floor was thick with sticky blood. Marty turned up his nose at the smell of urine and feces that he knew was the inevitable result of violent death. He had never been this close to a human victim, though.

Howard lay crumpled beside the woodstove like a wet towel. There wasn't nearly so much blood around him as there was around Terry. But the wide swath that led back to the door showed just how much blood the old man had lost. Marty stood up and tried to stop himself from shaking.

"El did this," said Stan, swallowing the huge lump in his throat. "Man. He's fucking crazy."

"Yeah." Marty couldn't quite get his voice to work.

"He cut their goddamned eyes out!" Stan's own eyes were wide as saucers.

"We're going to have to kill the son of a bitch," said

Marty. He noticed that Stan's knuckles were white on the grip of his rifle.

"Oh, yeah," said Stan.

"Calm down, Stan," said Marty.

"Yeah," said Stan. "I'm calming down, now. Getting calm."

"Breathe." Marty took a deep breath and let it out loud enough for Stan to hear.

Stan took one deep breath. Then another. A little color seeped back into his cheeks.

"We ought to cover them up," said Marty.

"Yeah," said Stan. "Right."

But there was nothing inside the cabin to cover the bodies with. They went outside and shuffled around, finding first a sheet that wasn't bloodied and then a blanket. They placed the blanket over Terry, gently draping it from her feet to her head, then put the sheet down over Howard.

Stan was clearly in a hurry to get back outside. But when Marty moved over beside him, Stan didn't budge.

"What?" said Marty, waiting patiently.

"I don't know. I just feel like we shouldn't leave them in the cold like this."

Marty knew what he meant. He and Stan were both in shock. Their minds weren't working right. Actually, the best thing to do would probably be to let the bodies get cold.

"We should build a better fire before we leave," said Stan.

"No," said Marty. "We don't have time. We don't know where El is or who else is alive. And, besides, they can't feel anything."

But Marty could tell by Stan's body language that this was going to be another sticking point.

"It isn't right we leave them here like this," insisted Stan.

Marty considered shoving Stan out of the way and just leaving. He knew that Stan wouldn't stay long in the cabin by himself. The trouble was he agreed with Stan. It didn't feel right to just leave them like this. He knew that it was insane, stoking a fire in the stove for dead people, but reason didn't have anything to do with it. Dead people didn't appreciate the flowers at their funerals either. But you still put them on the casket.

"All right," said Marty, leaning his rifle beside the door. "Let's get some wood."

3:00

DAWN HEARD THE FRONT door open and close and felt a draft slip beneath the bed.

El had gone outside.

She knew that he wasn't tricking her. For one thing, she was reasonably sure that he didn't know she was inside the store and, for another, she'd heard him still mumbling to himself when he shut the door behind him. She clasped the radio tight against her cheek and whispered into it.

"Micky, are you there?" She had the volume turned up just high enough that a mouse wouldn't have been able to hear it five feet away.

But there was no reply.

She wondered if the other radio had gone dead. Hers hadn't been on very long, but she had no idea how long the batteries were good for. Or perhaps Micky had moved somewhere out of range. Or she'd set the radio down and gone off to do something and now she couldn't hear it. Whatever the reason, Dawn had now lost contact with the only other human being in the village she'd been certain was alive—other than El.

The gray light of afternoon was barely able to cut through the thickening snow and filter down to the floor-boards. Her entire world was gray. She stared at the coiled springs in front of her face, smelling the age-old dust that felt so much cleaner in her lungs than the things she had been smelling all day.

What if something had happened to Micky?

I need to know what El's doing now.

If he's leaving, maybe I can get away.

But wasn't she better off just staying where she was?

After all, El hadn't found her and it seemed as though he wasn't going to. He probably still believed that he had wounded her and she was out in the woods somewhere, hurt or dead. Better to stay where she was and wait for help to arrive.

But when would that be?

And who?

Marty or Stan?

She didn't know the pair that well but what she did know of them didn't fill her with hope. They were like an old married couple, always bickering. They acted more like comedians than heroes. And they were probably all tucked away in their cabins, waiting out the storm beside their woodstoves, happily ignorant of what was going on.

Who then?

Micky?

She'd put all her faith in Micky and now Micky wasn't answering.

Damon?

Damon hated guns and, besides, she hadn't seen him in days.

Aaron?

The old man was more enigma than person, and he, too, lived far up the valley and didn't show himself much. And he was old. Real old.

Rich, the mail pilot?

He wouldn't be arriving for hours and El might murder him too.

She thought that she could probably make it through the night under the bed.

But what if El decided to spend the night in the store?

What if he slept in Clive and Rita's bed?

What if she lay awake all night, listening to El breathing, terrified to let herself drift off, lest she make some small noise and awaken to see him leaning under the bed, staring at her with those cold eyes? She wondered if he slept in his sunglasses.

She pictured him like that, lying back, sound asleep, no way to tell if his eyes were open or shut. That had to be why he wore them. Not to protect himself from the sun or the glare of the snow. Not to pretend to be anyone that he wasn't.

He wore the glasses like a mask.

So that he'd always look like he was awake.

Like he was always watching you.

It was no good waiting for the mail plane. El planned to kill everyone in McRay. Dawn knew beyond a shadow of a doubt that he had plans for Rich. And, so far El's plans seemed to have gone off without a hitch. All except the one he'd had for her.

El was outside somewhere and she had to find out what he was doing. If he left the store, she was going to look for some other place to hide. Better to bundle up and stay in the woods than here. She didn't want to think about hiding in one of the cabins, never knowing if El was going to show up and beat the door in.

With the day growing darker by the minute, Dawn once again forced herself out of her hiding place.

3:05

MICKY CLOSED HER EYES and prayed that Dawn was okay. The cub's saliva had chilled enough that a paper-thin layer of white was stinging her skin. The layer underneath melted slowly from body heat, and trickled infuriatingly in an icy stream down her cheek. The sow had stopped licking the back of her neck and had begun snuffling at her, shoving her muzzle into Micky's ribs. Several times Micky felt the sharp pressure of a claw point through her clothes.

But there was no tearing sound, no agonizing ripping through her flesh. The sow was just testing.

Micky opened her eyes again, just a slit, and saw that the cub was sitting on his haunches, regarding her and his mother curiously. He saw Micky's eye open and for just an instant Micky feared that he was going to tell his mother. She managed to squelch a chuckle—any movement or noise on her part might be all it took to turn a funny moment into a tragedy.

The radio had been silent ever since Dawn's last harrowing message. Micky hoped that the girl was well hidden and had the sense to remain where she was and stay off the radio. But she knew what it must be costing Dawn that no one had responded. She remembered her own helplessness at Dawn's age. Wondering if anyone would ever come.

Feeling betrayed.

And alone.

Feeling hunted.

Micky remembered staring out through louvered closet doors in her parents' store, as the man in the ski mask stalked her. The minutes like hours. Sweat dripping into her eyes. Breathing through tight lips. Everything seemed out of focus that day except his mirror glasses.

That and the odd way he held the shotgun.

For some reason the kid kept his middle finger on the trigger.

She didn't remember mentioning that to the police. In the chaos of the moment and her grief, it had probably slipped her mind.

But she could see it now as though she were viewing the scene through high-powered lenses. Focused tightly on the man's hand on the gun.

Her memory was a strange amalgam of uncontrollable images. The killer's finger. The flowers around her father's corpse. The smell of mums and chemical extender. Her parents' screams as they died. The rhythmic slapping of tennis shoes, padding room by room behind her as she crept on her hands and knees through the darkened shop. Wiping blood from her hands onto the tight weave of the carpet. The black-and-white lines of shadow and light thrown against the closet walls by the louvered doors. Like prison bars.

The wind died down and the snow fell in giant starfish flakes, so thick that everything beyond the cub's back was a kaleidoscope of white. Early May and McRay was in the middle of a blizzard. She knew that it might go on all night, or it might stop and the snow could melt under the blast of warm winds in hours, even minutes. The storm was as strange as the day.

She had no idea what to do now.

People around McRay were always talking about bears. But now it seemed all the advice she had been given on grizzlies wouldn't fill a decent paragraph.

Don't feed them. Don't get between a sow and her cub.

Make lots of noise and they'll usually leave you alone.

If one charges, play dead.

But she couldn't remember anyone ever mentioning what to do after you played dead or how long you might have to do it.

What's the attention span of a bear?

And why the hell are they still interested in me?

It occurred to her again that it would be very bad for her to be lying on the ground outside El's house if El returned home.

It was at least a fifteen-minute walk to the store, probably more in the snow. But El had Clive's four-wheeler. He could be anywhere by now.

How long has it been since Dawn called? Five minutes maybe?

The fact that the girl wasn't using the radio intensified Micky's fear for her. If Dawn wasn't talking, it probably meant that El was too close.

Would Dawn have time to make a final call if he caught her?

Is there anything I could do to help her if she did?

Micky tried to remember everything she had ever learned about hostage situations. But that mostly amounted to calling for superiors who would bring in professional negotiators and El wasn't taking hostages anyway. There was nothing she could threaten him with or promise him.

What do I do if the call comes right now?

Reach for the radio and risk having my arm ripped off?

Why was God doing this to her?

Micky promised herself an answer for that one sometime in the future. Someone was going to tell her why. She wasn't going to accept Milquetoast explanations from some psychiatrist. She was going to demand to know what kind of God would send three killers for the same woman on three separate occasions. Three men with dead eyes and powerful guns intent on killing someone they had never met.

Well, she had met El. If you wanted to call it *meeting*. But, really, she didn't know him any better than she had known either of the other two and that brought her full circle to her obsession with the repeating gunman.

Although it was impossible, her mind kept telling her that the exact same terror was happening again. That it was the same man behind all the killings. Just as she had known in the hospital that the gunman in the bar was the same man who had killed her parents.

Could he have gotten out of prison?

No way.

Did God have that sick a sense of humor?

Sure.

The same man.

Over and over.

Wasn't there an old saw about that?

Whom the gods would kill, first they make insane.

"I'm getting really tired of this shit," she said.

It was only when the cub snorted and fell over backwards that she realized that she had spoken out loud. A heavy slap on the back of her neck stung her and her head rocked enough to send a shooting pain down her spine.

But what she took at first to be the sow growling in surprise was actually the snarl of Clive's four-wheeler, somewhere off in the distance.

3:08

THE COZY FIRE WARMED Terry Glorianus's woodstove. Terry and Howard were tucked in beneath their shrouds. And Marty and Stan were halfway up the trail to El's cabin.

Stan still wanted to head right down to the store and find out what was going on but Marty had convinced him, barely, that they were better off inspecting El's place first. If El was there, then one of them would stake the place out while the other went to the store for help. If he was gone, then chances were he was already down to the store and they ought to check out his cabin to see if there was anything that might give them a clue to what he was doing. There was also the chance that he might have gone across the river toward Micky's place.

The snow fluttered across their cheeks, into their eyes and mouths, trying to soften a hard day.

Stan was following, as usual, and talking, as usual, and Marty really wanted him to shut up.

"What if you're wrong? What if it wasn't El?" said Stan. "What if El is dead in his cabin? Then what?"

Marty shook his head without looking back.

"Then I guess we'll have to find out who did it," said Marty.

"Who the hell else would do something like this?" said Stan, breathing heavily.

"How the hell would I know? Shut up! What was that?"

Marty could have sworn he'd heard a woman's voice again, just up ahead. But Stan was jabbering, and with the breeze and the snow and his own breathing, and the pumping of his heart Marty couldn't be sure. His muscles tightened and he slipped his finger around the trigger of his rifle.

"Hear what?" said Stan.

Marty gave him a look that would have melted rock and for once Stan was silent.

Marty pointed with his rifle, up the trail, and Stan got the hint, moving up close and walking silently behind.

They were only yards from the clearing at El's cabin.

"I thought I heard a voice," said Marty.

"At El's?" whispered Stan.

Just then, from the direction of the store, they heard the distinctive chatter of the four-wheeler cranking up.

"Want to wait and see if Clive shows up?" whispered Stan.

Marty shook his head.

"Maybe we should," said Stan.

"You're really pissing me off now," said Marty.

3 : 10

THE CUB WAS SO close to Micky's face that she could have licked *his* nose.

Her head was getting slapped around from behind, but not as roughly as before. Apparently the sow had reached the opinion that this human thing wasn't dangerous to her cub. Now the grizzly just wanted to know what made it tick.

Maybe she was getting ready to see if it was edible.

Suddenly something caught the cub's attention. He glanced at his mother, then back down the trail toward Terry's place, then back at his mother. There was a low growling from the sow and an astonished expression on the cub's face.

The four-wheeler buzzed in the distance, too far off to be exciting the bears.

So what were they looking at?

Perhaps it wasn't El on the four-wheeler at all.

What if it was Dawn?

What if El was coming up the trail on foot and Dawn had escaped on the four wheeler?

Did that make sense?

Micky didn't have time to decide.

The sow's growling increased to a roar.

Micky heard familiar voices and, ignoring the cub, she rolled over onto her back as she felt the sow rumble away.

Marty and then Stan emerged into the clearing. Micky saw their shocked expressions as the big grizzly tore down the hill at them like a runaway train with claws and teeth.

Marty lifted his rifle.

Stan tried to mimic him with trembling hands.

Stan's first shot tossed up a spray of snow at his feet. His whole body quivered as he struggled to work another round into the chamber of the bolt-action rifle.

Marty had his gun at shoulder level, sighting down it, squeezing the trigger. The gun bucked and he calmly chambered another shell as the huge grizzly seemed to sidestep, the bullet penetrating somewhere but not doing fatal damage. The big bear was slowed but not stopped. In the confines of the clearing, her roar of rage and pain sounded like a jet engine. Her enormous mass hurtled inexorably onward.

Stan managed to get his rifle up and fire but this time the shot was high, and then he was fighting with the bolt again.

Marty fired again, just as the beast reached them.

Stan was swept aside by the rushing mass of the animal, losing his rifle and falling into the trees. The bear landed on top of Marty and he struggled to pull himself tightly against the huge creature. He grasped at fur and hide, struggling to become part of the bear, while the bear clawed at his back and sides.

"Shoot her!" Micky screamed at Stan, who was climbing shakily to his knees.

Micky ran, slipping and sliding, down the hill, across the Teflon-slick snow toward Marty's rifle, lying on the side of the trail. Stan seemed dazed, staring with glazed eyes at the bear and Marty, dancing their deadly ballet.

Marty screamed as the long talons ripped through his flesh and cartilage like scythes. His head was tucked tightly beneath the bear's chin and she gnawed and gnashed, twisting her head viciously back and forth, trying to get her teeth into him. Marty's toes clambered for purchase in the fur along the hind legs and belly of the bear. And his fingers were buried in the pelt around her fat neck.

Micky fell but managed to get her fingers around the stock of Marty's rifle, as the bear stumbled right over her, dragging Marty along backward toward the woods.

She raised the barrel toward the massive hulk of hair and hide and teeth and talon but the bear kept turning and twisting and clawing like a hairy maelstrom. The animal's fur was covered in blood, Marty's and its own. And Micky was afraid that she had as much chance of shooting Marty as she did the bear.

But Marty kept screaming for someone to shoot and Micky knew that very soon it would no longer matter which of them she hit.

She pointed up at the writhing mass without searching for anything vital and fired. The gun bucked in her hand, the explosion stung her ears.

The bear reared back and shoved Marty away from her as though he were a piece of clothing she had inspected and found not to her taste. He dropped in a heap at the sow's feet. She shook herself off and staggered through the alders near Stan, as though the thick brush were made of cheesecloth. But she was lurching as she went and Micky noticed a wide trail of blood on the snow.

The cub barreled down the hill and rushed after its mother, squealing like a terrified piglet, and for an instant Micky felt sorry for him. She knew what it was like to see a parent shot. To hear the cries of fear and pain from someone you had always believed to be invulnerable.

But then she turned back to Marty.

He lay spread-eagled across the path. A flap of skin and hair had opened on the right side of his face from the top of his scalp down to his chin. The flap covered his eye and nose and exposed bright red muscle and white bone beneath. Marty's ear hung by a thread of skin and his right arm seemed to be twisted at an impossible angle.

But he was breathing.

Micky crawled over to him and gently slipped the large flap of skin back as close as she could to its normal position. His face seemed wrinkled then, as though he had too much flesh.

"We have to get him inside," she told Stan, nodding toward El's cabin. "He'll die of shock or hypothermia out here."

Stan didn't move.

"It is El, isn't it?" he asked.

"Yes," said Micky.

"He might be in his cabin."

"No. It's locked. He's at Cabels'. He killed Clive and Rita, and Dawn's hiding in the store."

"He killed Terry and Howard too."

"I know."

Stan glanced back down the trail, managing finally to crank another shell into the chamber of his rifle. "You're sure he's at the store?"

"I think he's using Clive's four-wheeler. I don't know exactly where he is right now. Stan, we have to get Marty inside."

"You think maybe he heard the shots?"

She thought about it. She was pretty sure that she had heard the four-wheeler after the last shot. More than likely El wouldn't have been able to hear the shots over the engine noise but there was no way of telling.

"I don't know." She pressed her finger against Marty's neck. His pulse was strong but his breathing was shallow.

Stan stared off in the direction of the Glorianus cabin. "He cut their eyes out. Jesus Christ. He cut out their eyes. We gotta kill him. Don't we?"

"Can you get Marty's shoulders if I carry his feet?" she said.

"I think so," said Stan.

They just managed it, though they had to stop for Micky to rest halfway up the slope.

Marty kept mumbling, trying to talk, dipping in and out of consciousness. Micky knew that he wouldn't be in a great deal of pain now. That would come later.

If he lived.

They got him up onto the stoop and both of them stared for just a moment at the padlock. No one in McRay locked their cabins. It was like a sign saying *Look at me! I don't belong here! I don't trust you!*

"Wonder what he's afraid of?" said Stan.

"Us," answered Micky.

She stepped over to the one small window and noticed that a blanket had been fashioned as a blackout curtain. Without hesitation, she broke the window with her elbow, then finished off the remaining shards with the sole of her boot. She ripped the blanket down and climbed inside, turning to lean out.

"Drag him over here," she told Stan. "You'll have to pass him in to me. We've got to get him inside."

Stan nodded and went to work. But, as he dragged Marty nearer the window, he stopped to stare at the snow behind him on the porch.

A broad swath of blood stained the virgin-white snow.

Micky swallowed a lump in her throat as she and Stan lifted Marty. There was definitely something wrong with his right arm. It was limp and pliable and she knew they might be doing irreparable damage by putting Marty's weight on it. As she dragged him backward into the room his feet hit the floor and Stan hurried through the window to help her.

The swirling snow followed him in.

The layout of the cabin was almost identical to Micky's. The woodstove sat in the far corner and, where her tiny kitchen would have been, El had a workbench.

But El's decor was a lot different.

Even with only the light through the busted window what they saw inside brought Micky and Stan up short.

"Holy shit," said Stan, turning slowly around.

Micky couldn't think of anything better to say.

Every inch of wall space seemed to be covered. There were rifles and carbines, shotguns and revolvers and automatic pistols. The back wall seemed to be dedicated to different types of assault rifles and machine pistols. Boxes of ammo were stacked to the ceiling in the far corner.

He has all of this and he's driving around with only a rifle and the pistol?

Why?

If he was planning on killing everyone in town, why wouldn't he gear up like Rambo and wade through McRay spraying bullets?

"How did he get all these guns without anyone noticing?" asked Stan.

"Nobody knows what comes in on Rich's plane," said Micky. "A box is a box."

Stan looked at the submachine pistols. "Are these legal?"

"No. But they're easy enough to get if you know who to buy from. My bet's El spent some time in prison. You make a lot of connections inside."

Marty groaned at Micky's feet.

"Light a lamp and put the blanket back over the window," said Micky tersely, dropping down beside Marty on the floor. Stan hurried to obey. He looked around and finally grabbed a short-barreled shotgun off the wall beside the door. He rehung the blanket, then laid the gun onto the bottom of the makeshift drape to keep it from fluttering open again. Snow still flitted in on either side but the wind no longer whistled through the tiny cabin.

Though she didn't want to do it, Micky had no choice but to roll Marty over and inspect the extent of the wounds on his back, where the bear had ripped and slashed. She could only imagine what those six-inch claws had done to the soft tissue. If they had entered below the rib cage, they might well have gotten his kidneys or spleen or gone even deeper. He might be bleeding to death and there was nothing that she could do. But the wounds, no matter how bad, could not possibly be as terrible as her imagination would make them, given time.

And Marty had no time.

Micky took a deep breath and rolled him over onto his side.

His jacket and shirt and long johns had provided no more protection than a layer of gauze against the ravages of the razor-sharp talons. The cloth was tattered and twisted and bunched together in bloody clots. Micky carefully rolled him over onto his stomach. She glanced up at Stan for help and saw instantly that he was trying hard not to vomit.

"Do you have a knife?" she asked.

Stan dug under his jacket. He fumbled open the clasp and handed her his knife, sinking to his knees beside her.

"Jesus H. Christ on a crutch," he muttered.

She opened the six-inch blade, sucking in another breath. Grabbing hold of the gummy, twisted cloth, she cut it away, tossing it on top of the broken glass in the corner. Blood still oozed onto the floor but Micky immediately noticed that there was no spurting.

That was a good sign.

Of course that didn't rule out internal bleeding.

She ripped and cut her way around Marty's clothing until he lay exposed from the top of his shoulders down to his belt.

Two claws had done the damage.

Twin cuts all the way through the skin and muscle ran from his lumbar vertebra diagonally up to the base of his right shoulder blade. Both were crimson and seeped with fresh, warm blood. Micky stared into Stan's eyes, willing him to focus on her, but he was refusing to look, staring instead at the floor.

"Jesus," he kept muttering, over and over.

She was afraid that he was about to go comatose on her. But his eyes were tuned in on something. She glanced over her shoulder. What she had taken to be a throw rug was in fact a gray animal hide. It looked familiar but, under the circumstances, it took her a moment to figure out what it reminded her of. The fur was mangy and she wondered why El would bother with it. There was nothing to commend it except the nearly perfect white blaze.

Scooter.

"Jesus," she said, echoing Stan.

She reached out with her left hand and grabbed Stan's chin, forcing him to look at her. "You have to find a needle and thread."

Stan ignored her. He knelt beside the pelt and ran his fingers through the ratty fur. He lifted the hide and poked his fingers through several large gashes. He glanced at Micky.

"He stabbed the shit out of that dog," he said.

"We don't have a lot of time, Stan," said Micky. "See if you can find alcohol or anything we can use for an antiseptic and some clean cloth, a sheet or something. And get a fire started."

It took too long for her words to sink in, but finally Stan set the hide down gently. Then he started rushing about, digging in cupboards, tossing plates and silverware and pots and canned goods aside. Now and then he stopped and stared at something as though he had discovered a treasure. Micky realized immediately that she had just told poor Stan to do everything. She pulled herself to her feet and started to help.

But two things slowed her.

She was exhausted. The stress of the past three hours had drained more from her body than a twelve-hour marathon. She felt as though she could barely move her limbs.

And El's cabin was such a strange place. It might as well have been the back side of the moon. Micky couldn't picture any person actually living in it for any length of time.

It wasn't just the hide of Clive's dog, lying on the floor like some obscene trophy. Or the fact that the house was more of an arsenal than a home. The whole inside of the cabin was . . . *wrong.*

As she knelt beside the stove and started methodically making a tinder teepee, she took in the first floor.

The interior was devoid of anything human.

Stan had cleaned out the cupboards and there were two pots and a small saucepan on the floor. Beside them sat one dish and several spoons, a knife and a fork. The shelves were well stocked but the food there seemed to be all pork and beans. The one chair, resting next to the stove, appeared to be the only furniture.

But how could that be?

Could El have sat for years in that straight-backed chair, contemplating the guns on the walls?

Or did he stare for hour after hour at Scooter's hide?

"Alcohol!" announced Stan, smiling nervously. He had opened a small cabinet beneath the counter. Inside were cans of chemicals, a few tools like needle-nosed pliers, and a hammer.

Micky took the pliers. They might come in handy for gripping the needle when she stitched up Marty's back. Over the workbench there was another, shallower cabinet, closed with a padlock that matched the one on the front door. On impulse she reached under the workbench and, running her fingers along it, came to the key on the nail she had intuited might be there.

"Gotcha," she whispered. She opened the cabinet and stared at four sticks of dynamite and several inch-long blue boxes that she didn't recognize. She was reaching for one when Stan grabbed her hand. She looked at him, surprised. He wasn't shaking anymore.

"Don't," he said.

"You know what they are?"

He nodded, eyeing the cabinet suspiciously.

"Yes. And I know where he got them from, too. Marty and I have been fighting over it for months. He swore that I misplaced the dynamite and the blasting caps. But I didn't. I figured he did it and was blaming me for his mistake."

"Shit," said Micky, thinking of what El could accomplish with dynamite.

"We ought to hide it," she said but Stan was still staring at the cabinet.

"Yeah," he said. "What's left of it."

"How much was there?" A sinking feeling started in her stomach.

"There should be eight or nine sticks more."

"What could you do with that much dynamite?"

Stan whistled between his teeth. "For starters, you could blow this cabin into toothpicks."

"Great," muttered Micky, turning back to Marty. "Go upstairs and try to find me a needle and thread."

She found the matches that Stan had used to light the lamp, lit another, and then the kindling in the stove. She carefully placed a couple of larger pieces of wood around the tiny fire and knelt beside Marty again, listening to Stan rummaging around upstairs. Her eyes rested on the narrow ladder that he had used to climb up into the loft and suddenly terror flooded her.

"Stan!" she shouted. "Stop what you're doing! *Now!*"

The floorboards creaked gently as Stan crept over to the edge of the landing.

His face was white again.

"What is it?" he asked in a tremulous voice.

"Be very very careful. Watch what you're doing. Can you see up there?"

Micky enunciated each word as though her jaw and lips were made of wood.

Stan nodded. "There's a little window."

"Watch for any kind of booby trap."

Stan's white face went impossibly paler.

"Right," he said.

Something else occurred to her as she stared around the barren downstairs. She glanced back up at Stan. "Are there guns up there too?"

"There's a lot of guns up here. And a wall full of knives too. There's a bed and an old trunk full of his clothes." Stan smiled shyly, holding out his hand. "But I found a sewing kit."

"Good," she said, waving him back down.

"I never saw so many guns," said Stan as he handed her the plastic bag of spools and needles and pins.

She shook her head. "Spree killers usually have hoards of weapons."

"So he planned this all out."

"Maybe not. They collect the guns because they feel inferior. Paranoid. The guns give them a sense of security. Of control."

"He's probably packing a machine gun," muttered Stan, staring at the wall behind the worktable.

"No. When I saw him all he had was the pistol and Clive's old carbine."

Stan frowned. "Why would he do that when he had all these?" He waved his hands around the room.

"Comfort," guessed Micky. "It's all about control. El feels comfortable with the pistol since he has it on all the time. These guns in here are just to make him feel safe at home. He probably feels most vulnerable here since he sleeps in the cabin."

"Then why did he have Clive's carbine?"

"I think he's afraid Clive might come back from the dead, take the gun, and kill him with it."

Stan's jaw dropped. "That's crazy."

"Yeah."

"What set him off in the first place, you think?"

"I don't know. Could have been anything."

She dropped back down beside Marty and finally succeeded in threading the needle with stiff black thread, dipping it in alcohol from the cap on the bottle, then sliding the clear liquid up and down the length of the needle and thread. It wasn't hospital procedure but she didn't have much choice.

"Stan," she said, staring into the wounds, building her courage. "Bring the lamps over here. Then get me the sheet off El's bed and soak it in alcohol."

He hurried to obey.

Micky let out a long deep breath and rested her hand on Marty's skin. It felt cool to the touch and she didn't know if that was because her hands were warm from starting the fire or if it was a dangerous sign of shock.

She put her head down close to Marty's face and lifted his eyelid. The pupil wasn't dilated and she thought that that was good. His jaw moved and she wondered if he was coming to. But then the movement stopped and she let the lid droop closed again.

Better he stays unconscious, at least until I'm done.

Stan was noisily jerking the linens off the mattress upstairs and Micky wondered how long El had been sleeping on them.

Might as well get started.

Marty's flesh looked like raw steak.

With a steady hand she gripped the bottom of the nearest gash and pinched. With her other hand she slipped the needle in, surprised at how easily it passed through the skin. She made a slip knot, drawing it tight, and then a square knot to finish it off. She cut the thread with Stan's buck knife, then repeated the process a half inch farther up the wound. By the time she had three sutures completed Stan was back with the sheet. Under his right arm were several books that looked like ledgers.

"They were under the bed," he said.

"Put them on the floor and get another knife. I need you to use it to make bandages and rags to clean up the blood and then put a pot of water on the stove."

She was going to have to keep Stan busy. If he stood for more than a minute staring at Marty, he would probably pass out.

When Stan began ripping the sheets, the tearing sound reminded Micky of the high-pitched whine of the four-wheeler.

Where is El now?

She studied the blanket that covered the window, barely riffling in the lowering wind.

"Stan," she said, quietly. "Stan, stop what you're doing."

The cabin went instantly quiet.

"Stan, I dropped Clive's radio out there. Dawn has the other one. You've got to go outside and find the radio. Okay?"

"Okay." Stan's answer was more whisper than speech. But he didn't hesitate. He was past her and out the window, closing the blanket behind him, before Micky realized that not only had she sent him out where El might be waiting, but there was a wounded bear out there as well.

But what else could I do?

She stood up and pulled back the blanket.

"Stan," she shouted. "Stan, be careful!"

3:20

ALTHOUGH IT HADN'T STOPPED her, the first shot had done the most damage to the old sow. The 260-grain lead bullet blasted the thin layer of fat left over from the past winter, broke her left collarbone, and clipped an artery inches from her heart. But she couldn't reach that wound with her tongue and it was the second shot that pained her the most. That bullet had entered beneath her ribs, ruptured her spleen, and lodged in her intestines, which were now slowly filling with blood.

She rocked a little on the hard ground, trying to find a position that didn't send needles of pain stabbing through her. Her breathing was short and quick and one paw quivered, scratching odd patterns in the dirt.

She didn't know she was dying.

But instinct told her she had to stay holed up and tend her wounds.

When the bullets ripped through her she abandoned all thought of her cub. She knew only that she had to get very far away from the guns that were tearing her flesh. She'd dropped the man and broken for the woods, crashing through eight-foot-tall alders as though they were crepe paper.

She ran blindly toward the sound of the creek, until she

crashed into it, stumbling and slipping and rolling her half-ton mass downstream.

She knew the area well.

Though she had a fifty-mile range, she seldom traveled more than ten from the valley. She was a garbage bear. She knew how to forage for berries and small rodents, how to catch salmon in the spring. But the easiest pickings were always the dump and the leftovers around the cabins and the trail. She had foraged around the same man's cabin for four years, always waiting until he was away.

Several times he had stalked her, trying to catch her at it. But he never had.

This time, because she was distracted by her cub, she had become careless. She had been intent on trying to listen for her offspring and eating at the same time.

The woman had startled her.

But the woman was no trouble and she bore no smell of the gunpowder that the bear associated with pain and death.

Then the men came.

The men and their guns.

She had been so preoccupied with the woman that she hadn't heard their approach.

She'd passed the last cabin, limping painfully. Ahead, she knew, the country opened up and there was one more cabin, then woods and then the river. She wouldn't make it that far. And anyway, she had finally remembered her cub. He would be searching for her.

She'd clawed her way up the bank, snapping aside the alders with her good shoulder, burrowing her way in deeply but not so deep that she crossed onto the trail again. She was close enough to smell it but she would not be seen here. After a time she heard the cub crying, and she managed a low roar from deep in her chest that sent ribbons of pain through her body. The cub found her and licked her face and she pushed him to her back so that she could begin licking her wounds.

The cub curled up against her, nuzzling nervously.

They'd be safe here.

Unless the men found their lair.

3:45

DAWN KNELT BENEATH THE window at the front of the store, her eyes barely above the log sill. The sun was behind the mountains but not officially down. That was four hours away. But the thick snow and the low light bathed everything in a ghostly glow. Dozens of times she was certain that she saw El, appearing, specterlike, out of the swirling flakes, only to discover that it was a trick of the light and the weather and her terror-filled mind.

She knew where El was.

She'd spotted him when she first got to the window, during a brief lull in the gathering storm. He was down by the bridge, again.

As soon as she heard the four-wheeler pulling away, she'd burst out of her lethargy and slid out from under the bed. She'd hurried down the stairs, careful not to glance over at Rita, and raced to the front window. She needed to see where El was going. She wanted to see if she had a chance to get away, to find a better hiding place.

El had blasted down to the bridge and stopped. He had a pack strapped on the back of the Honda and he took something out of it and walked across the bridge and then disappeared beneath it. Several times he appeared and disappeared, stopping once to retrieve something else from his pack, but with the increasing snow and the distance and bad light Dawn couldn't tell what he was doing.

She thought that she ought to tell Micky, though.

She looked once more, but El was still under the bridge, so she raced back upstairs to get the radio. But she didn't wait to get back down to start talking. It was wonderful to be able to speak again and not worry about being heard.

"Micky!" she said. "Micky! Are you there?"

No answer.

Was the damned thing broken?

There was a button on the front and when she pressed it the radio beeped.

Did that mean the battery was okay or was it a low-energy warning?

She had no idea.

Or, had something happened to Micky?

That thought froze her heart.

Micky was her only contact with another living human being. If something had happened to Micky, then she really was alone. Alone and helpless.

She didn't know anything about defending herself because her mother had never wanted her to learn anything about violence or murder or death. She was like a baby bird shoved out of its nest way too early, and now her protection was gone, and she had to fend for herself.

How?

Use your brain.

If you're like a baby animal, then think how animals survive! What would an animal do if it was in a situation like this?

Hide.

Take food and water from the store.

Find someplace in the woods.

Hole up.

She glanced out front again but she still couldn't make out the bridge. She watched the snow wraiths, dancing in the twilight. But there was no sound of the four-wheeler. She looked at the radio in her hands and made a decision. She couldn't just leave it on all the time or the battery would die for certain. She would try again, later. She twisted the knob on top until it clicked off.

Then she turned back to the store and went behind the counter to search for supplies for her lair.

3 : 48

ICKY STUDIED HER HANDIWORK and nodded.

Sixty-two black stitches now closed the two sweeping cuts in Marty's back. The wounds were puckered and red, but she had wiped away all traces of blood, and there was only a slight oozing from the wound that was starting to coagulate nicely. If he lived, he was going to have two very nasty scars, and she didn't know what she might have done to the muscle structure beneath, or if there was damage to the vertebrae or any other internal problems.

That was for a doctor to discover. She had done all that she could to save his life.

Stan knelt across from her, still ghastly pale. But since the wounds were closed he was able to look. And, actually, he'd been a great deal of help once he got back with the radio. He came rushing in through the blanket with no warning, frightening the shit out of her, waving his rifle and the radio in both hands.

"Someone was talking!" he shouted. "That's how I found it! I heard it in the snow!"

"Dawn?" said Micky.

"I couldn't make it out. I found it and called back but there was no answer." He passed the radio to Micky.

"Dawn," she said, depressing the send button. "Dawn,

are you there?" She repeated the message several times but all she got for an answer was boiling static.

Was that Dawn's last call?

Had El found her?

Had he crept through the store with his boots sounding on the floorboards, while Dawn cowered somewhere, waiting? Had the girl huddled in some corner, unable to move or breathe?

Stop it!

There had to be a million reasons Dawn wasn't answering. The obvious one was that El was too close and she had turned the radio off so that he wouldn't hear it. The thought that she or Stan might have just given Dawn away sent a chill up Micky's spine.

Dawn had made a connection with Micky. Her voice over the radio was like a call from the past. It had been eerie, as though, somehow, the radio were not connected to a sixteen-year-old girl, somewhere in the depths of the McRay valley, but to another girl, years ago, in a dark room in a dark building in Houston, hiding. Micky wasn't picturing Dawn Glorianus when she spoke into the transceiver. She was speaking to a young Micky Ascherfeld. Trying to reassure her that everything would be all right. Trying to let her know that help was coming.

As help had come in Micky's own past.

But was it too late for Dawn?

Was it too late for all of them?

Micky stared at the raw flesh and bone where the flap still hung loose on the side of Marty's face. She clicked her front teeth together, trying to make up her mind. Marty groaned. Stan looked at her expectantly.

It might be a long time before they could get professional medical attention for Marty.

Should she leave his face an open wound like that?

She'd swabbed it off as best she could with alcohol. Even unconscious, that had been enough of a shock to elicit a moan and a jerking movement of Marty's jaw. But she continued until it was all cleaned, going so far as to peel back the four-inch-wide flap and wipe off the bear hairs and grit.

But should she just leave it like that and bandage it?

"Stan," she said, "I think I ought to stitch up his face."

Stan just nodded as though he thought that decision had already been made.

"I'm not a surgeon, Stan. I could scar him for life."

A burst of hysterical laughter came out of Stan's mouth and she laughed too in spite of herself. She and Stan glanced down at the eighteen-inch cuts she had just sutured and then back at one another.

"All right," she said.

It had to be done. She was afraid that if she just bandaged the wounds, the skin might die before Marty could get professional help. At least if she sutured it together the skin had a chance of getting enough blood to survive. The surgeons might have something to work with to try to save his face.

The problem was that the skin hadn't torn cleanly.

At the base of the ear and at both ends of the tear, near the scalp and out along the jaw, the skin had ripped and stretched and the flap was ragged and uneven. She couldn't be certain that she was attaching skin to skin close to where it had begun and the needle she was using was straight, not curved like a surgeon's. It would be an horrific job, especially around the ear. A picture of the railroad-track scars on the face of Frankenstein's monster flashed in her mind and she wondered if Marty would come to hate her for what she was doing, every time he looked in the mirror.

Surprisingly, Stan swallowed his fear enough to swab Marty's face tenderly as she sutured. The skin was softer, thinner, more pliable than on his back and the stitching was easier. But the skin was harder to pull together tightly. And she kept catching the needle on muscle and bone. The stitches tugged and stretched at Marty's face, leaving slitlike holes that again reminded her of the old Boris Karloff movie.

"He's gonna be okay," said Stan. He glanced at Micky the way a ten-year-old kid might, looking at a vet over the body of his favorite pet. Guilt stabbed at Micky's gut.

"I'm doing my best, Stan," she said, feeling even more incompetent than before. She stared at the jigsaw puzzle of bloody skin and flesh.

It's just like glass.
Broken pieces.

Put them together so they're right.
That's all you have to do.
Hopefully Marty would live.
Hopefully he would be able to live with what she had done to him.

3 : 4 9

EL SAT ON THE four-wheeler with his back to the store and focused on the trail on the other side of the bridge.

The view of the far creek bank came and went but the storm seemed to be thinning a little. The sky was lightening in the east and his own tracks were clearly visible. He wanted more snow.

But he didn't want it the way other people would.

He closed his eyes and *wanted* it.

He *willed* the clouds down.

He *desired* the flakes to fall.

He'd done it before. Sitting alone in his cabin, in the dark, with only his face visible through a small opening in the blanket that covered the window. Sat for hours on end, drawing the weather down into the valley. He'd brought rain and wind, snow and sleet. And he knew he could do it now. He wanted the snow to cover his tracks.

But his powers seemed to have diminished and, as the flakes thinned out he stared through them, down the trail toward Howard's cabin. He'd heard shots before, when he was at work beneath the bridge, though he hadn't been able to tell where they were coming from because he'd left the motor running on the four-wheeler. His first thought had been that he'd been discovered. He ducked, whipping out the Ruger, cocking it and hugging the frozen gravel beneath the rough bridge posts.

His mind raced and icy tendrils of fear trickled down his spine. He breathed faster, sucking up the fear like a plant spreading its leaves to the sun, and his senses came alive.

First one shot.

Then another.

The echo slapped the mountains hard in the face but by the second blast he was certain that the shots were farther away than he had at first thought.

Close to Terry's place.

Maybe his own.

Marty or Stan. Not Micky.

She had only the Glock and he knew where everything in her cabin was kept. She was neat. Just like him. A place for everything and everything in its place. And only the one pistol.

As he realized the danger was distant, El's body and mind once again began to cycle down. His breathing slowed and the welcome fear slowly dulled. He felt almost like a windup toy running down. El's mind sometimes dimmed to the point of going out, like a guttering candle.

He could stare for hours at the wall and not remember what he had been thinking when he came back around. But he knew he hadn't been asleep. He hated sleep. Sleep left him hopelessly vulnerable. Defenseless. Sleep terrified El with a mind-numbing fear that even *he* could not enjoy.

Even when he was gazing in numb silence at the walls of his cabin he was *aware*. Aware in a way that other people would never understand, perhaps, but he knew that if anyone approached the cabin, he would know.

He kept the pistol in his lap, always.

He would be ready for them.

Ready to defend himself.

But sleep he could not control. It came on its own and it left on its own.

El hadn't slept in days. And he wasn't about to sleep now.

But he was recharging his batteries.

He leaned on Clive's rifle and Rita's shotgun, which were now strapped across the handlebars, and stared into the flitting snow. If anything moved on the trail, he would snap back to attentiveness. If anyone spoke, he would hear. If Marty or Stan came down the trail, he would move back to the safety of the store and wait for them.

But, for just a moment, he needed to stare into the snow.

4:05

MICKY AND STAN DRAGGED Marty over close to the stove, which now cast a comforting warmth, and covered him with a blanket from the loft. The railroad tracks of stitches Micky had created from his forehead to his chin bristled crimson, but there was little bleeding, and Marty was moaning more. She took that as a sign that he was strong and not going into shock, so they elevated his head and tried to make him as comfortable as possible.

"I'm going to the store," said Micky, standing and inspecting a Ruger carbine she pulled from the wall beside the door. The gun fired heavy-grained .44-caliber pistol slugs. She checked the chamber to make sure it was loaded.

"You stay with Marty," she said.

But Stan was already on his feet, shaking his head.

"We should wait here," he said.

"Wait for what, Stan?"

"For help," he said, nervously running his hands up and down his pants, though he had no blood on them. "We're all together here. We have guns. El's alone. We should wait."

"Stan, we can't just sit here and wait. Dawn's hiding down there at the store. She's all alone."

"You can't go down there by yourself," Stan said,

changing his tune completely. Stan was pliable, but it didn't look as though she was going to get out of El's cabin without him.

Still, someone did need to stay with Marty and, like it or not, she was trained to face an armed man and Stan wasn't.

Didn't that suck?

"I don't want to leave him by himself," Micky said, nodding at Marty. "He might go into shock."

"I wouldn't know what to do if he did. He needs help and the only way he's going to get it is if we call for it. The only place to do that is Cabels'."

"Stan. I don't want to argue."

"Then don't," said Stan, grabbing his rifle.

She remembered all the arguments she'd witnessed between Stan and Marty over the years. They'd seemed funny. This did not. But she sensed that she was not going to win no matter what she said.

"All right," she said, pulling aside the blanket and sliding out the window. She held it aside for Stan to follow. The snow was only an inch deep and the wind was warming fast. The clouds were already higher overhead and rising. If the temperature went up much more, the snow would turn to slush and be gone in less than an hour. But for now she could read their history in the thin layer of white. The staggering steps, the blood. She stared down toward where the battle had taken place and shuddered.

She slipped the radio out of her pocket and called Dawn again.

Still no answer.

"I don't want to go down that trail," she said, nodding toward the spot where the mauling had taken place.

The thought of passing the spot where the bear had attacked Marty sent a shiver up her spine. In her mind's eye she saw the frenzied attack again, the bear just a brown flash of fur and razor-sharp, blood-covered claws.

Stan looked down at the snow and shook his head.

"Me neither."

She slipped her finger onto the trigger of the carbine. "Where do you think the bear went?"

"No telling."

"Do you think she's alive?"

"Bastards are tough," he said. "But she was hit pretty good or she wouldn't have run off. She might have gone a long ways though."

"Or, she might be right through those trees. Waiting for us." Micky pointed the rifle barrel down toward the trail to Terry's.

"Yeah."

"We'll cross the creek," she decided. "We can follow the lower trail. It's more open. If the bear's around, we'll see her easier."

She started down the steps.

"Wait," said Stan, disappearing back into the cabin.

He reappeared, carrying the ledgers.

"Evidence," he said, hurrying down the steps.

"Of what?"

The books were trying to work their way out from under his arm. "I'll bet it's a diary."

Maybe.

Serial killers often kept journals. But she didn't think she and Stan needed evidence at the moment. What they needed was help.

"Leave them," she said, turning.

She glanced back over her shoulder to see Stan reluctantly slip the books under the porch. Then he hurried to catch up, panting alongside her.

Micky noticed how Stan kept glancing around, into the trees, then back over his shoulder. She was as worried as he was about the bear and about El. But Stan's face was open, curious, and frightened, all at the same time. And he stuck close to Micky. Very close. Again she was struck by his resemblance to a small, terrified child.

When they reached the creek, Stan waited for Micky's okay before sliding down the slope to the water's edge.

"How long have you and Marty been together?" asked Micky, trying to distract Stan.

"Twenty years," said Stan. "Give or take."

"Wow," said Micky. "I never realized."

She eyed the creek. It was a natural shooting gallery. Long and straight. It wouldn't take but a minute to cross.

But out in the middle they'd be balanced on slippery rocks, easy targets.

"I don't know what I'd do without Marty," said Stan.

Micky caught his eye.

"He's going to be all right, Stan."

Stan nodded, biting his lip.

"Really," said Micky, praying she wasn't lying.

4:15

EL SAT MOTIONLESS ON the four-wheeler.

The snow had stopped altogether and, although Dawn couldn't feel the temperature rising outside, she noticed the increase of natural light in the store.

She now not only had quite a hoard of food, and water in a plastic canteen, but she had discovered a better hiding place right inside the store!

The upstairs bedroom was little more than an enclosed loft with a polished spruce floor and a steep ceiling of tongue-and-groove pine over rough-sawn rafters. But before the ceiling reached the floor it had been intersected on each side of the eave with five-foot-high knee walls, and those, in turn, were covered with vertical tongue-and-groove boards. On the wall opposite the bed was a full-length hanging closet that was open to the room except for a six-foot section where Rita had draped a wool blanket.

Dawn had considered hiding behind the blanket but when she crawled inside she noticed that she could still see the door and, besides, all El would have to do would be pull the blanket aside and she'd be dead.

But as she was climbing back out of the closet, she tripped and knocked a box aside. And suddenly her hand wasn't on pine. It rested instead on a metal cabinet handle.

She slid her head in between Rita's coats and Clive's snow-mobile pants and found herself staring at a door, cut out of the pine siding that covered the knee wall. She tugged it open and discovered a dark, triangular tunnel that ran the length of the loft. The area was filled with cardboard boxes and stacks of more blankets and clothes as far as Dawn could see.

On the next trip downstairs she found a flashlight. She brought in cans of soda and candy bars from behind the counter. She moved the boxes around so as to make it seem as though the whole tunnel was filled with them, but in actuality there was a narrow maze for her to pass through to the tiny cave she had constructed at the far end. She could close the whole thing off with a false wall of boxes, clothes, and blankets.

It was perfect.

Even if El found the door, he might not search behind the boxes.

Not if I'm quiet.

But how would I know if he was inside the bedroom?

Maybe her hidey-hole wasn't perfect after all. In fact, even as she was stocking her nest she worried that she might not have heard his return from inside the well-insulated tunnel. She hurried back down to her spy station beneath the window.

But he was still there, down by the bridge, his back hunched over the handlebars as though he were regarding something incredibly interesting stuck to the front tire of the four-wheeler.

What was he doing?

4 : 1 7

MICKY'S LEGS STUNG LIKE fire. They were soaked to her thighs and the icy water sloshed in her boots. She and Stan trudged along the trail, Stan kicking noisily as he walked, his pants snapping. They were both trying to shake off some of the biting cold. But a warm Chinook wind already buffeted the valley. The temperature was climbing over fifty now, the sudden cold front come and gone.

The clouds dissipated overhead like frightened gray birds, the sky between them so deep that on any other day Micky could have lost herself in it. Thin snow still crunched underfoot, but it was quickly turning to slush. The sticky flakes that managed to cling to the rough bark of the tall spruces laced the trees with streamers of diamond threads. The forest glittered in a white-and-platinum embrace.

There was no blood on this snow. There were no open, gaping wounds here. There were no moans or guttural gasps or beastly roars. Right here, right now, it was almost possible to believe that nothing had happened in McRay. That it had all been a ghastly dream.

But, not that far behind them, lay Marty, clinging to life.

And, behind him, lay Aaron.

And, up ahead somewhere, there was El

"Stan," said Micky, "have you seen Damon today?"

Stan shook his head. "You think, maybe—"

"He wasn't in his cabin."

"He could be anywhere. I'm sure he's okay. You know Damon. He might be gone for days if he's prospecting. This is a good day to be gone."

"Yeah."

Micky kept the carbine at port arms, the red warning stripe around the safety button visible. Micky had reassured herself before leaving El's cabin stoop by ejecting all seven bullets and replacing them. They were large and heavy and solid in her hands. Bullets that could cut a man in half if he wasn't wearing body armor. And that, at least, she was certain El didn't have. Dawn would have noticed that. She would have commented on it. A man wearing full body armor in McRay would stand out.

Micky kept glancing around, and Stan stayed on the lookout, too. They didn't know where the hell El was and now there was a wounded bear somewhere in the neighborhood.

What next?

They were halfway to the clearing, past the Glorianus place, just about across from Howard's cabin, though it was still invisible over the lip of the creek and the trees.

On a whim, Micky reached down and turned up the volume on the radio. She only caught the last few words but she clutched at it, whipping it out of her jacket pocket.

"Guess you're gone . . ."

"No! Dawn! Are you there?"

"Micky?"

Micky's heart melted like the snow. Her knees went weak. Stan moved up even closer, listening.

"Yes! It's me! Where are you?" said Micky.

"I'm still in the store. I can see El."

"Where is he? Are you all right?"

"I'm okay. I found a hiding place. But I'm at the front window now. El's been down by the bridge a long time."

"The bridge? Can you see him?"

"Yes."

"What's he doing?"

"He's just sitting," said Dawn. *"He's on the four-wheeler with his back to me and he just sits and stares."*

That made sense. Micky remembered Wade saying once

that spree killers often led lives of spartan self-denial. They found little if anything in the world around them to take pleasure in. They were delusional but many times could not explain, nor want to explain, their delusions. She thought of the barren interior of El's cabin. The single chair and the blackout setup of the windows.

Was that how he lived all the time?

Sitting in that chair for who knew how long?

Staring at the walls?

She shuddered.

"Dawn, we're coming."

"*We?*"

"Stan and me."

"*Where's Marty?*"

"Marty's hurt."

"*El?*"

"No. We were attacked by a bear."

"*Are you joking?*"

It did sound outrageous, didn't it? No human being in his right mind would expect that so much could happen to the citizens of McRay on one day.

"No," Micky said. "I'm serious."

"*Wow,*" said Dawn.

That summed up the situation nicely.

"Dawn," she said, "Stan and I are coming down the lower trail. I'm going to put the radio back into my pocket and turn it down so I can barely hear you and I won't be talking because I need both hands for my rifle. Do you understand?"

"*Yes.*" There was fear in her voice. The girl didn't want to be left alone in silence again.

"I want you to tell me the instant El moves. Especially if it looks like he's heard us coming. Okay?"

"*Okay.*"

"Tell her to keep her head down," said Stan.

"She knows that," said Micky.

She could see the clearing, only thirty yards ahead. She steeled herself for the confrontation, gripping the rifle tighter, but not too tight. She gritted her teeth and forced her breathing to slow.

"We're going to have to kill him," said Stan. "Aren't we?"

"Don't let him get a shot at us, Stan. If he acts like he wants to surrender, okay. But watch yourself and don't let him get the drop on you or me. If you have to, do you think you can shoot him?" She stared into Stan's watery brown eyes, thinking that he hadn't even been able to shoot the bear that was attacking him. How the hell was he going to shoot El?

"Yeah," said Stan, swallowing hard. "I think so. Yeah."

"All right," said Micky, turning back to the trail. "Come on, then."

4:19

THE SOW NUDGED THE cub aside. He awakened but made no sound, sensing her mood. Her ears were peaked and her nose twitched as she sniffed the air. She was staring back down toward the creek, the way she had come.

The man's voice had snapped her out of her dull, pain-filled semiwakefulness. It was one of the voices she had heard before she was hurt, and a new sense of urgency dulled the pain. The man was back. Back with his gun. She struggled to her feet, grunting, and nudged the nosy cub back farther into the alders.

There were two voices now, and she recognized both of them.

Coming toward her, just across the creek.

4:20

A SLIVER OF LIGHT ENTERED El's brain. A thin, tentative thing that tickled his consciousness.

Off to his left.

It might have been caused by a familiar sound.

Faint as morning air.

Something requiring his attention.

He blinked.

Sensation seeped slowly through him.

Light in his eyes. Blue sky and pale blue snow reflecting it below.

Cold hands with fingers on cold steel. The gun and the handlebars.

His legs and butt stiff from sitting too long in an unfamiliar position.

The faint odor of woodsmoke.

Of gun smoke.

Of pine.

Of blood.

He licked his lips.

Salt.

Was that a voice, up the trail?

He turned to his left, unfastening the strap that held Clive's rifle without looking at it.

•   •   •

"He's looking your way," whispered Dawn into the radio.
No answer. Micky had said she wouldn't answer.

But did she hear? Micky said to keep telling her if El did anything.

"He's turning to look toward the trail." When Dawn let go of the button the radio gave a satisfying *squelch*, so she knew it still had power.

Micky stopped, just behind a small stand of spruce that blocked her view of the bridge and the store. Stan froze, directly behind her.

"How could he have heard us?" he whispered.

Micky wanted to slap him.

Was he an idiot?

She had no idea how El's hearing could be so acute. Maybe it wasn't. Maybe he was psychic. Maybe his brain was so different from a normal person's brain that he sensed them coming down the trail.

Does it matter?

She glanced over her shoulder at Stan but he wasn't looking at her. He was looking over *his* shoulder.

Across the creek.

The old sow didn't crash through the alders.

She fell out of them.

She stumbled down to the creek bank, through her rough-cut passage in the brush. Her left front leg gave out beneath her and she rumbled down the hill into the water like an eight-hundred-pound fur-covered cannonball. As she stood up on her three good legs she found herself staring directly into the eyes of one of the men that had hurt her.

And the woman.

For just a second the three regarded each other in shocked silence.

Then all hell broke loose.

4:21

M ICKY TRIED TO TURN at the same time that she raised the carbine.

But Stan pushed past her, breaking into a run. Micky panicked, fired one shot, wild, over the bear's head, and turned to follow.

The worst thing I can do is run.

The bear could easily overtake her.

She knew that the bear could rip her apart just as it had done to Marty.

But none of that stopped her legs from pumping like pistons, her feet slipping in the slush and mud on the trail, wet and frozen limbs forgotten. None of it quelled the sound of her own breathing and the pounding, splashing noise of the three-legged grizzly, huffing to make up the distance.

It was a race and Micky knew that it was a race that either she or Stan was bound to lose.

"He's getting the gun!" screamed Dawn, into the radio. "Micky! He's getting the gun!"

Micky caught up with Stan, shoving him along. She felt the thrumping feet of the bear behind her, saw El raising the rifle ahead.

"Oh, my God!" screamed Dawn into the radio.

The bulk of the bear knocked Micky aside, rumbled into and over Stan.

They were halfway to El, only thirty yards away.

El fired.

The bear gave off a high-pitched squeal and turned to face her new attacker, standing on her rear legs and looking twenty feet tall to Micky, who was flat on her back.

El fired again.

The big bear lurched, then crumpled like a badly folded map.

Stan started to get up and Micky discovered that she had had the wind knocked out of her. She could only wave at his back ineffectually.

El chambered another round into his rifle. He climbed off the four-wheeler and walked up deliberately.

No fear.

No nerves.

Just that cold stare behind those fucking glasses. Micky knew that at any instant he was going to pull the trigger while Stan was still dazed and in shock. Stan's rifle lay ten feet behind Stan, where he had dropped it as the bear bowled him over. She looked around for her own rifle. It was there, inches from her hand. She slid her fingers over the grip but El took his left hand from the rifle and waved at her to stop.

She obeyed.

When he was within two steps of Stan, El cocked his head, waiting.

Finally, Stan acknowledged him with a frown and a nod.

Micky saw Stan's knees give a little but he was holding up, staring down the long length of rifle barrel. The radio had gone mercifully silent. Micky prayed that, in the excitement, El wouldn't have noticed Dawn screaming.

When El was certain that he had Stan's attention, he moved around behind him, placing the tip of the barrel into the small of Stan's back.

"Push the gun away," said El, looking at Micky.

For a second she couldn't function. She stared into the glasses and everything went black. The voice was cold, emotionless and the face wasn't El's any longer. It was a face right out of her past. An impossible face that kept returning to haunt her present. But she shoved the gun away and stood when he told her to.

"Walk in front," he said. "To the store."

4:24

WHEN THEY REACHED THE front steps Stan took them all by surprise by bolting for the door.

Micky never had a chance to scream.

Clive's rifle bucked in El's hands and Stan fell forward, with a small hole in the center of his back between his shoulder blades. His hand dropped over the stair rail and he hung there, his face wedged against the balusters like a kid watching a party to which he is too young to be invited.

El pulled his pistol out and cocked it, holding it in his right hand, the rifle in his left. Bright red blood mixed with the slush and puddled beneath Stan. El turned away from him as though Stan were an uninteresting bit of fauna and not worth his time.

Micky looked at El and shook her head.

"I'm not going in," she said. She had to give Dawn time to hide. "You'll have to kill me here."

El's face was milky granite, the cheekbones nearly visible through his pale skin, his lips bloody slits. He was devastatingly calm. He waved the pistol up the stairs but she just stared at him, wondering what it would feel like when the big bullet tore through her. She hadn't felt the shot through her shoulder in Houston.

Will I feel this one?

Probably not.

Death might be merciful.

Life hadn't been.

"I'm not going to hurt you," El said, when he saw that she really wasn't going anywhere.

"Sure you're not," she said, staring at the blood that was soaking down around Stan's pants. But a little voice in her mind told her that she had known all along that El wasn't going to do it.

Of course not.

She stared into the glasses and knew what he was going to say even before he spoke in that revolting monotone.

Was there just the barest whine to it now?

The slightest sense of wounding?

Had her doubt in him touched something nearly human in El?

Was there anything human in El?

"I wouldn't hurt you," El said. "I did all this for you."

4:25

MARTY WASN'T CONSCIOUS.

But he wasn't unconscious, either.

He was in that curious state where pain was real, but it was an out-of-focus and distant real.

Were there hot irons pressing against his back?

Was there someone trying to twist his arm off at the shoulder root?

There was also the strange sensation that his face was on sideways, pulled too tight, as though the bones in his skull had expanded at the same time that his skin had shrunk like a piece of melted plastic wrap. The blanket scratched against his face like sandpaper.

He couldn't feel the fingers in his right hand, but his other hand clawed at the rough wood floor. When he opened his eyes he didn't recognize his surroundings but at least he seemed to be inside.

Where was Stan?

He tried to roll over and liquid fire shot up his back and exploded in his brain.

There was a clanking metallic noise and the soft warmth and light that flooded his face confused him. He stared up into flickering golden heat, inches from his face. His brain told him that he was lying up against a woodstove and he had banged into it, opening the door and exposing the fire inside.

He pushed himself away from the stove and flopped onto his side on the floor again, trying to focus. His head rested on fur. Gray fur. He blinked. Then he ran his fingers through it.

He'd felt it before.

Lots of times.

Scooter's white blaze was right in front of Marty's nose.

"Damn," he muttered.

So El *had* killed Scooter.

The son of a bitch was crazier than a bedbug.

Marty's eyes cleared a little more and he could barely make out the guns on the far wall.

"Shit."

Way crazier than a bedbug.

Why had Stan and Micky left him here? In El's cabin of all places?

What if the crazy bastard came back?

He spotted the lantern glowing on the counter and was drawn to it like a moth to a flame. He clawed his way up the side of the cupboard, pain shooting in lightning bolts up and down his spine.

What the hell do I want with a lantern?

But his mind and his body weren't communicating. He had wanted the light for something just a second before . . .

He knelt beside the counter, resting his cheek on the top, as exhausted as though he'd just scaled Everest. He reached for the lantern and only succeeded in knocking it to the floor. Coleman fluid spilled out and there was a nasty hiss as the liquid caught fire, racing across the floor back toward his blanket.

Marty passed out.

When he came to the pain was even worse than before. It surged along the skin of his back. His whole body throbbed with it. It was a few minutes before he dared open his eyes all the way and that was because he smelled smoke. Then he remembered the lantern.

Flames licked along the wooden floor and caressed the guns arrayed on the walls. His blanket was blazing and Scooter's pelt smoldered. The familiar crackle of wood burning—usually such a comforting sound—now sent terror pulsing along Marty's already overloaded nerves.

4:26

DAWN WATCHED EL LEADING Micky and Stan toward the store.

She couldn't believe that both of them had allowed themselves to fall under El's spell.

How did El do it?

Another bear attack?

It was just too unreal.

She shook herself out of her trance and slunk away from the window. Back into the hateful embrace of the store that she was coming to think of as her tomb.

It *was* a tomb.

She shared it with dead people.

She raced up the stairs and was halfway through the bedroom door when booted feet pounded on the steps out front and another rifle shot echoed through the store.

Either Micky or Stan was dead.

Dawn didn't wait to find out which.

She scurried back into her cave and tugged the hanging clothes together as best she could without getting them stuck in the door, which she then pulled shut. Flipping on the flashlight she'd found in Clive's workshed, and silent as a mouse, she crawled slowly through the maze of cardboard boxes. Finally, she clambered behind the last one and, tucking odd pieces of clothing and blankets around it, sealed herself tightly away.

The walls and the sloping roof were well insulated, and so was the floor, so that now she was surrounded by warmth and silence and fear. She clicked the radio on and off then on again to make certain that it was still working. A bit of static came out and she turned it up and set it on the floor beside her.

It occurred to her that there might be the smallest of cracks in her hideaway. Cracks that she might not notice. Not wanting El to see her light flashing if that was so, she turned off the flashlight.

Now she was alone in the dark and she wasn't coming out.

4:27

FLAMES DANCED HYPNOTICALLY, INCHES from Marty's face. He was vaguely aware that he was in danger and was trying to get his mind to function to remind him of what he had been doing before. He remembered the bear, barreling down on top of him.

But where was Stan?

Where was Micky?

He and Stan had come out of the woods and there was Micky and then the giant grizzly was on top of them.

What was Micky doing at El's cabin?

Why did they leave me?

He had only the vaguest memory of the attack. The flashing claws and the giant paw as powerful as the arm of a backhoe. Ripping at him. Tearing through his flesh. But it all seemed more delusion than reality.

The flame flickered and, through the wall of pain, the heat singed his face.

He drew back. A lightning bolt of pain discharged through the back of his neck and he screamed. When he did his body jerked and the burning blanket he had collapsed upon slapped him in the face. He screamed again and turned away instinctively, luckily rolling himself away from and not into the blanket.

But he was lying on his injured arm and the pain was so intense that it blinded him. He kicked himself away from the woodstove, trying to get up onto his knees, his vision returning but blurred. He reached out for the counter and struggled to his knees once again.

He managed to turn his head enough to see the blanket, ablaze in the middle of the floor and knew that he needed to drag himself outside before the whole cabin caught. But he couldn't make the muscles in his body answer his frantic demands.

The burning blanket was creating a thick, sickening smoke. As Marty's mind cleared, his lungs began to fill with the noxious fumes. He tried to stand up, lost his balance again, and, flinging out his good arm, knocked the small woodstove over onto its side. With horror he watched red-hot coals spill out onto the floor and set it afire where it wasn't burning already.

"Can't get a fucking break," he muttered.

He pushed himself off and crawled toward the door.

4:30

MICKY SAT IN THE rocking chair watching El.

For a man who had murdered nearly everyone in town he seemed obscenely composed. But that was typical of spree killers. She remembered the steady, sure movements of the man without a face in the dark massage room, calmly reloading, while all around there was noise and death and destruction and madness. She remembered the eerie sound of her parents' killer as he stalked her through room after room of the florist shop. He never spoke. All she remembered hearing was the rhythmic slapping of his tennis shoes across the concrete floor.

No problem.

Slap. Slap. Slap.

Slow and easy. Like a window-shopper, casually looking for his prey.

She never heard the faceless man in the bar speak, either. She hadn't attended the trial; the prosecutor had had all the testimony he needed without her. But in any case the man had never spoken and Micky had never seen his face. She hadn't been able to bring herself to look at him on television or in the papers. Not at him or his accomplice. But she knew that if she had, neither of them would have had eyes.

It was the calmness of the three that had paralyzed her.

The self-assured manner. It defeated her. And now El acted exactly the same way.

What can I do?

The Houston Police Department wasn't coming to her rescue this time. And they weren't coming to rescue Dawn, either. And sooner or later El would figure out that Marty was missing. Marty wouldn't stand a chance in his condition. El would slaughter him like a sheep.

Now El was doing something behind the counter that she couldn't see.

"Just stay where you are," he said, one evil lens of the shades peeking up over the bar top. "Be with you in two shakes." The rifle rested on the counter almost out of his reach but Micky had no notion that she could jump up and reach it before he pulled out his pistol and gunned her down. She glanced quickly around the mess, the ashy floor, the scattered boxes and broken jars, but there was no weapon in sight. El popped back up and there was something that might have been mistaken for a smile on his razor lips. In his left hand he had a roll of duct tape.

Walking calmly back to her, he ripped off a two-foot strip and bound her left wrist to the arm of the chair.

"Why don't you just go ahead and shoot me?" she asked.

"I'm doing this for you," he said, shaking his head and dropping to his knees in front of her to bind her left leg.

She kicked at his head with her right boot, putting everything she had into it. Her toe caught his temple and he fell back. But he still held the pistol, grimacing, staring up at her with a dazed expression. The glasses were cockeyed on his face and one eye was exposed. The kick had only dazed him. No way she was going to overpower him.

But Micky couldn't look away from the eye that was now visible.

The pupil was wide and dilated, the iris the color of gray stone. The lid hung loosely, as though he might fall asleep in mid-speech. And, just as she had suspected, there was nothing there. No window into El's soul. Just a lifeless, camera-like lens that viewed but did not reveal, analyzed but did not acknowledge.

El was a machine.

He ate.

He slept.

He killed.

Did he have sex?

Is that what this is about?

Sex?

Was he murdering everyone in McRay under the sick delusion that he and she could live happily ever after?

Killers often lived in fantasy worlds. The problem was that sooner or later their fantasies came up against the harshness of the real world, and then they were forced to make adjustments. Adjustments like Aaron and Terry and Howard and Stan. And many if not all of them were sexually frustrated because of real or imagined inadequacies so that, even if El got his wish and wiped out everyone in McRay but the two of them, pretty soon it all would go sour for him. He would be unable to perform and, thwarted by his own inability, he would turn his anger against her.

She would probably suffer a far crueler death than anyone else.

It was useless to try to talk to him but she couldn't help herself.

"You can't get away with this, El," she said, realizing her mistake even as she spoke.

His lips spread straight across his face so that he looked as if his cheeks had been slashed. He straightened the glasses and pulled himself to his feet, moving around to her side. With lightning speed he slapped her, backhanded. A burst of white pain blinded her and she tasted salty blood.

He bent calmly to tape her wrist. "My name is Eldred."

She nodded an apology.

He knelt beside the chair and jerked her leg back, taping it to the leg of the rocker.

"No one will miss them," he said, standing and inspecting his work.

"Of course they will," she said. "Clive calls in the weather."

"I'm going to do it," he said. "I have the key to the phone room." He jingled keys in his pocket.

But he seemed uncertain, as though that had not been part of the original plan and Micky wondered just how his brain did function.

What strange stew is simmering inside that skull?

Would it even be recognizable as thought to a normal person?

"They'll know it isn't Clive," she said.

"Clive passed away. I'm the new store owner."

"You don't think anyone will consider that odd?"

"Shut up about it," he said. His voice wasn't raised but she noticed a slight tenseness in his body and she pulled her head back, expecting another blow. But after a second he re-laxed.

He readjusted the glasses and she noticed that he wasn't looking at her face. He was focused on her jacket. She re-membered the radio and tried to shift inconspicuously to put it behind her, but he leaned over and slipped it out of her pocket.

He studied it, touching but not depressing the transmit button, and turning the volume and squelch controls slightly.

Testing.

"Where's Dawn?" he said.

"How would I know?"

He nodded at the radio. "I heard her."

Was that possible?

Could he have heard the girl on the radio from that dis-tance across the clearing, in the excitement of the bear at-tack and her own and Stan's sudden appearance?

Maybe.

She couldn't make the mistake of comparing his senses to those of an ordinary human being. El's senses might not be more acute, but he wasn't hindered by ordinary emo-tions. He'd probably felt no fear at all during the bear at-tack, merely been registering input like computer. The normal person would have blocked out everything but the most crucial info, his brain systematically shutting off in-formation that wasn't immediately necessary for survival. But El might well have been taking it all in for later review.

"I don't know what you're talking about," she said.

"Why are you being like this?"

"Like what?"

"I did this all for you," he said.

What did he want her to say?

Thank you?

Although the thought of apologizing to the monster standing in front of her made her physically ill, she knew that was exactly was what she had to do. She had to somehow go along with his madness long enough to get an edge. To get that one slim chance at survival that almost all victims received. Some seized it, some didn't. And some who did didn't survive. But if she irritated him now, he'd grow enraged and kill her anyway, and then Dawn would be alone.

Just as *she* had been alone.

That was unacceptable.

"Thank you," she said.

He stared at her for three long breaths.

Then he nodded and clicked the radio.

"Come on out, Dawn," he said. "Or I'm going to kill Micky."

Did I misread him completely?

Was he lying all along?

Could it be Dawn he wanted?

"Come on out, now," he repeated. "I'll take care of you."

He held the radio out at arm's length, and turned to stare down at Micky. A slow thin smile spread across his face.

No.

I was right.

He's lying to Dawn.

"She's in the store," he said, freezing Micky's heart. "Isn't she?"

She tried with all her will not to show anything, to maintain a poker face. But even that seemed a betrayal. She knew that El was reading her like a book because now his smile spread impossibly wide, slashing his cheeks.

"She is," he said. But instead of the pistol, he slipped the huge bowie knife out of his boot sheath and cradled the radio lovingly in the other hand.

"If you hurt her," Micky said, "I'll never do what you want."

"You'll come to understand," he said. "I knew you wouldn't at first. But you will."

He lifted the radio to his lips and spoke in a clear, calm voice.

"I know you're in the store, Dawn," he said. "I'm going to find you."

4:32

MARTY COULD BARELY HEAR above the roar of the fire. The smoke was too dense to see through.

It was so hot he was sure his hair would catch soon and the pain in his back and shoulder was another flame, almost indistinguishable from the raging heat all around him.

He had slipped flat against the floor again after he realized that the door was locked from outside and there was no way he could open it. Now he clasped both hands over his nose and mouth, breathing the little bit of air that was left in the cabin.

He curled into a ball against the door, his eyes watering, nose and throat burning from the acrid stench. The fire had spread across the floor and crept up the loft ladder. It was burning the worktable and running up the logs like liquid light.

He hadn't failed to notice the ammunition boxes in the far corner. Flames licked teasingly at the cardboard. He wasn't only going to burn to death. He was curled up next to a powder keg.

For the first seconds, after giving up on the door, he had rested against it, convinced that he was locked in and that now he was going to die, cooked like a goose. He had all but given up.

Now and then, though, he felt a gust of cold air on his cheeks.

He held up his hand and waited.

Sure enough, a puff of wind passed and he glimpsed a flicker of light. Fumbling with his left hand, he felt the rough wool blanket that blocked the window. Gripping it, he tried to pull himself up, but only succeeded in draping it down on top of him like a shroud. A gust of cool air rushed over him and he heard the fire *whoof* behind him. He threw the blanket aside and found himself staring up into blue sky.

The heat was so intense he couldn't breathe and the flames had caught the blanket and now they were reaching toward him with white-hot fingers. He ignored his pain, pulled himself up and over the windowsill, dragging himself onto the stoop and then down into the mud and grass at the bottom.

He lay on his good side, gasping, staring up at the front of the cabin as a burst of flame erupted through the window and hurtled skyward, spewing black smoke. Shells began to explode inside. Again the heat drove him back. He was about to pass out again. But he knew that he had to get farther from the house before he did, or he'd die for certain.

He dragged himself roughly through the slush, annoyed by the strange buzzing noise overhead.

Was it real? Or just another symptom of the damage the bear had done to him?

4:34

MICKY COULDN'T SEE EL but she knew from the sounds that he had completed his search of the workshed. She also knew that Clive's corpse was in there with him because El kept talking to Clive.

She had heard El open and close the padlock on the phone-room door, although how he thought Dawn might have gotten in there through a locked door, she had no idea. He was throwing things about and there was the sound of breaking glass again.

If I live, will that be the only sound I remember when I think of McRay?

Or will I remember Marty's moans? His screams as the bear tore into him?

Or Dawn's frightened call to me on the radio?

She had no idea where Dawn might be hiding. Like the other buildings in town, the store was built on short pilings and there was no cellar, not even a real crawl space, and all access would be from outside. Dawn's last call had been from inside the store and Micky was pretty sure the girl was still here. But she prayed that she was wrong. El was looking in places a cockroach couldn't hide, much less a teenage girl.

When El returned, Micky noticed a change in his attitude.

Just a little of the cocksureness was gone. There was more jerkiness to his motion, as though an invisible fly were darting about his face and he wanted to catch it with his tongue. He moved the big knife back and forth in front of him as he paced, like a blind man armed with a razor-sharp cane. He was looking under the counter, under the shelves, kicking aside boxes that wouldn't have held shoes, much less a young girl. And he kept babbling into the radio at Dawn.

Threatening.

Then cajoling.

Then whining.

Then threatening again.

Had any of those techniques ever worked for him?

Or was he so divorced from any experience with human society that he had no clue how to deal with real people?

Micky tried to picture what was happening inside his head, but she couldn't. There was no way to reason with him because he was reasoning—if what he did could be called reason—on some level that she couldn't reach, could never comprehend. He was calculating with figures that were skewed before they reached his brain, so the output had to be totally unrecognizable to anyone functioning in the sane world Micky lived in.

Maybe a professional psychiatrist could figure out what he was doing.

But it was beyond her.

What she did know was that part of his plan was unraveling and so was El.

As he continued to speak into the radio, she noticed that half the time he was forgetting to depress the button so that Dawn had to be getting very weird, half sentences at best.

And he kept glancing at his watch.

Micky tried to see the watch face.

It has to be late afternoon by now.

Rich will be coming in soon.

El was planning to kill the pilot. Micky was certain of that. And he wanted McRay to look as normal as possible when the mail plane got to town. Couldn't have bodies lying all over the place or people running around loose to warn Rich.

But Stan was outside, draped over the stair rail.

Dawn was inside and she and Stan were screwing up El's timetable.

El moved around behind her and she twisted painfully to watch. He was rummaging through rubber boots and sleeping bags, slashing them angrily with the knife, muttering into the radio.

"Dawn, come on out. You can't get away. And if you don't come out, I'm going to have to kill Micky."

Micky waited until his thumb depressed the button again.

"He's lying, Dawn!" she screamed at the top of her lungs.

The sound of her voice bounced off the rafters like a wounded bat.

4:40

DAWN KNELT IN THE darkness. Both fists pressed against her temples so hard her head felt as though stakes were being driven into it. She tried to shut out El's voice and the scream that had cut through the radio and echoed through the floorboards beneath her.

The scream had been so unexpected that Dawn dropped the radio.

It was lying only inches from her face, but she didn't want to touch it again. It had begun to feel slimy and creepy as El's disjointed speech oozed out of it into the tight confines of her man-made cave. Every time El spoke he seemed to be reaching out for her with scaly hands in the inky blackness, and each time he spoke she shivered.

Micky's scream had slashed through Dawn's fear and hit her with an instant new terror. It was as though Dawn had been listening to some horror story, told from a distance, and somehow her mind had grown numb to it. As long as it was coming from the radio it couldn't touch her, she didn't have to consider the fact that the man on the other end was only a few feet away, down the stairs. She could hold him at arm's length and, if she dared, could even click a button and shut out his voice.

But Micky's scream came out of nowhere, blasting through the tiny speaker and slicing through pine and insulation, to touch her heart.

The horror was real again.

And close.

4:41

MICKY'S NECK HURT FROM twisting around so far, but she was frozen, staring into her own double reflection in the glinting lenses above El's smirk.

The knife had stopped flitting. He cocked his head ever so slowly, looking over his shoulder, back toward the stairs. So he did hear it.

Micky had hoped that her scream had taken him by surprise. Shocked him. He had certainly looked that way when he whipped around to stare at her. She prayed that, after the scream, he hadn't heard the sound of something solid hitting the floor over their heads. Micky had jerked the rocker violently, pretending to try to free herself, knowing all too well she couldn't get away, hoping to disguise the sound that thankfully did not repeat itself.

But he had heard. She could see it in his face. In the turn of his head.

"I'm coming now, Dawn," said El, smiling into the radio. His voice was calm again and Micky wondered how a man could shift so quickly from one shape to the other, from nervous beast to self-assured killer. "I don't have a lot of time, though."

"What time is it, El?" said Micky, as calmly as possible.

"What?" He stopped with one hand on the stair rail, the knife swinging loosely by his hip. It was the first time she'd seen a curious expression on his face. Out of everything that had happened that day, was a normal question like the time of day the thing that could break through into that boiling cauldron he called a brain?

"I was wondering what time it was," said Micky.

He glanced at his watch again.

Was he going to tell her?

No.

And the question had been a mistake.

His lips went taut once more and the knife jittered in his hand. Without glancing back at her, he turned and started climbing the stairs again.

"The *time*, El!" she hollered. But now he ignored her completely. "El! Tell me what fucking time it is!"

His back disappeared through the bedroom door.

4:42

MARTY COULDN'T GET THE fucking buzzing out of his ears. The sound mixed with the muffled rattle of ammo exploding, reminding Marty of the sound of a wasps' nest that had erupted outside his bedroom window when he was a child. The angry insects hummed madly, splattering against the pane.

Now he had dragged himself almost to the tree line down the trail. There were patches of dirty blood on his palms and he glanced around and realized that he had pulled himself back to where the struggle with the grizzly had happened.

Today?

Yesterday?

His right arm was useless. The pain there and in his back throbbed with enough power to knock the wind out of him when it reached the high end of a wave. He was getting the feel of it, though. It rolled over him slowly, pulsing with his heart. As though the nerves throughout his torso and arms were all attuned to the blood flowing through his veins, and the pain would thrum to a roaring crescendo, building, building, dragging him to the brink of darkness and then rolling over him, then easing for a minute or so, leaving only a dull, mind-numbing ache throughout his body.

But the buzzing was driving him crazy. Like mosquitoes on amphetamines. And it was growing louder. Not mosquitoes. Bees. Infuriating and dangerous and something that he needed to focus on if only the damned pain would let him breathe.

And of course there was the fire.

Even as far away as he was from the cabin he felt the heat. Smoke poured through the window and around the edges of the door and out from under the eaves. But he welcomed the heat now. The cold ground was sapping what little strength he had and he knew that he had to find the strength to get up and find shelter.

He needed help.

He tried to push himself up to a kneeling position but it was like trying to lift a truck. He had no strength and the bloody muck between his fingers would give no purchase. His hand kept sliding out from under him. He lay there for a moment, cheek on the back of his hand, catching his breath, letting one more wave roar through and out again and listening to the goddamned buzz.

It grew to a thrum.

Then a high-pitched scream.

And suddenly he knew what it was.

The sound roared over and away and he was fighting again, ignoring the pain, his fingers clawing for a grip in the icy gravel. His chest felt like burning bands of iron but finally he was on his knees, swaying drunkenly. It was all that he could do to remain upright. His body wanted to fall first left then right. Each time he overcompensated and it took all his strength to keep from falling onto his face again.

Upright, he could see the fire better. Evidently there was an upstairs window out back. A tall, thin flame, like a giant butane lighter jet roared heavenward there. It struck Marty as beautiful. Like a sign from God. He watched the flame lurch and whip in unseen currents of wind, swirling and mixing with the dark puffs of smoke.

The buzzing returned.

He tried to get to his feet.

But that was a mistake.

One knee buckled and he fell forward, landing hard on his wrist.

He balanced there for interminable seconds wondering how much more pain he could be asked to endure. This new one was a lightning flash, shooting up his wrist, into his elbow, and clawing through his shoulder. He bit his lip hard and pushed himself backward, perching precariously again on his knees.

The plane approached from up the valley. Marty could hear the buzzing getting closer and just when he thought that it would clear the top of the cabin, he began to wave wildly. He couldn't even keep his eyes open. The pain shut them and he wondered if he was biting through his lip. But he heard Rich roar over and he prayed that he had been seen.

One last wave and his strength vanished, and he felt himself slipping back down into the muck.

4:44

A FLOORBOARD CREAKED.

Dawn slid her hand silently along the floor and, finding the radio, quietly clicked it off. She didn't need it anymore. El was in the bedroom. The radio wasn't going to help and if he spoke and heard himself, it would give her away.

She knelt on the floor, her right side pressed against rough studs and itchy insulation. Her left side touched cardboard boxes. Her elbows clasped her knees and her forehead rested on the back of her hands on the floor.

For what seemed an eternity, her entire world consisted of the incredibly loud *thrump* of her heart.

Then she heard El rummaging around in the clothes closet. She expected to hear the door opening immediately, but for some reason it didn't. There was an occasional bump or squeak but not the distinctive wood-on-wood sound that she knew the tightly built door made.

What's he doing?

Surely he wouldn't search the bedroom closet. There was no place for anyone to hide in there.

She could hear him talking and assumed that he was still speaking to her on the radio. There was something that might have been anger or frustration in his voice but it was not the anger of a normal person.

Then she heard it.

She felt it.

And, in her mind, she saw it.

The little hidden door opening.

El's head, slipping through into her tunnel.

The mirror glasses taking in the narrow space, the stacks of boxes and old clothing.

Dawn held her breath and waited for him to speak and when he did, she bit her lip and stifled a sob.

"Dawn?"

There was nowhere left to hide.

She remembered the way he had lifted the big knife over her mother.

Dawn could feel it, ripping through her flesh, cutting and breaking through her rib cage, slashing her organs. She shivered in the darkness. Every muscle in her body quivered but somehow she made no sound.

"Dawn."

The voice was so calm. So unthreatening.

How could it be attached to something so evil?

"Dawn, honey, I know you're in here. Come on out, now."

She heard the door scrape open. Cloth rustled as El struggled through the narrow opening. Something snagged and ripped and he cursed. Another creak and then he was in. His presence polluted the air around her. The evil pressed against her paper sanctuary like a dark river of blood.

"Leave her alone!"

Micky's scream came at Dawn from all directions at once.

"Goddamn you, El! Leave her alone, you bastard!"

Dawn pressed her head down so hard onto her hands that her fingers ached. She wished that Micky would stop screaming. When Micky was screaming Dawn couldn't hear El.

Is he closer?

Or has he stopped, listening to Micky?

A floorboard groaned and Dawn knew that he had crept closer.

"Come on, Dawn," he coaxed, ignoring the shouts from

below, speaking calmly, as though he hadn't even heard them. "Come on. Don't make me come in there and get you."

He was closer now and she heard the sound of cardboard crunching and then being shoved around. Part of her cave had just disappeared.

Then another.

She tried to picture in her mind what he was doing. How long it would be before he could move the last box and then be staring down at her over the top of her useless cardboard fort. He was cursing and she heard the sound of slashing and ripping and labored breath. It must be hard for him to move the boxes around. It was a tight space even for Dawn and El was so much bigger than she.

And there was another noise too.

A dull buzzing from outside.

Like a swarm of bees.

"You hear that, El?" screamed Micky. "You hear that, you bastard?"

The slashing stopped and the buzzing grew louder but Dawn was so terrified, so paralyzed that, although she knew that she should recognize it, she couldn't place the sound.

"That's Rich, you shit!" yelled Micky. "He's going to see Stan's body! He'll report you to the troopers!"

Could it really be?

Could they be saved?

But Dawn felt the boxes beside her sliding away.

El was on the other side trying to remove the tightly packed sleeping bag and blankets.

She was like a mouse that had stared too long into the eyes of a snake. All she could do was wait for the boxes to crumble, and she knew that she would lie right where she was without even looking up, as El drove the big knife into her quivering back.

She wouldn't be able to look into his face. A dull, unreasoning part of her brain had wrested control and told her body that if she stayed where she was and didn't do anything, nothing could happen to her. She tried to convince herself that her only safety lay not in playing dead but in becoming nothing.

She focused on the pain in her lip and in her hands and the air trapped in her chest as the buzz grew louder again, climbing into a roar that sounded and then echoed away down the valley.

"He's seen Stan!" screamed Micky.

Why doesn't Micky shut up?

She's just going to make him angrier.

But the box stopped moving.

Dawn could feel the weight of El's hand resting against the wall of cardboard, pressing it into her ribs.

She knew that all he had to do was drive the big knife into the box and he could slash all the way through and cut her into little pieces along with the boxes. He could poke and jab the nasty blade through like a magician sticking swords in a basket, only she wouldn't appear at the end and take a bow.

"Five o'clock," came the machine voice.

Dawn opened her eyes and she could just make out the grain of the wood under her hands. She didn't dare move or make a noise.

What about five o'clock?

"Early. Why is he early?"

Rich.

He's talking about Rich.

But Rich wasn't always on schedule.

"He's calling Anchorage now!" shouted Micky.

"Shut up!" shouted El, echoing Dawn's thoughts.

"Calling the troopers, El! They'll shoot you down like a dog when they get here!"

"Shut the fuck up!"

He pounded the boxes and Dawn was crushed against the wall but she was deadly silent. El couldn't know she was right on the other side. For all he knew there could be ten more rows of boxes. She didn't feel safe but a ray of hope entered her heart.

"Shoot you down and take pictures without your fucking glasses, El!" Now El slammed the boxes again so hard that the sleeping bag fell across Dawn's back and more light seeped in.

El hadn't brought a lantern or a flashlight with him. He was searching by the faint illumination that made its way through the clothes closet and into the tiny door. To El it must have seemed incredibly gloomy. But to Dawn it felt as though a searchlight had just fallen on her and she was close enough to El now to smell his body odor. It had a musky, animal scent.

She held her breath, not wanting to disturb the bag.

A heavy rumble shook the floor, walls, and ceiling. From inside the tunnel it sounded like distant thunder. But thunder was a once-in-a-decade event in interior Alaska. Dawn had never heard it since moving to McRay.

No.

That was dynamite.

"The bridge," she heard El mutter.

His voice was right in her ear.

A heavy silence hung over the store and then, from the distance, the buzzing of the plane returned.

"Hear that, El?" taunted Micky. "Rich is circling. He's seen Stan. Did you hear that explosion? Whatever you just blew up, Rich saw it. Your timetable's off, El! You're all finished!"

"Shut up."

Dawn couldn't help but flinch. It sounded like El was right in her face. His voice was so near he had to have seen the sleeping bag move. The boxes crunched against her again, and then there was the sound of El crushing his way, cursing, back through them.

He was leaving.

4:50

MICKY HAD MANAGED TO shift and hop around until the
rocker faced directly up the stairs. But the El that came
down them was not the same El that went up.

His face was ashen. The knife jerked in his hand and his
other hand was so tight on the grip of the pistol—still hol-
stered—that his knuckles were bone white. His head
whipped left and right, trying to follow the plane's flight
through the walls and ceiling as though it were a mocking-
bird, diving on him to protect its nest. His chin was tucked
down into his chest, accentuating the odd impression.

But there was no blood on his knife.

And Micky had heard no scream.

She had to assume that he had not yet found Dawn.

For her own sanity she had to believe it.

Because if he had murdered Dawn, she would not be able
to live with the guilt. She had failed her parents. She had
failed the dancer and then Wade. She had even failed Aaron.
And finally, she had failed herself. But she wasn't going to
fail Dawn. Somehow, she was going to get the girl out alive.

And then, as she watched El's back disappearing up the
stairs, she had felt as though even that bit of salvation was going to be denied her. She had screamed to distract him, never
believing that it would work. But her screams were all she had.

And he had been diverted.

At least for now.

The problem was that she had no idea what El would do next.

He was staring directly at her, and with his stiff motions and the gleaming knife in his hand, he reminded her of Jack Nicholson in *The Shining*.

Should I talk to him?

He'd told her to shut up.

Would I be better off obeying?

Outside she could hear Rich's Supercub circling the clearing.

Even if Rich hadn't spotted Stan's corpse, he'd be wondering why no one was coming outside to greet him. If the explosion had been El's cabin, as she suspected, then that, too, would surely have set Rich's antenna buzzing.

What had happened at El's?

Had Marty somehow blown himself up?

Or had he intentionally destroyed the cabin as a warning to Rich?

She didn't think Marty was in any shape to accomplish that but she prayed it was so. Still, a part of her mind warned her to prepare for the worst.

She watched El, waiting.

"Five o'clock," he said, shaking his head.

What was he talking about?

"Five o'clock," he repeated, hurrying past her to the window.

He craned his head, watching the plane circle overhead.

She was hoping that he would do something stupid, like going out front and shooting at Rich. It was damned near impossible to hit a moving plane and do much damage with a revolver and Rich was certain to see El and realize that something had gone terribly wrong in McRay.

But El just waited.

Would Rich land? Or would he call Anchorage and then circle, waiting for help?

That would be the sensible thing to do. The thing a lone officer might do. But Rich wasn't a police officer. He was a mail pilot in a remote bush village. He might very well land at the strip and come in to investigate.

Of course he'd call Anchorage first.

Wouldn't he?

She heard the plane disappearing to her right and over her shoulder. She could see El leaning hard against the front window.

To her dismay, he slipped the knife back in the boot sheath and retrieved the rifle. He turned to stare at her and she gave him what she hoped was a hateful look.

"I'll be back," he said. Again the voice was deadly calm but she noticed that his hands were still shaking.

Nerves or fear? Or both?

She didn't say anything. She wanted him to leave.

God help her, she wanted him to go out to the airstrip after Rich so that she and Dawn would have a chance to escape. She prayed that Rich would see El and fly away, but beyond that, she just wanted El to take his knife and his gun and get out long enough so that she and Dawn could make a break for it. She knew that if they could get away, the two of them could make it out into the woods. They could hide long enough for the authorities to come, even if it took days, even if Rich hadn't made the call.

If they could just get away from El.

5:00

EL STEPPED OUT ONTO the front deck of the store.
He glanced at Stan, draped motionless over the railing.
Why had the plane come before five o'clock?

El knew that the mail would be arriving at five o'clock because that was the way he had planned it.

Howard had surprised him by appearing unexpectedly at Terry's, and Dawn's running into the creek hadn't been planned either. But both of those events had been fortuitous. He just put Howard in Terry's cabin and assumed that Dawn would bleed to death deep in the alders.

Everything had been going according to schedule.

He had destroyed Howard's guns and prepared the bridge for when Stan and Marty either happened along or came to find out what the noise was about. And he was ready at any time to confront Micky if she showed up.

But what he hadn't expected was the bear and Stan and Micky, charging him out of the woods.

His first thought was that Stan and Micky had somehow trained the bear. The animal was attacking *him*. But, even as he pulled the trigger, he had already realized that the big grizzly was in fact attacking Stan. There was a pang of disappointment when he knew that he could have let the bear do his work for him but it occurred to him that the animal might have attacked Micky too and he just couldn't chance that.

Bears were just too unpredictable.

Bears were crazy.

And that was when things started to go wrong.

He had planned to shoot Stan inside the store. But Stan had surprised him by making a break for it. Still, that was no problem. All he had to do was tie Micky up and drag Stan into the shed with Clive.

But then he discovered that Dawn wasn't dead in the woods. That she was alive, somehow inside the store . . .

And the explosion.

What the hell was that?

Five o'clock!

The mail plane was supposed to show up at five!

El slapped the pistol grip so hard a ribbon of pain shot up his arm.

He had planned to be finished at the store in time to take a leisurely ride out to the airstrip and wait for the plane to arrive. He had gone over the scene again and again in his head because, of the entire plan, only the killing at the airstrip could have an almost certain chance of going off exactly. And it needed to go off exactly.

Because only Clive and Rita or Rich could talk to people outside of McRay.

Was Rich nervous now?

Had he spotted Stan?

El glanced at Stan's body and his mind twisted and turned in that strange way that it had of molding events to fit El's reality.

No.

Rich had seen nothing.

Rich would have no warning.

He wouldn't have heard shots fired.

Wouldn't have heard the ammo going off out front of the store.

He'd land and when he saw El sitting on Clive's four-wheeler he might wonder why Clive wasn't there to meet him, but he'd be more curious than alarmed.

I'll wait and wave like a good old boy, while Rich unloads the mail.

Then I pull up under the wing and shoot him dead.
Five fucking o'clock.

He strapped Stan's and Micky's rifles on the handlebars along with Rita's shotgun and rested Clive's rifle clumsily on top of them, keeping it in his left hand as he gunned the four-wheeler with his right thumb. The ungainly pile of weapons made the Honda damn near unmanageable but he felt that he needed all the guns now. He had to have them near him.

El smiled.

With any luck at all, Rich's curiosity would kill him.

5:02

MICKY LISTENED TO THE four-wheeler rasping away with the closest thing to relief she'd felt all day. She stared up at the landing and prayed that she had been right.

There was no blood on the knife.

El hadn't said anything about finding Dawn.

She'd heard no screams. No struggle.

And he hadn't come back down the stairs muttering to Dawn's corpse.

But of course now Micky was duct-taped to a chair. Trussed like a Christmas turkey. That presented a little problem.

"Dawn!" she screamed. "Dawn! Can you hear me? El's gone."

Silence.

"Dawn! It's all right! He's gone. Answer me!"

Silence.

Am I wrong?

Is the girl dead after all?

No.

She can't be

Micky refused to accept that possibility. She knew exactly what was happening.

She'd been Dawn.

The girl was paralyzed. Just as she had been.

And Micky knew that her own paralysis had cost people their lives, no matter what the police said. No matter what the shrinks said. No matter what Uncle Jim or Damon or Aaron said. Hiding had saved her life. But there had been a dreadful cost.

"Dawn!" she screamed again. "You have to listen to me! He's gone but we don't have much time!"

5 : 0 5

DAWN COWERED UNDER THE sleeping bag, still unable to believe that El wasn't tricking her. Wasn't waiting with raised knife for her to move. Her eyes were closed so tightly that the lids hurt and tears leaked onto the backs of her hands. There was nowhere else to go, nowhere to run, nowhere else to hide.

She heard Micky screaming but she tried to block the cries out. She couldn't believe that El was really gone and, even if he was, what could she do? There were no guns left and she wouldn't have the courage to face him with one if there were. He had killed everyone in town but her and Micky and now he was going to kill Rich.

What did Micky expect?

Dawn just wanted to sleep. She wanted to keep her eyes closed until her mind went blank, and then everything would be all right. Then nothing could hurt her. She would just disappear and, if she ever came back, things would be better. The police or someone would have come and taken El away or killed him.

I hope they kill him.

She pictured different ways for him to die. She wanted him to suffer the way her mother had suffered. She wanted them to cut him up into little pieces and then burn the pieces.

Go to hell.

She remembered old Howard, staring straight into the barrel of El's gun and saying that. She wished that she had Howard's strength. She wished that she had had the guts to pop up in El's face like a nasty Jack-in-the-box and rip his glasses off his face and spit out that same curse. She knew she'd be able to hear Howard for the rest of her life.

Go to hell.

"Dawn! You have to help me!"

Micky's shout cut through the cobwebs in Dawn's brain.

She closed her eyes even tighter and tried to close her ears as well.

What does she want?

Should I go?

What if it's a trick?

What if El's holding a gun to Micky's head, making her call me?

He would do something like that. Then when she showed herself, he would squeeze the trigger and blow Micky's brains out right in front of her eyes. Before he came for *her*. Came up the stairs again with that robot face and those alien eyes and that ugly knife. Came to cut and stab.

And kill.

"Dawn, honey! He's gone. I know what you're going through! But if you hide, he'll come back and, even if you live, you'll hate yourself! Help me!"

What is she talking about?

Why won't she shut up?

Dawn already hated herself.

She didn't need Micky to tell her about it.

She moved her left hand, ever so slightly, gently lifting the bag a half inch off the floor.

Then she listened.

No movement.

No breathing.

It was only her mind that insisted that El was still lurking over her.

But that didn't mean that her second guess was wrong.

He might very well be holding the gun to Micky's head or the knife to her throat. Making her call out.

But Micky wouldn't do that.

Dawn's eyes opened just a slit when she realized that.

Micky would never call for her.

She'd let El blow her brains out first.

And another little voice told her it wasn't likely that El would hold a gun to Micky's head because an inkling of El's plan was starting to seep into her mind.

He hadn't killed Micky the way he had her mother or Howard.

He had left Micky alive in the store and hunted Dawn instead.

Because he expected Micky to stay with him when everyone else was dead.

He was in love with her!

Or whatever passed for love in his screwed-up brain.

He wasn't going to kill Micky.

And if he wasn't going to kill Micky, then Micky was her only hope.

Dawn lifted the bag enough to glance over the one box that still barred the tunnel. A feeble light shone against the rafters and exposed pink fiberglass insulation.

But no shadow.

She drew a deep breath and pulled the bag off her back, biting her lip at the slithering, silky noise of it. A mouse probably couldn't have heard it but the sound of it in the confines of her tunnel made Dawn wince.

"Dawn! Please, honey! We don't have much time!"

The voice was pleading and Dawn wondered if Micky could really help or if she was only giving up her hiding place so that she could die sooner.

Maybe Rich has a gun.

Maybe Rich will kill the bastard.

"Dawn!"

I'm coming! she thought, mouthing the words silently.

She crept ever so slowly around the last box.

5:06

EL STOOD AT THE end of the short gravel runway. To his left, through a narrow stand of spruce and birch, he could barely make out the muddy flow of the Kuskokwim in full spring swell. The river was so wide that he couldn't see the far shore.

The four-wheeler was hidden in the trees.

The mail plane had circled once overhead, close enough for him to see Rich's face in the pilot's seat. The Supercub was a powerful little machine, favored by bush pilots for its lifting ability and the fact that it could take off and land on a postage stamp. But most of the planes were well over fifty years old and as it cruised overhead now the engine didn't sound much larger than the one on the four-wheeler. El was tempted to pull out the pistol and blow the little aircraft out of the sky.

He had to tie up all the loose ends.

Rich was the only remaining connection to the outside.

The telephone was no problem.

He'd overheard Clive before, sending in the weather report. El had contrived to be there on numerous occasions when Clive reported in with it and he knew exactly what to say. He had considered pretending to *be* Clive but thought better of it. He would simply say that Clive was busy and then tell them later that Clive got sick and died.

People died in the bush.

It was to be expected.

Over time, he would report that everyone in McRay had died.

If anyone asked.

It never occurred to El that Rich might be missed. Things that didn't fit neatly into his plan weren't ignored. They just didn't exist.

Rich circled again, tilting the plane at a hard angle.

What is he doing?

Land the damned thing!

El stepped out into plain view.

He smiled broadly and waved.

5 : 08

D AWN STUCK HER HEAD out into the murky twilight of the bedroom.
It blinded her.

She covered her eyes and waited for them to adjust, her ears as keen as a rabbit's.

Micky had stopped shouting. Maybe she had given up.

Or El was making her be quiet.

The thought froze Dawn in place, half in, half out of hiding. She knelt there for a long minute, listening.

What if he's down there, in the store?

What can I do?

Go back and hide?

El was going to find her sooner or later if she did. She let out a long deep breath and pulled herself as quietly as possible to her feet, creeping one step at a time across the floor, not wanting to make the boards creak the way El had.

She stopped just short of the bedroom door, standing on tiptoe, trying to peek over the edge of the landing. She could see the light from the front window and new footprints marring the carpet of ash. The door was half-open. If El was gone, he hadn't bothered to close it. A shaft of light forced its way inside as though it had to struggle against the darkness that El had created.

Dawn took another tentative step forward and her eyes met Micky's. Then Micky's eyes closed and slowly re-opened. She was nodding to herself and smiling.

"He isn't here, Dawn," Micky said in a hoarse voice. "Please come and cut me loose."

5:09

THE PLANE ROARED OVER El's head, descending fast, the engine sputtering.

El watched as the wheels splattered gravel and the plane fishtailed and then straightened, the flaps dropped and the engine idled. Rich slowly rolled to a stop at the far end of the runway. The motor revved once more and Rich made a 180-degree turn and then there was silence.

El blinked.

He had expected Rich to taxi back to him.

Why had the plane stopped at the other end of the airstrip?

He didn't know whether to walk casually out to greet Rich or to wait.

His fingers tapped the walnut grip of the pistol nervously.

The plane just sat there, its windshield reflecting the low sun into his eyes.

Walk over? Act nonchalant and wait?

This was the kind of situation that El wasn't good at. He hadn't planned for this.

He nudged gravel with the toe of his boot and chewed his lip.

Nothing moved on the far end of the runway.

What was the bastard doing?

A pleasant chill started between El's shoulder blades.

Was Rich on the radio?

Was Micky right?

El didn't have any idea of whether or not the plane's engine had to be running to use the radio but on reflection he assumed not. He stared up at the high peaks and wondered if Rich could contact anyone.

Maybe.

El sauntered toward the plane.

When he had gone ten paces, the side door of the Supercub popped open and a couple of booted feet hit the runway. But the window in the door reflected light just like the windshield and the sense of menace behind the twin mirror surfaces sent a pleasant tingle of fear up El's spine. He couldn't see a face to match the feet and he wasn't expecting the sound of the bullhorn that brought him up short.

"That's far enough!"

The voice was harsh and nasal over the electronic amplification. It croaked away through the trees like the call of a solitary crow.

El tried to smile and wave but just when he needed it his voice failed him.

Was that a gun barrel between the door and the plane?

He glanced around.

He wasn't on the strip proper. Instead he trudged through the spongy muskeg beside it and it was maybe twenty yards to the nearest trees.

He glanced back but it was equally far to the four-wheeler, where the loose rifle rested against the seat.

Get your voice! Say something!

But El wasn't accustomed to shouting. Mumbling was what he practiced.

He waved again stupidly and took another couple of steps forward.

"No farther!"

The voice was even harsher but fear had crept into it.

Did Rich have a gun or was he bluffing?

More than likely he did have one in the plane.

He'd be a fool not to, considering where he flew.

In that case, El decided, it was time to trust fate.

He waved again and, sidestepping in case Rich did have a gun, he drew the pistol and began to fire as he advanced.

5:10

GUNSHOTS RANG THROUGH THE open door.

Dawn was on her knees clawing at the duct tape with raw fingers. She couldn't seem to find a loose edge or peel the tenacious tape and Micky urging her on only frustrated her the more.

Both of them stared at each other as another shot echoed off the mountains.

Micky closed her eyes and cursed.

"Find a knife," she said. "Anything sharp. Hurry."

Dawn shook her head.

"You have to, Dawn," said Micky. "Go!"

"He took all the knives. He even took Rita's scissors off her sewing machine. I looked all over."

Of course, thought Micky. *No guns. No knives. No sharp objects or anything that might be a weapon. All the weapons in McRay belonged to El now.*

Think!

She stared at the blue mountainside through the window and tried with all her heart and her cunning to come up with a way out of their dilemma. El was only one man. Surely they had a chance at least to beat him. Their ancestors had defeated wooly mammoths with only stone tools and courage. Eskimos had been hunting polar bears with little more for millennia. And El's brain was dangerously out-of-whack. That had to give them a tiny edge.

Or did it?

Had it saved any of the others?

Weren't those shots proof that he had just murdered Rich?

But all the others had been surprised. They hadn't known what was coming.

She and Dawn *knew*.

And they had a few minutes at least to try to escape. If they could get out the door before El returned, then her idea of hiding out until help arrived might work. Forget looking for a weapon. Forget facing El. Just hide and wait and let the authorities deal with him.

The sun reflected off the snow on a peak outside and prismed through the window directly into her face. The sharp pain closed her eyes and she cursed softly. But when she opened them an idea was written on her face.

"Break the window," said Micky. "Get a shard and cut this tape."

Dawn leaped to her feet to obey. She searched quickly through the wreckage that El had wrought. Beneath a pile of blankets she discovered an ax handle. She rushed straight up to the window and, without hesitating, made a home-run swing. The crack and tinkling sound took Micky back to the crash at the bar. And, for a second, all she could see was Wade's hand, hanging lifeless from the window of the police cruiser.

Dawn leaned on the handle, surveying the pieces of glass that had fallen out onto the front deck. Micky shook her head. The wood frame held deadly-looking triangular shards, radiating from the center point where Dawn's blow had landed. The transparent daggers ranged in length from eight inches to two feet long, and they angled slightly outward, a crystal shark, snapping at the world.

Micky struggled against her bindings. "Get gloves or a cloth! Something to protect your hands. Quick."

Dawn vanished behind the counter.

Two more shots rang out. Different.

Then another.

Then a plane engine, revving into life.

5:11

E L CROUCHED BESIDE THE four-wheeler, nursing the wound in his right calf.

The prop on the Supercub stirred loose gravel at the far end of the runway, and already the plane was starting to roll. El leaned the pistol on the front right fender and fired off the last three shots in the cylinder in rapid succession.

The plane picked up speed.

El had sensed Rich getting ready to fire before he caught the glint of Rich's scope and that intuition and the flash of light set off something in his brain. He didn't hear the shot that hit him in the leg and spun him like a broken-field runner, didn't know that his dance had probably saved his life when Rich's second shot went wild, past the spot El's head had been only a split second earlier.

El stumbled stiff-legged back to the four-wheeler and cowered behind it, trying to catch his breath.

The pain hit him then. Not hard.

Not yet.

But it would and he couldn't look at his leg.

No way.

He didn't mind other people's blood.

But he couldn't stomach his own.

Micky would have to fix it.

After he took care of Rich.

He shoved the empty pistol back into his holster and reached across the seat for Clive's rifle.

The plane was almost on him.

He wondered if Rich could get a shot out the window.

Probably not. He had to fly the plane.

El grabbed the rifle by the barrel and started to drag it across the seat.

A violent explosion erupted in his ear. Hot vibrations rattled through his palm, up his arm, into his shoulder. He dropped back against the engine of the four-wheeler as the rifle clattered onto the gravel on the far side of the Honda.

He shivered so hard his teeth chattered.

A dull burning sensation started in his right hand and when he wiped his hand across his face bright ribbons of blood blurred down his cheeks.

5:12

DAWN JERKED AT A twelve-inch piece of glass, her hands wrapped in a terry-cloth towel.

Overhead the rumble of the plane rattled the rafters. Rich banked so low over the store that Micky was certain the landing gear would rip through the roof.

So Rich was still alive.

But if El had been killed, surely Rich would have come into town to search for survivors.

Dawn clasped the piece of glass in the wad of cloth and, respectful of the cruel edges that gleamed in the half-light, hurried back to Micky's chair. Micky stared at the jagged shard and noted the bad break, the bulblike, prismatic edges that heralded a microthin, razor-sharp edge. Dawn had chosen well, whether she knew it or not. The *scalpel* would cut duct tape like butter if the girl didn't slice right through Micky's arm.

Dawn ever so carefully cut the bindings on Micky's left side, slicing gently where the tape stuck to the chair and not Micky.

Micky marveled at Dawn's control. Fear welled behind the girl's eyes. But it stayed back there, held tightly at bay, her hands taut but not shaking. When Micky's arm slid free she reached out and slipped practiced fingers around the glass. Taking it out of Dawn's willing grip, she sliced the tape from her other arm, then her feet.

The plane circled.

Dawn studied Micky and something passed between the two of them before the girl fell into Micky's arms.

Micky wanted to hold her forever. She felt strong lungs pumping against her and warm tears burning her throat. She stroked the girl's hair gently.

"We have to find out what he's doing," Micky said.

Dawn nodded.

Both of them edged cautiously over to the shattered window, peering out cautiously into the dregs of the day. Rich circled again and Micky waved, though she didn't believe that he saw her.

No sign of El.

"He's waving back!" said Dawn, pointing toward the sky.

The noise from the plane echoed in the clearing, a chainsaw buzz that grated Micky's teeth. But it was a welcome pain.

She glanced quickly across the open area out front, judging their chances of making it to the distant sanctuary of the trees before El could return. But, as she was calculating the odds, Dawn continued staring intently at the plane, her hands shading her eyes.

Rich was no longer circling.

He was diving toward the trail to the strip.

Micky tried to decide if there was an oddness to the sound of the plane.

Something off.

Then there was a rifle shot from the trees.

The plane veered sharply away to the left and its engine noise faded.

The sound of the four-wheeler took its place and Micky saw it nose out of the trees.

She turned back toward Dawn. The girl stood stiff, her mouth open, staring across the clearing at El.

"Upstairs!" screamed Micky, shoving Dawn backward. "Now!"

5 : 13

THE PLANE BUZZED AROUND like a fucking mosquito.
Why doesn't he land or get the hell out of town?
El wanted Rich either to go away or die so that he
would be out of El's brain forever. Already the memory of
Terry Glorianus was dulling. Clive and Rita were merely
momentary frustrations. That was the way his brain functioned. El dealt with the here and now.

He could plan in a limited fashion. The future was a
vague notion to him, though he could function in it in his
own way. But the past tended to be irrelevant.

He just wished that there would be an end to the goddamned plane because he knew that when it went away he
wouldn't be bothered by it anymore and he could get back
to Micky.

Micky would fix his leg.

That was how his brain was working right at that moment, as he approached the clearing. He had already forgotten the heated manner in which he and Micky had parted.
She was back in the place in his mind she had inhabited for
the past few years. She was his girl. Micky would take care
of him and love him once the other distractions around
McRay were taken care of.

He had visualized that scenario for years, until it became

so real to him that he *had* to act on it. The others were going to kill him. He knew it. He'd known it for a long time. Rita and Clive, Howard and the others. Every time he'd met them he'd had his hand on his pistol. Ready. Waiting for them to make their move.

The plan hadn't just sprung into being.

Nor had he sat over long months meticulously jotting down his timetable.

It coalesced over endless winter nights, like a slow, recurring dream.

Until he had trouble believing it hadn't already happened. The only reason he was certain that he wasn't in the dream now was that it wasn't repeating the way it was supposed to.

Rich was supposed to be dead by now.

And Dawn.

Then the others would come calling and fall right into his trap.

By a little after six he and Micky would be having dinner together.

The plane buzzed over his head as he entered the clearing and he stopped, raising the rifle and firing off two more quick shots. He cocked the lever action but the gun was empty. He tossed it into the muskeg and plucked at the bungees that held the other rifles. But he was shaking and the fingers of his wounded hand wouldn't obey him. He gave up on the tied guns but fumbled the pistol into his left hand.

It was empty.

He forced himself to calm down.

His right hand throbbed and his fingers were stiff as boards. He had shot himself through the center of his palm and he kept thinking how Christ-like that made him. But he couldn't look at that wound any more than he could force himself to look at the bloody hole in his calf.

The plane swooped like a mad bomber, making El duck with each pass. But he managed to eject all six empty shells and reload. As Rich dived at him again, El used both hands and took a quick potshot at the underbelly of the plane. His wounded hand slipped along the cylinder and he accidentally advanced one of the unfired shells.

He cursed and fired twice more at the plane, pretty sure he had put a couple of holes in it, then reached across and shoved the pistol back into the holster. But, when he tried to throttle up with his wounded right hand, he flooded the four-wheeler.

He cursed again, pressing the start button until his thumb ached, but the Honda was dead. In disgust he climbed off, giving the machine a kick with his good foot, sending a blast of pain up that leg.

He spit into the slush and hobbled toward the store.

5:14

MICKY PRESSED HER BACK against the half-open door to the bedroom.

Dawn was in her hiding place again. One gleaming eye peeked balefully through the door at Micky, who held the ax handle aloft like a batter waiting for a fastball.

"Micky!" whispered Dawn, sliding one thin finger through the crack in the door and pointing at the top of the handle. "He'll be able to see it!"

Micky glanced up and nodded, dropping the dense hickory wood onto her left shoulder.

"Close the door, but not all the way," she hissed, watching Dawn comply. "If I tell you to run, you run, got it?"

No answer.

"If I tell you, you run right past me and out the door and don't stop running. Do you understand?"

"I don't want to leave you."

"You do it, understand?" Micky's face was hard but her eyes were soft.

"Yes." The voice was a mouse squeak.

Micky twisted her fingers around and around the smooth handle, flexing her muscles, preparing for the swing. The handle felt silly as a weapon but it was all she had. It would have to do.

Her mother and father.

Wade.

The dancer.

Aaron.

All the others.

All lost.

Not Dawn.

Dawn was going to make it out of this, no matter what it took. No matter what it cost.

Outside the plane continued circling but seemed to be maintaining more of a distance. Rich must have called for help by now. But getting help from Anchorage would take two hours at least, maybe three. He was probably staying in place above them so that he could guide the troopers to El when they came. She wondered how long the little plane could stay in the air.

Micky heard a grunt and a curse from downstairs and at first she thought that it was Marty. It didn't sound like El. Something hit the floor hard and then something else rattled across the room. Either El was enraged that she had gotten away or he was hurt. She prayed it was both. Anything to disrupt his thinking. To distract him. Hopefully he'd believe she and Dawn had gotten away and he wouldn't bother to search the store.

"I know you're up there!" he shouted. "You stupid bitches! You tracked ash all the way up the stairs!"

Micky stared at her feet in horror.

Neither she nor Dawn had worried about the ash as they rushed to the window. And when they knew that it was futile to try to make a break across the clearing, they'd both run upstairs without thinking. A muddle of footprints milled in the center of the bedroom. Faint tracks led over to Dawn's hiding place. Micky closed her eyes. When she opened them again they were damp with tears of frustration.

"Stupid bitches!" El screamed. His voice cracked.

He was definitely hurt. He alternated between a screech and a whine, accented by gasping breaths.

But he was getting closer to the stairs with each step and Micky tensed like a spring on a switchblade. She heard the distinctive *click* of the single-action pistol being cocked.

If she hit him right, he'd go down like a brick and she

wasn't going to let him up. Her muscles flexed and loosened, flexed again. She'd hit him over and over, crush his skull, break his neck, smash his rib cage, until he was dead and she could pull off the mirror glasses and see what was behind them.

You hear me, God?

I'm going to see what's in the bastard's eyes.

You owe me that.

The first stair tread creaked and there was a wrenching noise, as though El were ripping the railing away from its bolts.

"Shit." It was more a groan than a curse but Micky heard the creak of another stair tread.

The little door opened a hair and Micky shook her head violently. The movement stopped. Dawn was watching and Micky knew exactly what the girl was feeling.

No problem.

For the first time she mouthed the words so that Dawn could see and read her lips.

Another creaking tread.

Another curse.

There was an odd unevenness to El's tread. A hesitation that shouldn't be there, as though he were climbing with one leg then bringing the other up to meet it and, when he had to take the next step, when he put all his weight on the wounded leg, that was when he grunted. Either he had fallen from the four-wheeler or Rich had shot him.

Two quick steps, then a gasping breath.

One more.

How many risers are there?

Surely ten or more. Maybe twelve.

How many has he taken?

Four?

Five?

She couldn't remember. But he was close. His breathing sounded like it was right on the back of her neck. But he hadn't reached the head of the stairs.

Not yet.

She slowed her own breathing and listened.

"I did this for you," said El. It was the cry of a wounded

child, a spoiled kid who has been punished for something he is convinced he is not guilty of. "For us!"

The thought that he had been there, in his cabin, all that time, dreaming of her, thinking of her, having God alone knew what fantasies about her, made her sick. Then a switch clicked inside her mind and she saw El, as clearly as though she were watching an old black-and-white movie.

Inside her cabin.

He had been there before.

She knew it the way that she knew that she would take the next breath. The way she knew that her heart would beat.

And the fury in her brain exploded into a violent, white wrath.

"You have to help me, you bitch!"

Creak.

She saw El sitting in her chair.

Touching her glasswork.

Saw him on her bed.

Pictured him . . .

Her fingernails dug into the ax handle.

Creak.

This inhuman monster had been in her house?

Through her private things?

This piece of refuse had fantasies about *her*?

This *thing* was going to murder Dawn?

He was right on the other side of the door now. There was a rattle of pain in each of his gasping breaths.

The ax handle no longer felt silly in Micky's hands. It felt like a war club.

"I'm hurt."

The whine again. Grating like broken glass against her soul.

"You're *supposed* to help me."

Come on in.

I'll help you.

The floorboard creaked.

Micky tensed.

Did the hidey-hole door move a fraction?

Another footstep and the toe of his boot appeared. He was only inches away, separated by a wooden door that would not stop a bullet. Micky was tight as the hammer on a pistol; the ax handle no longer rested on her shoulder but lifted, an inch from her left temple, poised. She glanced at her feet and noticed a thin trickle of El's blood, snaking across the floor. She blinked slowly in satisfaction.

Take another step.

Just one more fucking step.

"Come out, you bitches!"

The sudden ferocity of the scream, the blind hatred behind it, jolted her and she almost gasped.

"Come out!"

The scream clawed its way out of the bottom of El's lungs. Apparently he thought that both she and Dawn were in the hidey-hole.

The pistol shot rolled like thunder around the small room. Metal hangers rattled as an old coat danced against the other clothes. Splinters of pine flittered through the air. Micky was stunned.

Had he hit Dawn?

Micky's muscles were metal bands. Her fingers were so tight on the ax handle that they ached.

Take one more fucking step, you monster!

Suddenly she saw his back as he lurched two steps toward the closet. She stepped out and carved a vicious swing at the side of his head, determined to slam the heavy end of the handle against his temple.

But El fired again.

The shot rocked him backward and the ax handle connected farther down the handle. The force was dulled and a nasty vibration shot up Micky's arms.

El staggered away, swinging around to bring the pistol to bear on her. She focused on the gun rather than his head, bringing the handle up and down swiftly, aiming for his wrist as the half-inch hole in the barrel spun inexorably around.

The handle impacted El's wrist at the same instant that his finger tugged the trigger.

The explosion again rocked the room and Micky felt the white heat of a bullet strike her in the left shoulder, driving the wind out of her, slamming her backward and to her knees.

But rage sustained her.

Not this time.

You might have me.
But you aren't getting Dawn.

The strength had deserted her left arm. She could barely grip the ax handle.

But El had dropped the pistol. He staggered, struggling to remain on his feet. One more blow and he might go down for the count. But she couldn't reach his head and she only had the one uninjured hand. In slow motion, she watched El slip the big hunting knife from his boot with his left hand.

She brought the handle of the ax up between his legs with all the power she possessed, happy to see his look of annoyance turn to surprise, then pain.

El dropped heavily to both knees and, just as exhaustion and pain overwhelmed her, Micky slung the handle backhand and caught him hard on the right side of his neck. He crashed facedown onto the bloody floor.

She dropped onto her worthless left hand and, when it would not support her, slid down onto the floor, her face inches from El's mirror glasses. She wanted to rip them from his face but her arms would not obey her.

"Get out!" she tried to scream at Dawn. But there was no breath in her lungs.

She sucked in air and tried again but her voice was scarcely a whisper.

"Dawn! Get out! Run!"

She heard a tiny creak as the little door opened.

Dawn pressed against the wall, as far from El as she could get. Micky tried to nod but it was all she could do to summon up the energy to keep breathing and her vision was foggy.

"Get far away," said Micky. "Wait until help comes. Don't come out until then. You understand? Don't come out for anything!"

Dawn disappeared around the corner of the door as Micky slumped to the floor.

5:20

MICKY CAME TO, BOUNCING down the stairs on her butt.
Excruciating pain radiated outward from her shoulder and a blistering agony inflamed the back of her head. She clawed at the railing as El dragged her along violently, by her hair.

He wasn't breathing anymore.

He was gasping.

When they reached the first floor, he dropped her like a sack and leaned against the wall, jerking the knife from his boot. His face was contorted, unrecognizable. An ugly lump swelled in front of his left ear and his cheekbone seemed to be somehow out of place.

Did I do that?

The Ruger was back in its holster.

But the knife swung like a metronome in his hand.

"Get up." There was a cold anger in his voice now.

Hatred?

No. Something more.

Betrayal.

Micky didn't move.

"Get up!"

The scream was sharper than the knife. She recoiled from it but tried to stand.

The pain in her shoulder lashed up the back of her neck and melted into the fire at the back of her head. She nearly blacked out again. Warm blood oozed between her breasts, soaking her shirt. More pain rocked through her as El's boot slammed into her ribs.

If I pass out, he'll kill me.

She focused on his smudged glasses as she pulled herself up the bannister post, drawing power from her rage. But even standing she was stooped from agony and from the instinctive urge to cradle the wound in her shoulder. She was pleased to note that El wasn't standing quite upright either, although whether that was a symptom of his leg wound or the blow to his manhood she didn't know. Or care.

He lashed out with his crippled right hand and caught her backhanded across the jaw, splattering more blood onto her cheeks, driving her out into the room.

She needed to run.

And now was the time.

El was limping and oozing blood down around the ankle of his boot.

But she could see that he had more strength in reserve and, even with his leg wound, she wouldn't get far. Besides, she had to give Dawn time to get away. The thought that the girl was now safe from El gave Micky solace.

Dawn's one I haven't lost.

El smashed her face again. She spun against the sales counter, gripping the bar top with both hands. El grabbed her hair, lifted her head, and slammed it onto the wood.

Blinding white pain flared behind her eyes, and a sickening crunch sounded as her nose broke.

"Fuck you," she managed to lisp through bleeding lips.

"Fuck you," said El, stabbing the knife down into the counter and punching her hard in the side of the face.

The blow drove her two feet farther down the counter. Her ribs throbbed and she knew that she was losing a lot of blood where the heavy magnum bullet had ripped God knew what kind of hole in her shoulder. The lightning agony from her broken nose melded with the gunshot wound and the cracked ribs and the wrenched muscles until she was one quivering mass of pain.

He's going to kill me now.

El tugged the big knife back out of the wood of the countertop.

Now.

But at least Dawn got away.

Dawn crouched alongside the bottom step across from Stan. She scrunched up against the logs, her eyes on the plane that circled high overhead.

Inside she heard El dragging Micky down the stairs.

Dawn could hear the blows and the cursing. Hear something hitting the bar.

And she knew that El had changed his mind.

He's going to kill Micky.

Just like he did Stan. Just like he had Clive and Rita.

Just like he had Howard and her mother.

Why does the plane keep circling?

Why doesn't Rich come down and help?

He should be doing something.

Not her.

She was only a sixteen-year-old girl.

No one could expect her to do anything.

She hadn't done anything to help Howard. She hadn't done anything to help Clive and Rita. Or Stan.

She hadn't done anything when El murdered her mother.

And it's my fault.

I should have done something.

Micky had told her to run. Told her to hide. Micky was an adult.

When help came she would tell them what Micky had said.

Had said.

As though Micky was already dead.

But she wasn't dead.

Not yet.

Micky isn't dead!

Run!

Hide!

She glanced quickly around the clearing.

She wasn't going to run out front where El could see her. Better to slip around the back of the store, and maybe head up toward Marty's and Stan's cabins. Way up the valley.

El's muttering filtered through the front door. Low. Unintelligible. And once again it had that terrifying machine quality to it. It was the way he talked when he was about to kill. Micky's scream ripped through the clearing like rope scraping over a cliff. Dawn felt herself falling away with it.

Micky had helped her when she didn't have to.

Micky could have gone along with El until help came and Micky would probably have survived.

Dawn glanced over her shoulder at the four-wheeler, deserted at the edge of the clearing; at the rifles still strapped tightly on the handlebars.

El slumped against the counter, holding the knife inches from Micky's face. She had the strange sensation of being able to see both sides of the blade at one time. One view was the knife itself. Then there were the twin reflections in El's glasses.

"I did it for you," said El, pressing against her.

She slid away from him, along the bar.

"You did it for yourself, El," she hissed.

Anger flamed again in his cheeks and the knife slashed.

She braced herself, waiting for the icy blow, the cold metal burn as the blade tore through her. But a low *twang* vibrated in her ears, and once again El struggled to pull the knife out of the countertop.

Micky wanted to lash out, grab him by the hair, and smash his face in. But she had no strength left.

He slithered along the counter until his body touched hers again.

"I wanted it to be just us," he said, running the razor edge of the knife ever so lightly around her throat. The shallow cut left a stinging warmth in its path, merging with all the other pains that cried for her attention.

"Now, I'm going to kill you," he said. "Just like the rest."

"Get it over with, you worthless fuck."

She snatched off his glasses, grinding them into the countertop. For just an instant she glimpsed something in his eyes that she had not expected to find there.

Something human.

Then she noticed that he was having trouble focusing.

His glasses were prescription.

He had to have them.

She couldn't help herself. She laughed in his face.

The mad killer.

The man who had decimated an entire town.

Myopic.

A nearsighted Manson.

Micky Ascherfeld, dead at the hands of a mass murderer with bifocals.

She was only sorry that he wouldn't see her smile before she died.

She spread her hands wider on the countertop to keep her balance. She wanted to face the bastard standing. El pushed himself off from the counter, preparing to strike.

Micky's right hand slid across the glass that Dawn had used to cut her free.

Dawn clawed at the bungee cords holding the rifles across the handlebars of the Honda. Her hands shook so badly she couldn't grip the hooks to free them. But she wasn't going to let El kill Micky.

I can't.

She glanced back toward the store and gasped as Damon splashed through the creek. He clawed his way up the slope and ran stumbling across the clearing.

"Where's Micky?" he gasped. With one hand he held his side, with the other he helped unravel the tangled straps. The guns clattered to the ground. Damon scooped up Rita's shotgun.

"In the store. With El. He's going to kill her." Dawn reached for a rifle. But Damon grabbed her shoulder.

"You stay here." He spun and dashed toward the store.

Dawn leaned against the four-wheeler, praying that Damon would make it in time. With all her heart she wanted to see El laid out dead. She wanted to spit in his face. But any second now she expected to hear Micky scream as El buried the knife in her.

Dawn tried to catch her breath as she glanced back down toward the bridge.

Micky slashed wildly with the shard and blood spurted from the gash on El's left bicep.

The glass dug through her palms all the way to the bone. But she had to strike before El could. She slashed again, ignoring her own pain.

I have to finish him.

Her second cut was deeper than the first. The shard grated across the cartilage and tendon of El's arm.

He screamed. It was a cry of rage and pain and betrayal.

He punched her and the pain blinded her for an instant. But his knife hand hung useless at his side.

He backed away from her as she swung the glittering dagger again and again.

She lurched toward him, hacking. Slashing. Swinging wildly to keep him off-balance, to stop him from reaching for the pistol.

He squinted, limping away, trying to fend off her attack with his wounded gun hand without getting cut again. They were two bloodied fighting cocks, worn to the point of collapse, but still intent on the kill.

El stumbled back against the rocker, fumbling the pistol out of its holster. He gritted his teeth as he pulled back the hammer with his thumb, aiming the gun at Micky's face. She stopped in mid-slash, the glass glistening crimson in the low-angled light through the windows.

I'm dead.

But all I need is the time to drive the shard into the bastard's heart.

One misstep. One heartbeat. One eyeblink.

One split second.

El's lips drew back across his teeth and his myopic eyes narrowed. His finger tightened on the trigger. The door crashed open and El glanced over his shoulder.

The fading light silhouetted Damon in the door. He stood silently on the porch, pointing Rita's shotgun at El.

Micky swung the glass underhanded, ramming the shard deep into El's midsection. The hammer on his pistol fell on an empty cylinder as the jagged sliver sliced through his gut and then curved upward, piercing his left lung. The gun crashed to the floor. El clawed at the glass as blood gushed from the wound.

He dropped to his knees, staring fixedly at Damon with a stunned, childlike expression.

"It's over," Micky gasped.

"I didn't hurt her," said El. "I wouldn't hurt her."

Damon fired through the open door. El was blasted back against the woodstove and Micky slipped in the ash and gore, fighting to stay on her feet. Horror shattered Damon's face. He rushed inside, dropping the shotgun against the windowsill, hurrying to catch Micky before she fell.

Helping her into the rocker, he knelt in front of her. He ripped her shirt open, wadded the tail and held the cloth against the gunshot wound in her shoulder. She reached up and pressed her hand over it.

"Hold that tight," he said.

He glanced at her bloody hands. "Jesus, Mick."

She thought he was going to throw up. Instead he tossed his jacket onto the floor and tore off his own shirt, wrapping it tightly around her other hand.

"Where have you been?" she asked.

"Where I always am." He sounded guilty. He hadn't been there when she needed him. "I heard shots. I headed down to the claim but Stan and Marty were gone. Howard was gone too. Then I went to Terry's place." He gave Micky a look and she nodded.

A board creaked on the porch out front and they both turned to see Dawn standing in the doorway, backlighted by the sun.

"I'm okay, Dawn," said Micky, as the girl slipped through the door.

"I told you to wait," said Damon.

Dawn edged over beside Micky, across from Damon.

"Aaron's dead too, Damon," said Micky.

Damon nodded, as though he expected as much.

Micky bit her lip. The adrenaline drained away and the day settled on top of her with the weight of a mountainside.

"After I found Aaron, I went to your cabin first to warn you," she told Damon.

He ever so gently touched her nose and white pain flared. "Broken."

"Duh!"

"Sorry. Anything else I should be worrying about? I don't see any other holes. If not, I'm going to go flag down Rich. We need help."

"I'll be all right," said Micky. Her heart, which had been pounding mercilessly all day, was at last beginning to slow.

"Why did you run through the creek?" asked Dawn.

"What?" said Damon, frowning.

"Why did you wade across the creek?"

Damon shrugged. "Something didn't look right on the bridge."

"El sat down there a long time," said Dawn.

"I thought he might have booby-trapped it," said Micky. She had trouble holding her head up. "El stole dynamite from Marty and Stan." The thought of Marty clutched at her heart. "Marty's hurt bad. We left him in El's cabin."

"I think El's place blew up," said Damon.

"Maybe Marty got out," said Dawn.

"Maybe," whispered Micky, not believing it.

"I'm going for help," said Damon, starting toward the door.

"He would have cut our eyes out," muttered Dawn, turning her attention back to El's corpse.

"What?" said Damon, turning in the door.

"He cut their eyes out," said Dawn, not looking up. "And then he cut them up."

"Don't talk about it, Dawn," said Micky, trying to get the girl's mind on something else. Anything else. She didn't want Dawn spending the rest of her life focused on this day, the way she had been focused on her own horror for so long.

"Their eyes?" said Damon. "He cut out their eyes?"

"You found Terry?" asked Micky. She didn't want to say any more with Dawn right beside her.

"Yeah," said Damon, still staring at Dawn. "After that I came right here when I heard the shots over by the airstrip."

"And you didn't notice?" said Micky. She remembered Stan's horror. The look on his face when he recounted the gruesome discovery. How could Damon have found their bodies and not have noticed?

"Someone set Aaron's house on fire," said Micky.

"El," said Damon.

"He didn't burn down anyone else's cabin."

"Maybe he didn't have time."

Did that make sense? El had seemed so confident until he got flustered over Rich arriving early.

"Maybe he was never there," she said.

"How could he not have been there, Micky?"

"Maybe El never went to Aaron's," she said, feeling even weaker than she had before.

"That's crazy, Micky."

"Is it?"

Dawn had turned to watch them. Micky noticed the curious expression on the girl's face. The bright eyes. Dawn's lips parted slightly, her cheeks sagged. "You didn't want me to come inside with you," she said, glancing from Damon to El's corpse.

"Where were you all day, Damon?" asked Micky.

"I told you. I was looking for the goddamn mine."

Micky nodded. "You went to see Aaron. Didn't you?"

"Why would I go see Aaron?"

"That's what I want to know. Why did you kill him, Damon?" She knew in her heart that it was true. El had never gone to Aaron's cabin. He had no need to. Aaron seldom came down into the lower valley anymore. El knew that he could kill everyone down below and then attend to the old man at his leisure. And Aaron had had his eyes. El would never have left the old man whole like that. "Why did you murder Aaron?"

"That's crazy, Mick," said Damon. But he sidled over and lifted the shotgun from its resting place. Micky's heart pounded like a drum. Her breath caught in her throat.

"Aaron had both his eyes," she hissed.

"Maybe El was in a hurry."

Dawn edged away from Micky. Damon took two steps closer to the rocker.

"You didn't get what you wanted from Aaron," said Micky. "Did you?"

"Don't be silly. You know I wouldn't hurt a fly."

"You shot El."

"He was going to kill you."

"No, he wasn't. He was already dying. Were you afraid he'd say something to give you away? My, God! *I didn't hurt her.* El said, *I didn't hurt her.* You told him not to hurt *me!*"

"He would never hurt you! He was obsessed with you. I can't believe you never saw it."

The enormity of the horror was impossible to fathom. It was one thing to accept a psychopath like El going on a killing spree. It was another to comprehend Damon murdering someone. But she understood one thing immediately.

"You made El do it," she said. "Somehow you started this. Why, Damon? How?"

Damon aimed the shotgun at her chest.

"I never meant for this to happen, Mick. Not any of it."

"Don't point that gun at me, Damon."

The sadness in his face was more frightening than rage.

"I never meant for it to happen," he repeated. "The old bastard wouldn't tell me where the mine was."

She couldn't believe that it all came down to that. All the deaths. Not just in McRay. But every death in her past. Had they all been about money?

The kid robbing her parents' store.

The pair of sociopaths rampaging through Houston with the stolen armored truck.

Now this.

But as she stared into Damon's eyes she knew that she was mistaken. This wasn't about money. Stan had been right. For Damon it was all about the *finding*. He had to know where the mine was. And he was so obsessed with his quest that he'd been willing to kill for it.

"There is no mine," she said, quietly. "It's a myth."

"There is! It's here. The son of a bitch wouldn't give it up! I don't know what happened. We were yelling at each other and the old bastard grabbed his rifle. Honest to God, I never meant to kill him, Mick. But he pointed the gun at me and I jerked it away and pointed it back at him. The next thing I knew the damn thing went off. Honest to God! That's how it happened."

"So you set Aaron's cabin on fire to cover up his murder. But then you got worried that someone investigating the fire would discover how Aaron died. So you started El on his killing spree."

Another realization struck her. "You knew all along," she whispered. "You knew El was dangerous and you've always told me that he wasn't. You've been planning this for years!"

"No!" he shouted. "I knew about the guns, sure. But El could have been controlled. I *was* controlling him. It was me that kept him from hurting anyone all this time."

"Aaron crawled out. I found him across the clearing."

"No way."

"He would have burned to death."

"I didn't mean to kill him," he repeated. But the thought of burning Aaron alive seemed to touch something human in Damon. His eyes softened a little. The shotgun dropped a notch so that Micky wasn't staring directly down the long dark barrel.

Dawn took a step backward, out of Damon's peripheral vision.

"How did you start El on his spree?" asked Micky.

She understood now. Damon knew that if he could get El to kill someone, then everyone would assume that El had murdered Aaron as well. Two separate killers in one day in a town the size of McRay would be just too unbelievable.

"It wasn't like that. I didn't mean for him to kill anyone."

"Really? And what was going to stop him?"

Dawn reached down and quietly retrieved El's pistol. Micky wanted to signal to the girl somehow. To let her know the gun was empty. But she didn't dare draw Damon's attention to Dawn. He might just spin around and kill her.

"El trusted me. I was the only one who talked to him. All I had to do was tell him that everyone in McRay hated him. That they were planning on killing him today. He ate it up. Said he'd known it all along. Said he knew just what to do."

"You set him loose like a mad dog, Damon. You're as bad as Vegler." She spit out the name and Damon looked as though she'd slapped him in the face. "Vegler made you sick. And now you're no better than he is."

"I didn't mean for anyone to get hurt," Damon whined.

"So you made sure El thought that I was his friend," said Micky.

"I did, yeah. But I knew he wouldn't hurt you anyway. I didn't *think* he'd hurt you. He already had plans for you."

"I'll bet."

"I wasn't going to let him hurt anyone. It was all a mistake."

"A mistake? Damon! Six people are dead!"

The shotgun shook in his hands. "I followed El to Terry's place. I still had Aaron's rifle. I was going to stop El before he hurt anyone. Kill the son of a bitch. I was!"

"Then why didn't you?"

Dawn raised the pistol with both hands. She pointed it at the back of Damon's head.

"The fucking gun jammed. I was running down the trail after El and I went to cock the rifle and it got stuck. The bullet was all crumpled inside and I panicked. I'd just got to the edge of the clearing when I heard Terry screaming. I saw Dawn running into the alders, and then Howard showed up."

"And El killed him."

"Yeah."

"What then?"

Dawn gritted her teeth, pulling the hammer of the pistol with both thumbs.

Micky tensed.

"I followed El," said Damon. "Waiting for my chance. But the son of a bitch kept wrecking all the guns. He smashed Howard's before he threw them into the woods. He even burned all of Clive's ammunition."

Micky thought of the Glock, resting in a pile of melted plastic. But she shook her head.

"El's place was full of guns."

"And there was a bear there. I damn near walked right into her."

"I wish you had."

"Don't say that, Mick."

"What are you going to do now?"

His eyes hardened again. His finger tightened on the trigger. "I can't go to jail, Mick. You know I can't. I'd go crazy."

"You're crazy now, Damon. They'll catch you. The cops will go over every inch of this valley with a fine-tooth comb. They'll figure out what happened."

"I'll be gone by then."

Dawn clicked the hammer back on El's pistol, but Damon never looked away from Micky. The smile that crossed his lips was as sad as his eyes. He raised the shotgun again.

"I love you," he said, speaking directly to Micky, ignoring Dawn, "but I can't go to prison. You know I can't. I'm sorry."

"You never loved anyone but yourself," said Micky.

Dawn pressed the cold barrel against the back of Damon's head. "You killed my mother," she said.

"That gun is empty," said Damon.

Dawn pulled the trigger.

Two shots roared.

CLOSING TIME

THE TOP FINIAL OF the swaying rocker hung by a splinter. Micky let out a long, slow breath, cautiously searching herself for new wounds. But there were none. Dawn helped her to her feet and they both stepped across Damon's body, heading for the door.

The girl's face was deathly pale and her eyes were wide. Micky knew that she had to reassure her before she went into shock.

"Thank you," rasped Micky. "You saved our lives. You didn't just run and hide like I did when I was your age."

They staggered out onto the landing and leaned on the railing. Neither of them looked down at Stan.

"I was so scared," wept Dawn. "I thought Damon was right. I thought the gun was empty."

"So did I," said Micky, wondering if her luck was changing. She searched for Rich, over the trees. "At least you won't have to live the rest of your life not knowing if you could have done something."

"My mother," said Dawn. "I didn't do anything."

Yes.

What do I say to that?

"Dawn, there was nothing you could have done. You were alone. You didn't have a gun."

"You're losing a lot of blood," said Dawn, staring at Micky's shoulder and making a face.

Micky peeled back the blood-soaked cloth. The bullet had clipped her collarbone and left an open track across her shoulder. She didn't think an artery had been hit or she would have been dead already. But if the bone was completely broken, it was going to mean more painful rehab.

"I'll be all right."

"What can I do, now?" asked Dawn.

"Flag Rich down," said Micky, knowing it was important to keep the girl busy. She pointed out into the clearing. "He'll come down for you."

Dawn did as she was told and Micky noticed the girl's shoulders straighten when she had a job to do.

I haven't saved her yet.

Not if she blames herself.

I won't allow that.

Rich dipped his wings in a final pass and disappeared over the trees toward the strip.

Dawn glanced back toward the store, awaiting further instructions.

"Go get him!" Micky shouted. "It's up to you."

OPENING DAY

MICKY SAT ON THE concrete bench in the center of the vast open rotunda that was the entrance and focal point of the new Wellsgate Mall, on Houston's ever-expanding west side. Behind her a fountain played the high keys as water tinkled and gurgled along the blue-tile runway that fed an indoor jungle.

Shoppers hurried past, eager to be the first into stores that offered spectacular savings on Grand Opening Day. High-class home furnishings, state-of-the-art electronics, and upper-end men's and women's fashions, including a fancy negligee store that men kept not quite glancing at. Outside, the temperature was nearing one hundred. But inside, the world existed forever at the meat-locker chill Texans loved.

Micky ignored the bustling crowd. Instead, she studied the stained-glass skylight overhead, half the size of a football field, showering rainbows on the floor below. It had taken her two years to complete the giant work and her fee was more than many artists earned in a lifetime. But more than the money, she was proud of the work.

She noticed shoppers stopping in their feverish search for bargains to follow the train of light upward from their feet, staring in wonder at the glass above. The sheer size and complexity of the work gripped them. The changing light from outside brought the glass to life, shimmering and flickering as though electrified. On every face, Micky saw awe, wonder, and, occasionally a nod of understanding.

That gladdened her.

Her heart was in the work.

It had a brooding quality that caught the eye, like a roll of distant thunder over an unseen horizon. But as the noonday sun approached zenith, the darkness was diminished, then subdued, and ultimately defeated. Then the ceiling of glass glowed with an inner fire, radiating hope and renewal.

Rebirth.

That was what she called it, although only the few who read the small brass plaque beneath the You Are Here map would ever know that. Micky Ascherfeld's name would never be a household word. But she was all right with that.

"It works," Micky muttered, thinking of what it had cost to get to where she was.

She thought of Marty. She'd received a couple of letters from him in the four years since the murders. He'd been in the hospital six weeks longer than she was but then moved right back to McRay. He'd laughed off his scars, but couldn't laugh off the loss of his best friend. But Micky had been gladdened to hear that a family with two young boys had moved into the Cabels' building. At least he wasn't by himself any longer.

A couple of months after that first letter, Marty wrote again. He sent her a piece of ore with an inch-thick layer of bright yellow gold in it. And a copy of a deed to the mine naming her and Dawn as coowners with him.

There really was a mine.

Damon had been right.

Aaron had known where it was all along.

Almost as soon as Marty returned to McRay he began working his claim again. A year after he got back, he had hiked up to Aaron's to see if there might be a shovel left in the old man's toolshed. Even without Stan, Marty was still going through shovels. He said he felt guilty about busting the lock on Aaron's storehouse. But he needed the tool and the place was going to pot anyway. When he kicked open the door he nearly fainted.

It wasn't a shed at all. It was the entrance to the lost mine.

Aaron must have discovered the mine years before, hidden in the underbrush. He'd built the lean-to to disguise it. That was why he moved out of Micky's cabin down by the store and high up into the valley.

Not to get away from people.

To be close to his mine.

She smiled, thinking of the old man knowing all along. What a great joke he must have thought that was.

Micky tried to spot the stone in the center of the window above but it was invisible at that distance.

Dawn had moved in with her aunt in California after the murders. But she had become powerfully attached to Micky. So after getting out of the hospital, Micky had moved to San Francisco to be close to the girl. Their continued relationship had been good for both of them. As she grew up, Dawn developed all her mother's dark beauty with none of the aura of tension and fear that had been Terry's constant companion.

Micky built a studio and sold her works through a local gallery. Eventually she took on commissioned work as well. But she refused to go back to her old style. Instead she opened herself to new, wilder forms that bubbled up from some deep wellspring within. With each new piece her reputation grew, until she'd received the commission to do the skylight for the mall. For that she had had to move back to Texas and lease a large warehouse space. By that time Dawn was eighteen and had enrolled in the University of Houston.

Micky had insisted that Dawn see a professional therapist in San Francisco and continue seeing one in Houston. But Dawn never failed to point out Micky's own refusal to submit to therapy.

The light through the abstract glass danced at their feet and Micky watched it create strange new patterns.

"*You're* my therapy," she said.

When she realized that she had spoken out loud she blushed, then smiled, not sure whether she was talking about Dawn or the skylight.

She wiped a tear from her eye and held the glittering liquid, like shattered glass, in her palm, watching the droplets come together again, forming one whole. Then she tilted her hand and let the teardrop spill into the waterway.

She smiled at her own reflection and the mirror image of the ceiling overhead. She could easily imagine Dawn's face beside her.

"Maybe both of you," she whispered.

ABOUT THE AUTHOR

Chandler McGrew was born and raised in Texas and lived for a number of years in Alaska. He now resides in the mountains of Maine, with his wife, Irene, daughters, Amanda and Charli, and a dog and cat, all of dubious disposition.

Turn the page for a preview of
Chandler McGrew's newest thriller

NIGHT TERROR

Coming soon
wherever Bantam Books are sold

NIGHT TERROR

SILENCE HUNG OVER THE darkened house like a shroud. Outside the window, the moon peered through skeletal pines. Gray-black clouds scudded across the sky, rats leaving a sinking ship.

Audrey Bock screamed.

The agonizingly long shriek resounded in the confines of her bedroom, and then away down the hall, like the caterwaul of a hellbent train.

Her husband, Richard, bolted upright, fumbled for the lamp. Something clattered to the floor.

Audrey screamed again, a wail of abject terror. Beneath the fury of her gut-wrenching cry, like sand shifting beneath a wave on a deserted beach, other sounds struggled toward the surface.

Richard cursed.

His fingers clawed at the bedside table.

A thin breeze fluttered the curtains.

The light finally flicked on as Audrey screamed yet again.

She stared straight ahead through unfocused blue eyes. Her back pressed stiff against the headboard. Her knees tucked tightly to her chest. Her short blond hair was tousled. Her hands flapped wildly in front of her face, warding off some unseen menace.

Richard clutched her, following her gaze across the harsh shadows of the bedroom, into the hallway, barely lit by the bathroom night-light.

"Let him go!" Audrey shrieked.

"Honey, there's nobody there." Richard shook her gently. "It's a dream, Aud. Wake up. "

"She's got him, Richard!" Audrey cried, so loudly that Richard winced. "She's got him!"

"Honey, it's a bad dream. Wake up!"

"Leave him alone! Leave my baby alone!"

"Audrey!"

She clawed at the sheets, but Richard tugged her back as she struggled feebly in his arms.

"She's got him," she said, in a voice suddenly far too calm.

"You're asleep. You've got to wake up."

"She's going to kill him. She's got my baby!"

Richard couldn't understand how Audrey could have her eyes wide open and still be sound asleep. This was nothing like one of her nightmares.

"I've got to go!" She fought him. Stronger this time, but still unable to break free.

"Honey, if you don't wake up I'm going to put you in the shower." He wasn't sure that was such a good idea, but he didn't know what else to do. Perhaps just the threat would work.

"Don't touch him!" she screamed. This time she broke free. She stood beside the bed, wobbling, gesturing into the hallway.

Richard slid across the bed and wrapped her in his arms again. She was a head shorter than he was and weighed barely ninety-five pounds. He lifted her easily and carried her into the bathroom.

The vision followed them through the house, focused directly in front of Audrey's eyes. She clawed at the empty air. Richard lowered her gently into the tub and she cringed in the far corner, quivering, as though the icy water had already been turned on.

He stared into her eyes and fear surged through him. "Audrey, please."

He'd seen eyes like those before.

Eyes of madness.

He remembered his mother's screams. Remembered her begging him to save her from the demons that he could not see. He remembered other eyes as well. Tara's patients. And the inmates at the institution in which his mother spent her final days. Richard was more afraid of madness than of almost any other terror on earth.

Almost.

He turned on the tap, expecting another cry from Audrey as the cold water struck her.

But her silence was worse.

She quailed in the farthest corner of the tub. The water plastered her hair to her head. Her chin rested between her knees and she shivered so violently her teeth chattered.

But still she stared straight ahead at the evil visible only to her.

Richard knelt beside her, spray soaking his pajamas. He stroked soggy hair out of her face. "Aud, it's a dream. It's just a bad dream. You have to wake up."

"It isn't a dream." Her voice was mechanical, inflectionless.

He lightly slapped her cheek. "It is."

She looked into his eyes and for the first time he thought that she could see him.

"She's here!"

He gripped her shoulders and shook her. "No one's here, Aud."

"She's got him." Her tone was hesitant now. Confused. Her emotions were mercurial, unstable.

"Wake up, honey," Richard said. "You're almost awake. Come on. Stand up."

"I am standing up."

"No, you're not. Come on."

He lifted her to her feet and she wrapped her arms around him and fell into his soaking embrace. They huddled together beneath the icy spray for several minutes. Until her breathing eased and her heart slowed.

"I want him back. I need to help him," she whimpered.

"I want him back too, Aud." He held her at arm's length and looked into her eyes. "Are you with me now?"

She gave him a curious look.

"Are you awake?" he asked.

"Yes."

"Good. Let's get you dried off."

She stood compliantly as he removed her dripping nightgown and toweled her dry. Then he kicked off his own sodden pajamas and dried himself.

"Let's go back to bed," he said, exhausted.

But she stood as still as a zombie and he realized that wherever she was, she wasn't completely back yet. He lifted her like a small child, speaking calmly to her all the time, and carried her back to bed.

Audrey awakened to the smell of frying bacon.

She stretched languorously, shocked by the feel of linen against her bare skin. She lifted the sheets and stared at her nude body. She had gone to bed in a nightie. No question about that. And that was the last thing she remembered.

She grabbed her robe out of the closet and followed the smell of breakfast into the kitchen. Richard was a great cook when he wanted to be. Better than she was.

Richard glanced up from the electric griddle as she entered.

"How do you feel?" he asked.

"Sleepy. What time is it?"

He glanced at his watch. "Nine-thirty."

"Why'd you let me sleep so late?"

"It's Saturday. Besides, after last night I thought you needed your rest."

She took the coffee that he offered and dropped into a chair. "I slept like a log. But I woke up with nothing on."

"You don't remember anything?"

"Remember what? Did we have a wild night?"

"You had the worst nightmare you've ever had."

"Really?"

He set his coffee cup beside the griddle. "I had to put you in the shower to wake you up. That's why you were sleeping nude."

"You're kidding."

"I'm not kidding. It was awful. I couldn't get through to you. You just kept staring into space and screaming."

"Screaming?" She couldn't believe it. She was tired. As though the deep sleep she had gotten had done her body no good. But she didn't remember waking in the night. And she certainly didn't remember a shower.

"You kept shouting for *her* to let him go."

Neither of them questioned who the *him* was. Neither of them needed to mention that today was the first anniversary of Zach's disappearance.

"I can't believe I didn't wake up in the shower."

"You sort of woke up, after a while. You talked to me, but it was like you were speaking through a wall. I carried you back to bed and you finally went to sleep again."

"That was it?"

"You woke me a couple of times and I thought you were going to do it again. I talked to you and you went back to sleep. But you were stiff as a board all night."

"I'm sorry."

"There's nothing to be sorry about. I wish I could have done something."

"You did something by being there."

He slid a plate of bacon and eggs in front of her and she picked at it.

"Maybe you should call Tara," he said.

"No." Tara was the last person she wanted to call. Tara understood why Audrey chose not to see her anymore. Being around Tara or speaking to her reminded Audrey of just how much besides Zach she had lost.

"Then call Doctor Burton."

"I don't need a doctor."

"You need something."

"What about you?"

"I'm okay." He carried the griddle to the sink and stood staring out into the backyard.

"I'm getting better," she whispered. And she believed that. She hadn't been weeping every day, standing in the front window staring out across the lawn. She hadn't awakened in the middle of the night to go tuck Zach in in what? Six months?

She could see Richard working his way up to saying something and she knew what it would be. She just didn't know how he would phrase it this time.

"I don't want another baby," she said.

His neck reddened.

"You can't replace my son," she said softly.

Richard turned slowly to face her. "Audrey, having another child doesn't mean we're replacing Zach."

"Then what the hell does it mean?"

She shoveled bits of egg around on the plate, staring at the pattern in the yolk. The fork felt strange in her hand. Soft. Her entire body felt weird.

What was that?

A panic attack?

She willed her breathing to slow, concentrating on her pulse.

Richard sat down in the chair next to her. "I loved Zach just as much as you did."

She glanced up and saw that he had already realized his mistake.

Her voice was a heavy stone, poised to crush both of them. "I still love him."

"So do I, Audrey."

"Then why didn't you say so?"

"I only meant that we have to go on living."

"I'm living. You're living."

"No, we're not. We're just frozen in time. Waiting. Audrey, we've done all we could do."

"He's out there, somewhere," she whispered, barely able to breathe. "He needs me and I can't find him. Someone took my son."

"Our son."

"I want him back."

"I want him back, too, Aud. But we have to face the fact that we may never get Zach back. There hasn't been one call. No one saw him taken. He could be anywhere."

She dropped the fork onto her plate. The handle was bent.

"Why didn't they call?" she asked. "Why didn't we get a ransom note?"

"You know why, Aud. The police told you why. Zach wasn't kidnaped for ransom."

"No!"

"Honey, calm down."

She stared out through the open back door. "The bastard stole my son right here. From our home." That burned. The fact that Zach had been taken from a place where he should have been safer than anywhere else in the world. When both she and Richard were home. It inflamed her guilt and her rage. But it also angered her that Richard was right. They had done everything there was to be done.

They had contacted the Oxford County Sheriff's Department immediately. The police and game wardens searched the area with dogs for days. She and Richard had run through the woods with the searchers, shouting Zach's name, searching for him beneath every deadfall pine, in every dry gully. The woods surrounding the house were deep Maine forest and the farm to market roads spider-webbed the mountains.

The sheriff sent out a File 6 Missing Persons Report by teletype to all law enforcement agencies, including the NCIC, the National Crime Information Center. Audrey and Richard had placed ads in local newspapers, paid for spots on radio stations, put professionally printed posters in stores and gas stations. They had even spent most of their savings hiring a private investigator out of Boston.

All in vain.

There were no clues.

Zach had wandered into the front yard to play while Audrey worked in her back garden and ten minutes later he was gone.

One year ago today.

How dare Richard think of another child?

"He's alive," she said.

Richard didn't respond.

"He's alive," she repeated.

Audrey stood now, staring out the back door into her garden.

She hadn't set foot in the backyard since the day of Zach's disappearance. Her perennials had survived but they were coming back wild and uncultivated and the areas that would normally be planted already with young annuals were filling with spring weeds. She hated seeing it like that.

Audrey's garden was an extension of herself. Tara had explained the rudiments to her, bought horticulture books for her to study—until Audrey outgrew her teacher and began to instruct Tara. Audrey found solace and rebirth in the nurturing of plants. She had transferred a lot of those feelings to her love for Richard and Zach. But there was something different about her love for gardening. When her hands were immersed in the soil her mind emptied and all her training took over. For that brief period of time all that existed for her was the tiny ecosystem that she had created.

The garden called to her now. She longed to smell the rich soil. To feel her fingers working through the damp earth. To hear the sound of crickets and birds.

But when she rested her hand on the doorknob, it felt frigid to the touch. Hostile. As though her garden dreaded her return as much as she feared returning to it.

So what do I do?

Spend the rest of my life inside this house?

Until I'm pacing from room to room in an old housecoat like some hag out of Dickens?

Until I turn into a bodiless spirit, living on memories and rage?

Still the door would not open.

An odd tingling tickled the very back of her mind.

Why should I be afraid of my own garden?

But it wasn't just her garden she feared.

It was the door itself.

It wasn't the place.

But the passing into the place.

It was that irretrievable step from the past year into this new one.

A year without Zach.

Last year Zach had been with her.

This year he wouldn't be.

She glanced around the kitchen. Sunlight glinted on the blue countertops and white vinyl floor. The dishes were washed and stacked. The laundry was dried and put away. The house was spotless. There was nothing more to be done inside. No more living to be accomplished. If she remained in the house it would not be to live but to die.

She clamped down hard on the knob and opened the door. Without hesitating on the stoop, she strode out into the backyard.

The day was warm and golden. The air was redolent with balsam fir and lilacs, just beginning to flower. A pair of robins performed a mating dance on the lawn near her storage shed. One of those perfect spring days that made Maine winters bearable.

One year ago she had been right here. Down on her knees in the dirt. A sudden inexplicable sense of doom had overcome her and she had risen to her feet and raced to the front of the house, calling Zach's name.

On the grass at the edge of the lawn, where the ground dipped into the roadside drainage ditch, lay Zach's baseball bat. His baseball was never recovered.

She opened her shed and discovered her tool bucket just inside the door. Carrying it to the center of her garden, she slipped on her kneepads and knelt. The familiar position and the smell of damp earth revitalized her. But at the same time the familiar scent threatened her determination. She took out her garden claw and scratched at the weeds that were making inroads into her carefully planted perennials.

She stared at the tines of the claw as they traced finger patterns in the dark soil, as though the tool were guided by someone else's hand. Suddenly her determination to break free of her mental prison was shattered by fear and grief.

What am I doing here?

How could I possibly come back to this place?

She bore down on the tool, burying it deeply, jerking it along. The rasping sound grated on her ears.

I'm here because I have to be.

Because if I wander aimlessly through the house for one more minute, I'll go mad.

Because if I don't come out here and do this then Zach's kidnaper wins.

Because then the son of a bitch takes both my son and my life.

Wasn't that what Richard was trying to do as well? Beat Zach's kidnaper? Beat him by burying himself in his work every day? Beat him by having another child?

Audrey couldn't bear that thought.

Even if another baby wasn't a betrayal of Zach, how could she possibly consider having another child? How would she ever keep him safe?

One year today.

She remembered Zach cavorting around her that day. He was more full of life than any six-year-old should be. Shouting and tumbling. Grass stains on his T-shirt. Sunlight glinting in his eyes. The yard barely contained his exuberance. She and Zach were impossibly close, even for a mother and son. She always sensed when he needed her. When he awakened in the night. With each passing day their closeness had grown and evolved until Zach had often finished her sentences for her.

The vision of another child flashed through her mind.

She blinked.

The image was gone as quickly as it appeared but its shadow hung just behind her eyes. It was a picture of herself at the age of nine or ten. Bright blue eyes and a cockeyed smile. She was holding a small doll in her hands as though in offering.

Suddenly, like a knife, jagged pain slashed through her abdomen. Lightning struck, blazing outward in fingers of golden fire.

She clutched at her belly. Her teeth chattered. Her hands shook where they grasped her light cotton blouse. She struggled to get to her feet, then decided against it, digging her kneepads into the soft loam of her garden instead.

The agony was volcanic. Intense. It electrified every nerve ending in her body. Sparked her synapses like strands of flickering lights on a Christmas tree. The pain flowed over and through her. Minutes later, when it finally drained away, she was weak as a kitten. She clutched her arms tightly about her, like a long distance runner fighting a cramp.

The day seemed dimmer, out of focus.

What the hell was that?

Never in her life had she experienced such pain. Not even during childbirth. And the pain had struck so suddenly, out of the blue.

What in the world could have caused it?

Just as she began to relax from the first attack, another wall of flame crashed down upon her. Pain raged through her like an out-of-control fever. The agony was a chemical explosion that erupted inside her body and burned its way out through her skin.

She glanced frantically at the unplanted earth, wondering if she should lie down and hope for the terrible seizures to pass.

Dare she do that?

No.

Maybe something was horribly wrong inside. Maybe she was bleeding internally or something had ruptured.

She needed help.

She remembered the birthing techniques she had learned years before. She took short, shallow breaths and tried to relax.

After an eternity, the second attack passed. She struggled to her feet and stumbled across the lawn toward the door, praying to get inside before another blast of pain struck.

She was halfway up the back stoop when the agony lashed her yet again. Worse than the first two. Much worse.

Her fingernails clawed the wood banister. The muscles in her arms tightened into steel bands. She doubled over. Her cheek rested on the splintery stair rail, one foot on the landing, one on the top step. She eyed the door, only two paces away.

Her body shook so violently she was afraid she might collapse in a heap of boneless jelly. But as the pain eased once more, she staggered into the house.

She dragged a kitchen chair over to the wall phone, not wanting to be caught standing when the next attack struck. She knew more were coming.

She grabbed the phone and pressed the autodial button for Richard's office. He answered on the third ring.

"Help me. Oh, God, it hurts so bad" was all she managed before the next wave of pain thundered over her and left her moaning into the receiver. She heard Richard, as though from a great distance. Telling her that he was on his way. That he was calling the hospital.

The phone crashed to the floor.

The pain rose inside her. It swelled like a molten rush of lava. Burned its way through her, singed her body, torched her soul.

As the wave crested, she drifted far away, deep down inside herself. Reality dissolved into thin echoes of sound and sunlight and the surflike pounding of her heart. She thought she heard, for just an instant, a child's voice.

And the sound of a child's feet, pattering along.

She opened her eyes but she was alone.

She didn't know if she had been delirious for minutes or hours. But the sun hadn't moved and neither Richard nor the paramedics had arrived. And the pain didn't seem to have lessened all that much.

What was that voice she'd heard?

She closed her eyes and clasped both hands again across her belly. She drew her knees up to her chest, her feet rested on the edge of the chair.

Pattering feet again.

The voice.

And then darkness.

BANTAM MYSTERY COLLECTION

____57204-0 **KILLER PANCAKE** Davidson • • • • • • • • • • • • • **$6.99**

____57719-0 **MOTHER TONGUE** Holbrook • • • • • • • • • • • • • **$5.99**

____57235-0 **MURDER AT MONTICELLO** Brown • • • • • • • • • **$6.99**

____58059-0 **CREATURE DISCOMFORTS** Conant • • • • • • • • • **$5.99**

____29684-1 **FEMMES FATAL** Cannell • • • • • • • • • • • • • • • **$6.50**

____58140-6 **A CLUE FOR THE PUZZLE LADY** Hall • • • • • • • • **$6.50**

____57192-3 **BREAKHEART HILL** Cook • • • • • • • • • • • • • • **$6.50**

____56020-4 **THE LESSON OF HER DEATH** Deaver • • • • • • • • **$6.99**

____56239-8 **REST IN PIECES** Brown • • • • • • • • • • • • • • • **$6.99**

____57456-6 **A MONSTROUS REGIMENT OF WOMEN** King • • • • • **$6.99**

____57458-2 **WITH CHILD** King • • • • • • • • • • • • • • • • • **$6.50**

____57251-2 **PLAYING FOR THE ASHES** George • • • • • • • • • • **$7.50**

____57173-7 **UNDER THE BEETLE'S CELLAR** Walker • • • • • • • • **$6.50**

____58172-4 **BURIED BONES** Haines • • • • • • • • • • • • • • • • **$5.99**

____57205-9 **THE MUSIC OF WHAT HAPPENS** Straley • • • • • • **$5.99**

____57477-9 **DEATH AT SANDRINGHAM HOUSE** Benison • • • • • **$6.50**

____56969-4 **THE KILLING OF MONDAY BROWN** Prowell • • • • • • **$5.99**

____57533-3 **REVISION OF JUSTICE** Wilson • • • • • • • • • • • • **$5.99**

____57579-1 **SIMEON'S BRIDE** Taylor • • • • • • • • • • • • • • • **$5.99**

____58225-9 **REPAIR TO HER GRAVE** Graves • • • • • • • • • • • **$5.99**